NEME

C000181990

MARGARET CLIFFORD

Falcon Books

First published in 1998 by Falcon books.
An imprint of M & N Publishing Co. Ltd
1 Northumberland Avenue, Trafalgar Square
London, WC1N 5BW

Paperback ISBN 1 899865 08 X

TABLE OF CONTENTS

THE ARRIVAL

Leaping, Twisting Flames of Fire
Entwined within the burning pyre
A Devouring, Searing white hot Kiss
The embrace of the Avenger "Nemesis".

M.C

1

CHAPTER ONE: THE ARRIVAL

YEAR 1692. SALEM, MASSACHUSETTS

"The air was heavy and oppressive with the pungent smell of burning flesh. Salem was ablaze with the purging of sorcery.

Martyn Millar, Appointed Witch-Hunter General. Denouncer of all evil. Oblivious to the nauseating attack on his nostrils, studied the sky with a feverish interest.

A pall of smoke hung low over the common, reaching out with long dark tendrils as if reluctant to leave the reason for its being. Nevertheless, the heat from several still smouldering fires was forcing it upwards until it merged with the gathering cloud."

"This! Is symbolic. I am witnessing the Power of Good, force the Power of Darkness away from the earth. With me as the mediator." He smiled in deep satisfaction at the egotistical thought.

He was about to "cleanse" his nineteenth offender.

His fists clenched into a tight knot. Just thinking of the act brought an eager tingle of anticipation to his senses.

He turned to face the village. His piercing blue eyes burning like twin fires. The fires of Hell.

Folding his arms, he watched the howling mob of villagers approaching him. A scowl marred his handsome features as the raucous sound assaulted his hearing.

"The scum turn my mission in life into a fiasco" he muttered fiercely to himself. He turned his head from the crowd for a moment, only facing them again when he had calmed his anger.

The villagers drew slowly near, the crazed lust for death showing in the faces of some as they careened around jeering and shouting obscenities.

Millar's lip curled in disgusted loathing as his keen eyes surveyed the crowd until he found what he was searching for.

Two men dragged a terrified young girl between them. Her bare feet cut and bleeding. The marks of several beatings evident on her features.

Millar's expression, totally devoid of pity, never faltered as he witnessed the girl's feeble attempts to ward off her tormentors.

He thought of his own daughter, his beloved Sarah. Not much older than this unfortunate misguided creature, and thanked God that she was a good and pure girl.

A screeching sound like that of a cat invaded his thoughts.

"An hysterical woman had run forward hurling more obscenities at the girl, who tried in vain to shrink back as the woman spat full in her face. Yet another attempted to rip the girl's dress from her body, screaming to see the third nipple. The girl was spared this degradation as, at a nod from Millar, one of her captors struck the woman a savage blow sending her reeling into the crowd and bringing several of them crashing to the ground with her."

Millar had no wish for the crowd to see the girl's perfectly formed and unblemished body.

The trio reached the post, ready piled with brush and timber. Millar stood with his back to them as his associates secured the girl.

Holding his arm aloft, a hush gradually descended over the crowd.

His ice blue eyes burned into those closest to him.

The crowd backed away, a flicker of fear passing nervously from one to another.

Millar allowed a small humourless smile to play about his lips.

"Yes scum." The voice so soft only he could hear it.

"Fear me for I am to be feared."

Slowly he turned to face the girl. An expectant hush fell over the crowd. When he was sure he had their full attention, he spoke in a loud clear voice.

"Rebecca Allen, this is your final chance to repent and confess your dealings with the Devil."

The girl raised her bowed head, soft grey eyes meeting his.

Millar felt a sudden pounding in his heart. "What was it... What could he see in those pleading eyes... Innocence. Hell and Damnation! She is trying to place me under her spell."

He averted his eyes quickly, careful not to allow the crowd see his momentary panic.

The girl spoke in a softly cultured voice.

"As God is my witness, I am innocent."

Her long golden hair fell about her shoulders forming a halo around her face. The emotion in her voice lending credence to her words.

The crowd stepped back even further. Looking at each other. Afraid of the vision this girl created whilst protesting her innocence.

Not so Martyn Millar. He felt the anger rising inside him again, anger directed at himself, for he too had felt the fear clutch at his heart.

3

His anger gave strength to his voice.

"So be it." His gaze never leaving her face.

"Fire her. And may God have mercy on your blackened soul."

Four men put blazing torches to the pyre and the crowd watched with baited breath.

As the flames hungrily devoured the dry timber, the girl of barely eighteen years, cried out again. "I am innocent. Oh God, I am innocent."

Millar stared dispassionately.

The first fingers of flame curled around her body. She threw her head backwards in a convulsion of pain. Eyes rolling wild with agony. Millar seized this opportunity.

"See" he shouted triumphantly. "See her face. Now you will hear her call on her Master."

Eagerly his eyes searched her face, he waited for the curses to reign down on him. Curses he had heard so many times before, he was now immune to them.

Her eyes caught and once again held his.

"You are a murderer" she screamed, pain contorting her mind and body. "I will be avenged. You will suffer Martyn Millar. Your own will avenge me. Your own will be my Nemesis."

"As her last words were torn from her tortured body, a pendant suspended on a chain around her neck caught the light of the flames.

A pendant carved with inscriptions that had been termed the symbol of her witchcraft.

The blinding glare shocked Millar for a second. Shielding his eyes from the brilliance. He watched fascinated as the white hot pendant burned onto her body over her heart."

The village clock tolled the hour of six. As the chimes faded away, Millar became aware of the silence that had descended over the crowd. He allowed his eyes to travel over them making no attempt to conceal the utter contempt he felt for them.

"Superstitious fools all of them," he muttered. His own fears already forgotten.

After satisfying himself that the girl was dead, he turned again to the crowd and spoke to them. "Return to your homes in safety. The Devil's Advocate is no longer with us."

The crowd slowly began to disperse, no longer exhilarated. Their recent frenzy diminished into subdued murmurings. Some casting cautious glances, first at the still burning pyre, then more furtively at

Millar, quickly lowering their glance lest he saw them.

Millar missed nothing. The humourless smile played on his lips as, bowing mockingly to the crowd, he turned on his heel and headed for the village tavern beckoning the two officials who acted as observers of justice to follow him.

"The tavern was unusually quiet but it suited Millar that way. Ignoring the over zealous attentions of the landlord trying to draw him into the dank looking and dimly lit interior, he seated himself at a small table outside. His two companions joined him after ordering ale for the three of them. The two men then proceeded with the necessary paperwork."

Millar watched without interest and taking a deep draught of ale the moment it was delivered, he relaxed, wiping his mouth with the back of his hand, a satisfied smile on his face. He allowed his thoughts to dwell on his latest triumph. The arresting of Rebecca Allen.

"The girl's father had been out of town when they had forced an entrance into their home and accused her of witchcraft. That was a great pity for he was surely more guilty than the girl, but he would be back and then... Millar smiled sadistically at the thought."

"Vincent Allen and his daughter were a strange couple. Even stranger was the collection of papers and artefacts that had been found in the house along with phials of liquid and containers of ointments which they claimed could cure people of certain illnesses."

Not anymore. Millar smiled again as he brought to mind a vision of the smouldering pile of rubble that had once been the home of these devil worshippers.

His thoughts returned to the girl. He usually took his pleasure from the young and pretty females. They were always willing in the hope that it would save them from burning. Millar frowned as he remembered his attempts with Rebecca Allen. She had merely stood and gazed at him, one hand clutching the pendant hung low on a chain. The moonlight streaming through an opening in the prison wall capturing her naked body in its beams, giving her beauty an ethereal appearance. Even now he didn't know why he had turned away and walked out of the room.

An uneasy feeling that he could not ignore had struck at his heart. He had vented his unease, his fear and lust on the willing bodies of two other unfortunate victims of his Cleansing Ritual. A title he gave to the burning of the victims whose misfortune it was to fall into his hands.

Throughout the trial, Rebecca Allen had been silent except to insist on her innocence occasionally. Her last words hadn't troubled him, he had heard far worse, after all, she was the nineteenth witch he had brought to justice. "Still... They had been disquieting words, no witch had ever had that effect on him or the crowd before."

One of the officials looked up from his writing, a curious expression on his face.

Millar gave a small embarrassed laugh realising he had spoken his thoughts aloud. "It's nothing Silas. Just musing."

A commotion drowned out his words.

"Where is Master Millar."

The dishevelled figure of his stable boy was pushed in front of him. The boy was obviously greatly agitated.

"The Mistress has sent me for you sir. She says for you to come home immediately."

Millar gave the youth a look that silenced any further words from him and finished his ale before standing. "Alright boy, I will come with you now."

For his wife to send for him at such a time could only mean urgent family business and he did not permit his affairs to be discussed on the street.

He walked the short distance to his home in silence. The boy, trying to keep pace with his master knew better than to speak again unless spoken to.

The moment Millar entered the house, his wife threw herself into his arms. "Oh Martyn," she cried. "It is our daughter. She is gravely ill. Come quickly. See for yourself."

"Millar climbed the stairs, his wife at his heels and entered his daughter's chambers. His blood froze at the sight that greeted him. Two maids were struggling to hold his daughter firmly on the bed. Her eyes had rolled upwards so only the whites could be seen. Her head moving side to side. Long red, gold hair in total disarray. Lips parted as if in a scream, yet no sound escaped them. He reeled with shock, grasping the door joist to steady himself."

"What in God's name." He shouted. Startling one of the maids into loosing her grip on the girl's arm, who was then rewarded by a violent blow to her head by the now flaying arm.

Millar swiftly walked to his daughter's side. Much as he loved his two young sons, this girl meant more to him than any other living creature.

"Have you sent for the doctor?" he managed to say at last.

"Yes. Yes. He should be here now."

Sounds from downstairs confirmed his wife's words.

The doctor came straight up to the girl's room. Taking one look at

6

her, he ushered all but her parents out. Once loosened the girl threshed around wildly on the bed. Millar had once seen the inside of a lunatic asylum... He paled and visibly shuddered at his own mental comparison. **This was his daughter.**

"How long has she been like this?" The doctor's voice startled him.

"Not long" the distraught mother answered. "Since just before the village clock struck the hour of six."

The doctor gave Millar an alarmed look, but said nothing. He bade them both hold the girl while he administered a strong sedative which took effect almost at once. Satisfied that the girl was now sleeping, he stood and motioned Millar to step out of the room with him, leaving Mistress Miller sobbing quietly over her daughter.

Once outside the door, Millar grasped the doctor's arm.

"What is wrong with my daughter?" he demanded.

The doctor shook his head. "I wish I had the answer to that question, sir. It appears to me that Sarah was struck down at the exact moment in time Rebecca Allen said she would be avenged."

Millar stared at the doctor... (What in God's name was he listening to...) He backed away, smouldering anger clouding his eyes.

"I do not believe what I am hearing." His voice was dangerously calm. "I expected better from you. You are an educated man."

The doctor merely stared at him in silence.

Millar's calm exploded. "This is the kind of superstitious nonsense the rabble on the streets would say." The thunder in Millar's voice matching the furious expression on his face.

"Is it?" the doctor persisted, holding up his hand. Determined to have his say before Millar threw him out of the house as he surely would. "I have attended every burning including this one. I have heard you cursed many times, but I have **never** heard words like of which Rebecca Allen used... She did not curse you. She made a plea for vengeance. She said "Your own would avenge her. Your own would be her Nemesis." I beg you sir to listen to me, for the sake of your family."

Millar pushed the doctor violently away from him. "Go. Leave my house. I never wish to see your face again. You are finished in this village... Do you hear me... Finished."

The doctor, his face pale from the attack, shrugged his shoulders. "Very well. I hope for your family's sake, I am wrong." He hesitated as he was about to leave. Plunging his hand into his pocket, he pulled out a chain. "This is the girl's pendant. It did not burn." He held it out to Millar. "I think you should....."

"How... dare... you." Millar. His face white with fury lashed out with

7

his fist, sending the pendant flying to the ground. "Give it to the devil who spawned her." Turning on his heel, he strode back into his daughter's room, closing the door firmly behind him.

"Millar watched the dawn turn the darkened sky into a deep rose pink. Shadows under his eyes giving his face a gaunt appearance. A low moan made him turn swiftly in his daughter's direction. She was still at rest, heavily sedated."

The moan had escaped from his wife fitfully sleeping in a chair.

"Studying her heavy features, sagging in sleep, he felt a rare surge of pity for her. He had no love for her. It had been an arranged marriage. Having come from a prominent family, she was acceptable in higher circles. Also she had come to him with a handsome dowry. To her credit, she pad presented him with a beautiful daughter and two attractive sons. Not that she had contributed much to their appearance. She was a plain woman. Her only saving grace being her eyes. Her eyes were the most beautiful emerald green Millar had ever seen. Wasted on her, Millar had always thought unkindly. His Sarah had inherited those eyes. With her mother's eyes, his features, hair colour and stature, she was indeed a stunning beauty..."

"So had been Rebecca Allen!" Panic seized him. Why had he thought that? He gazed at the sleeping girl and felt the first deep stirrings of real fear...

As the dawn broke fully, Sarah stirred restlessly, her mouth forming words but again no sound. Millar crossed the room and knelt beside the bed. She was trying to speak. He bent close so as to hear her, the sickly smell of laudanum heavy on her breath making him grimace.

She uttered just one word... "Nemesis"...

Millar fell back, terror clutching at his heart. "No... Sarah... No!" At the sound of his voice, Sarah sat upright. Eyes wide, staring like a crazed animal. Millar's face was ashen. Her eyes had changed colour. They were a startling vivid turquoise. "I am Nemesis" she said and fell back in a dead faint.

"The mutterings on the streets were once again witch talk. This time it was Millar's own daughter who was being hounded. Some were saying Rebecca Allen was innocent as she had claimed and Sarah was the one who should have burned. Millar knew he could not afford to ignore the gossip. He had to move his family to safety before the villagers decided they were brave enough to turn on them. He knew that only the fear of himself kept them at bay. So, with the help of a couple of trusted friends, he secretly filled a wagon with food and water and purchasing as much of the sedative as he could, he left the village and started on the long journey to Pennsylvania where his brother lived."

Sarah had to be constantly sedated. Millar noticed each time she became agitated, her eyes would change colour. To his horror, he found he was afraid of her. Afraid of his own beloved daughter. He wept bitterly at the realisation.

When they were almost at their destination, he took his wife to one side. "As soon as we reach my brother's home, I am leaving you and our sons and taking Sarah away."

She started to protest, but he silenced her.

"Sarah is still in danger, but I fear she may also be dangerous." His wife sobbed quietly knowing that her husband spoke the truth. She too was afraid of Sarah and the two boys would not venture near the sister they had once adored.

"I must take her as far away from Salem as possible. It may be her only chance of recovery."

So, on arrival at his brother's home, he bade his wife and sons goodbye, saying he would send for them. But deep inside, he knew he would never see them again.

"For over a year Millar travelled. First with wagon trains, then alone. He and his raving daughter were shunned. People hated and feared them. Wherever they went, tales of unexplained deaths preceded them. Millar himself had witnessed one terrifying death."

"He shuddered as he recalled the stranger demanding money from them, brandishing a vicious looking knife. Sarah had slowly stood and looked at him. No word had escaped her lips. No evidence of fear on her face. Her eyes had changed colour. They had first become turquoise. Then so blue... He had seen lightening spring from them.

The stranger had stared at her. Unmoving like a scared rabbit. A look of pure terror fixed on his face. Millar stared at the two of them. Then to his horror, the man had burst into flames. In seconds, he was an inferno.

Millar dropped to his knees and was violently sick. This was something he had no control over. He looked at Sarah with renewed fear.

Sarah merely glanced at the remains of the man she had just annihilated then lay down in the wagon as if the effort had exhausted her.

Millar hastily covered the smouldering remains with earth."

After that episode, he tried to keep her away from towns and people.

9

Afraid of what other horrors she may be capable of... Afraid of her.

On several occasions, Millar heard of a man who was searching for them. He decided that these tales were invented to frighten him. Keep him away from the towns, but his last attempt to buy laudanum proved it to be fact.

"He had been travelling behind a wagon train. Out of sedative and Sarah's madness driving him to despair. He might not have seen the small town but for having to stop and give Sarah a drink. That's when he saw the dim lights."

At first he thought it was the wagon train. He almost cried with relief when he realised it was a town. He bound and loosely gagged Sarah repeated telling her he was sorry, knowing that it didn't penetrate her senses anyway. Then he walked into the town.

Dusk was falling. He could make out an ale house more by the sounds of muted revelry coming from it than by sight. He saw a woman hurrying towards him. He spoke as she neared him.

"Excuse me madam."

The woman stared at him, then looked around frantically.

"I do not mean you any harm madam. I merely wish to enquire if there is a doctor or apothecary in town."

She relaxed a little. "There's no doctor. But you could try Brennen's down the street, he sells most everything."

She hurried away without another word or a backwards glance.

Millar walked in the direction the woman had pointed and came to a dark looking building with the name Sean Brennen painted over the doorway. As he entered the dimly lit store, a bell tinkled his presence to the owner.

A voice with a soft Irish accent asked. "Can I be of assistance to you sir?"

"I need laudanum." Millar answered, moving closer. "Or anything that will sedate a sick person."

The Irishman stared at the figure in front of him. The face was that of an old man. But the voice suggested younger. "Are you ill sir?"

"No. No, my wife is with child, I want to be sure I have something for the pain when the time comes." He knew exactly what he looked like. He had seen his reflection.

The storekeeper reached into a cupboard. (The man was obviously lying. None of your business Sean Brennen,) He took out a small phial placing it on the counter.

"Is that all you have?"

The anxiety behind the question confirmed Brennen's suspicion. He carefully placed another phial on the counter. "That's all I can let you have sir."

As Millar hastily paid for and picked up the laudanum, the bell signalled another customer. Millar heard the resonant tones of an obviously educated man.

"I wonder if you could help me. I am looking for a gentleman travelling with his daughter. A refined couple, but the girl may be sick. I have heard they were travelling with a wagon train that passed here recently."

(Hardly ever get two strangers in one night.) Brennen kept his thoughts to himself.

Millar, grateful for his haggard, dishevelled appearance, gave the owner of the voice a quick glance. A tall bearded man stood almost blocking the doorway. Millar shook his head and pushing past the stranger, he rushed out into the welcome darkness.

(The bearded one may not have noticed the flash of fear in Millar's face, but it did not escape Sean Brennen's observant eye.)

Once again Brennen kept his thoughts to himself. (A man didn't last long in these parts unless he minded his own business.)

Millar hurried back to Sarah. Convinced that the man was a witch-hunter as he himself had been. He too had spent months tracking evil doers down when necessary. Fear gripped his heart as he quickly sedated Sarah. He watched the wildness leave her face as she slipped into sleep.

"Seated with his head resting in his hands, despair washed over him. He was sick of having to steal away in the night. He knew now what it was like to be the hunted instead of the hunter. Each day was a torment. He did not know how much longer he could cope with Sarah or the hostility of frightened people who did not understand. But if each day was a torment, then each night was a living nightmare. For every night since leaving Salem... Martyn Millar had burned in his dreams."

"The town was now several days behind him. Maybe weeks. Millar had lost all sense of time. He stood beside the wagon clutching at a torn map given to him by a holy man. This man had told him to take Sarah to The Great Salt Lake, saying that the air and salt would purify her mind and body which he believed to be possessed. Now with the sun burning down on him, he stood swaying. A broken, ill and disorientated man. He was lost and dying.

Embracing his daughter for the final time, he collapsed and died at her feet. He died not knowing that he had passed the Lake two days before. He had not even noticed how strangely quiet and withdrawn Sarah had become. No longer needing medication.

"Sarah Millar. Now twenty years old, looked down at her dead father. A solitary tear coursed its way down the thin contours of her cheek to her chin. The droplet falling almost in slow motion, reflecting the rays of the sun like a pure crystal and landing on Millar's upturned face.

For a brief moment, there was a shadowy glimpse of her former self as she saw that the tear was caught in the hollow beneath one of his now sightless eyes.

She grieved for her father's suffering. Then it was gone.

She turned away and walked deeper into the desert. Walking until she could walk no further. She was unaware of the small cave she stumbled into, being more dead than alive now. Laying down, she closed her eyes for the final time.

"Two lone Indians witnessed both deaths, then disappeared from the scene like silent shadows."

"The girl was dead. Yet the head moved like a grotesque marionette.

Nemesis did not die. She could not die. She stirred angrily, trapped inside the girl's skull. Cursing the fact that she had been obliged to attempt entry into the girl's mind too fast thus sending her insane.

She sighed deeply. There was something about this place that made her weak. She knew she was becoming dormant. Inertia drifted over her in ever increasing waves. Dulling her thoughts. Threatening the very essence of her being. She would have to be patient."

"Damn the infernal mortals. My time will come."

The disembodied voice echoed menacingly around the cave...

"My time will come. I <u>will</u> have my revenge. I will teach all mortals the true meaning of fear... I will present them the wrath of.............. 'Nemesis'".

THE AWAKENING

Dreams are rudiments of the great state to come.
We dream what is about to happen.
Taken from "The Dictionary of Dreams"

By Gustavus Hindman Miller.

CHAPTER TWO: THE AWAKENING

THE GREAT SALT LAKE DESERT, UTAH.
YEAR 1972. SUNDAY MAY 7TH

"The old man slammed the hood of the pick-up shut, securing it with a thump of his fist.

"Let's see if you'll start now... you... blasted heap of rust." His words echoed in the emptiness of the desert. He glanced uneasily over his shoulder... at the entrance of his gold-mine, then jumped into the cab. Holding his breath... he turned the ignition.

"Come on... come on," he whispered desperately.

The engine burst into life. A gleam brightened the rheumy eyes.

"That's it old girl... I knew you wouldn't let me down."

The engine coughed, spluttered... then whined into silence.

Frantically, he tried the ignition again and again... Nothing. He glared at the transmitter placed on the passenger seat.

"Fat lot of good you are" he shouted at it. "First time I've ever needed you... and you blasted well won't work."

Climbing out of the cab, he gave the truck a parting kick before walking over to the shack. Gloomily he pulled a beer from the cooler box.

"Maybe Al will try raise me on the transmitter... When he doesn't get through... he'll come out... Yeah! Course he will, it's his job isn't it?"

He threw a stone viciously, watching it ricochet over the rocks.

"Don't be a blasted idiot. How many times has Al Jackson played hell with me for switching the damn thing off. How many times have I told him to mind his own bloody business, that I don't need busy bodies. How many times have I told him I don't need a transmitter. Well, I was right... it's no bloody good anyway."

He threw another stone, noticing his shaking hand.

"Stop talking to yourself Bailey... Do something positive... go get that damn truck started... then you can get out of here."

He glanced at the lengthening shadows, a look of fear passed over his face. "Damn it! I should have checked the truck yesterday... or this morning instead of working in..."

14

His eyes flickered towards the mine. "Instead of working in there." He shuddered and attacked the engine of the pick-up with renewed vigour. The sun had gone down when he finally gave in.

"Hellsfire! I can't find a blasted thing wrong with it". He threw a spanner at the truck. The clang sounded deafening in the silence of the desert, reminding him of how much alone he was. Again he glanced nervously around him, close to tears.

"Looks like I'm stuck here for another night... Maybe even more." He shuddered again and walked slowly back to the shack.

The oil lamp gave off a warm glow, making him feel safer in the one roomed shack. A look of annoyance crossed his face.

"Since when do you need to feel safer, Pop Bailey." He spoke the words aloud.

"Since yesterday," he answered himself quietly.

Taking a diary out of an old trunk, he seated himself under the lamp and started writing. When he had finished, he picked up a book and tried reading, eyes wandering occasionally to the window.

"Damn it!" He threw the book onto the camp cot. "How the hell can I read... I can't concentrate... I daren't sleep..."

He suddenly jumped to his feet... "The transmitter... I should have brought it in... I could have worked on it... maybe got it going... Yeah."

He got as far as the door, hand resting on the handle. He shut his eyes tightly, head shaking.

"Can't go for it now... too late... too tired... too dark."

He slumped down on the cot, running his hands over his face.

"Got to rest for a while... just a little while... mustn't sleep."

"Percival Oswald Philious "Pop" Bailey, lay back mentally vowing to keep his eyes open.

His eyelids drooped, unable to prevent the desperate weariness that crept over him. He drifted into an uneasy sleep, tossing and turning. He awoke with a start crying out. Then drifted into sleep again.

MONDAY MAY 8th.

"He stirred. A grimace slowly changing the peaceful expression on his face into a mask of sheer horror.

He felt the now familiar prickle of fear at the nape of his neck creep down his spine with the insidious stealth of a slow moving reptile, creating an icy chill that settled deep into the pit of his stomach.

A low moan of despair escaped his lips as he struggled to sit upright, banging his head sharply. His movements were restricted. He was entombed alive in a satin lined coffin.

Panic ripped through his body like an explosion. He lashed out at the lid with both feet. Screaming in fear.

"Damn! Damn! Solid oak." He knew it was solid oak. Hadn't he chosen the timber himself for this casket?

Suddenly he felt the casket begin to move. He could hear the soft whirr of machinery as he was slowly propelled forward.

Forwards to... "Oh my God. Forwards to What..."

"Jesus Christ!... No!..."

He began beating on the lid with his fists. Desperate frenzy lending him strength.

"Let me out... I'm alive... **I'm alive!**"

The casket came to a shuddering halt and there was silence.

The old man listened. Staring wildly into the blackness of the coffin. Heart pounding. Breath tearing from his tortured lungs. Hands bruised and bleeding.

The sudden whoosh of flames brought a terrorised shriek from deep inside him. **He was being cremated alive.**

"The heat and smoke was suffocating him... What could he hear!... Laughter. Crazy maniacal laughter."

The casket exploded. The inferno engulfed him. He was burning. Not in a crematorium but in... "Jesus the mine's on fire... I'm trapped."

He threshed around in agonising pain... hitting rough walls that tore the flesh from his burning body.

"Oh God let me die..." Flesh blistering. He burned, yet still he lived. The crazy laughter rose in volume. It grew stronger. It burned into his soul just as the flames burned into his body and still he lived.

"Oh God have mercy... For pity's sake, please... LET ME DIE."

Bailey sat bolt upright. Sweat pouring from every part of his body, tears streaming down his lined face. The sheet on his camp cot was wet. The strong smell of urine filled his nostrils.

"Oh God no... I've pissed meself again..."

Sobs wracked his tired frame. He lay back and finally gave in to the hopeless misery that had been building up inside him for days. It erupted violently from him. His body convulsing with every sob. Eventually he lay quiet. Staring mutely at the ceiling of the shack. Slowly he sat up, exhaustion making him feel weak. Sitting on the edge of the cot, legs dangling limply, he rested his grizzled head in his hands.

"Sweet Jesus, I must be going crazy. It's finally got to me. This God forsaken place is sending me insane."

He gazed through the window at the unfriendly terrain. Nothing but sand as far as the eye could see and he was stuck here... alone.

No transport. No transmitter.

Three nights running he had been terrorised by this nightmare of burning alive. Each dream more terrifying than the last. This time it had woken him twice through the night.

"Feel so weak now. Got to get away from here." he muttered to himself. "Must get to Caplin somehow and see the doc."

His eyes rested on the diary laying on the floor where it had fallen the night before, he picked it up studying for a while then carefully made another entry. The room spun around him as he rose unsteadily to his feet. He glanced into the yellowed mirror hung on the wall opposite him... and shuddered.

A drawn haggard face stared back. A stranger's face.

He closed his eyes tightly, swaying as he did so. The fear was tearing him apart, robbing him of his reason.

"Am I **really** going crazy? Is this how it starts?"

Opening his eyes, he looked again into the mirror, hoping for an answer. The hollow eyed reflection of a man marked for death, gazed back mockingly.

Arms hanging loosely by his side, shoulders stooped, he walked unsteadily outside, unable to cope with the physical and mental change he could see and feel in himself.

"The late afternoon sun struck his face making him wince. The shock of realising that he had slept most of the day scarcely registering. Pouring water into a battered tin bowl, he undressed and washed himself, shivering in spite of the warm sun on his body. He dressed and sat listlessly in a rocking chair.

He sat staring trancelike at the entrance to his mine. His hooded eyes seeming to sink deeper into their sockets.

The sun dropped low in the sky. A light breeze ruffled his hair, bleached white with constant exposure to the merciless hot desert sun.

An empty beer can rolled from the rock it had been carelessly placed on. The sudden noise brought Bailey's mind back from the blank void it had been travelling through."

"I'm not crazy," he said bitterly. "By God... I'm **not** crazy."

The sound of his own voice startled him. Reaching down, he angrily drew a can of beer from the cooler box and took a long drink of the now tepid fluid. Grimacing at the taste, he threw the half empty can in the direction of his mine.

"This mine's been my life for the last thirty years. Mine and Sam's. It's the only life I know. Now... Sam... What's happening to me? For godsake... What's happening to me?"

He closed his eyes tightly again trying to shut the horror out.

"He and Sam had loved the life. The regular monthly trips to Caplin where they would get stink roaring drunk, (spending many a night in jail). Caplin had been a shanty town then, they had watched it grow into a pretty little township. The beginnings of a smile touched the corners of his mouth as the memories flooded back, easing the fear for a short while."

"Those were the days Sam. Those were the **real** days." He opened his eyes and stared at the mine. A look of pure terror flitted across his face.

"There's nothing wrong with me. It's the mine. There's something hellish in there. Christ... I can feel it."

His thoughts drifted uneasily back to yesterday morning...

"He was busy replacing worn props. Sam had been a stickler for safety. "Those props are your life partner, take great care of them," was Sam's regular warning.

Pausing for a while, he wiped his forehead with the back of his hand. "The mine's damned hot. Unusually hot."

He glanced around nervously, staring into the shadows. Sweat was running down his back. His vest clinging to him in wet sticky patches. The uneasy feeling that he was not alone gradually crept over him again, same as it did yesterday, only more intense.

He turned ice cold with terror.

"Don't be such a damned idiot." he muttered angrily to himself.

"He couldn't shake the feeling off. He knew there wasn't another soul around for miles, yet he was being watched and whatever it was, he knew damn well it was dangerous. Every fibre of his tense body told him that. He'd never experienced anything like this in his life. He tried to ignore it but every sound he made caused the hairs on his arms to rise.

"Maybe the dreams are a... warning... Warning of what, you old fool."

He pulled a rag from his pocket to wipe his sweating palms, a small screwdriver clanged to the floor, bringing his raw nerves to screaming point.

He couldn't stand it any longer. Throwing his tools down, he started to run."

"The wide fissure in the rock face brought him to an uneasy standstill. He studied it for a moment. It hadn't been there the day before. He knew every crack, every dent and scrape in this mine. He knelt down to take a closer look and was alarmed at the heat escaping from it, too great for him to touch."

"Now I know why the mine's so hot..."

The fear struck at him again, the mine wasn't in a volcanic area, he and Sam had checked and double checked. Geographically, the mine was sound.

"God only knows what's causing this heat."

He swayed dizzily as he rose to his feet, staring hypnotically at the fissure. For one long and terrifying moment he felt as if he was stood at "The Gates of Hell."

Nothing short of an earthquake could stop his headlong flight. He didn't stop until he stood panting, leaning on the shack wall for support."

"I know what I'm going to do now. Throw everything into the pick-up and get the hell out of here...."

"He shuddered as his thoughts came back to the present. He felt ill. He couldn't stand the nightmares and the constant fear. Every ounce of energy was being drained from him. He hadn't eaten for three days. His head sank down to his chest... a defeated man. Tears brimming in his eyes threatening to flow once again. That's when he caught sight of the desert rat watching him intently. Head on one side."

The two gazed at each other in silence for what seemed like an eternity.

"Hello fella," Pop spoke softly so as not to alarm it.

The rodent continued studying him.

"You hungry?" Pop slowly reached into the cooler box and brought out an apple. Equally slowly, he reached into his trouser pocket and took out a penknife. Slicing of a piece of apple, he gently tossed it to the waiting rodent who proceeded to demolish it, never once taking its unwavering yet fearless gaze from the human.

Pop stared back at it, welcoming the diversion from his grim thoughts. When the piece of apple was gone, the rodent crept boldly closer, sniffing the air. Surprised, Pop threw more apple and was relieved when the creature came even closer. He was desperate for company. Any company.

"Come on fella, I won't hurt you."

19

The desert rat moved calmly nearer.

Pop ate a piece of the apple himself, talking constantly to the desert rat as if it could understand.

"It wasn't you in the mine. It isn't anything animal or... human. Christ... why did I say that? That's crazy talk. You know I'm not crazy, don't you. Even food wouldn't draw you this close if I were crazy." By this time the animal was sat at his feet like a pet dog.

"I know it isn't my imagination. I know there's something in that damn mine."

"Pop stared at the animal in amazement as it continued to gaze unafraid right into his eyes. It seemed to be... listening to him. He'd never known such boldness in these normally timid creatures... Strange."

He pushed the thought away and held out the last morsel which was nimbly accepted, and rose shakily to his feet.

"I might be knocking on a bit, but I've still got a damn good pair of legs... I'm walking to Caplin. I'll be there by morning. Better than staying here. I can make it."

The decisive note in his voice made him feel stronger. Straightening his shoulders with determination, he gave a tense, yet expansive smile to the desert rat.

"Thanks for listening my friend, you've been a great tonic."

"The animal twitched his whiskers and with a piece of apple firmly clutched in its paws, it rose upright on its hind legs staring into Pop's eyes. Its head rolled to one side, not once but three times, almost as if it were beckoning him to follow."

Pop felt a knot of tension in his stomach, he stared back disturbed by this strange behaviour.

The animal gave the man a last look and scampered away.

Opening the trunk where he kept his most treasure belongings, Pop's eyes fell on a weathered brown hat. He picked it up carefully.

"Sam," his voice barely a whisper.

"Sam had been his lifelong friend and partner. They had dug this mine out practically with their bare hands in the early years, enduring hardship along with the good times. They had done it together."

He sat down on an upturned milk crate. Alone with his thoughts.

"He had been alone ever since Sam had died a little over two years ago. His friends in Caplin had wanted him to give up the mine then and move into town, but Sam had always been convinced that one day they would make a big strike. So out of loyalty to the memory of his friend, Pop had stayed on alone. It was Sam who had nicknamed him Pop.

"Lord above! Your folks must have had a helluva bust up when they named you!" he laughed. "I reckon I'll just call you Pop."

A sad smile softened the weary face as a tide of memories came flooding back. "I'm sorry old partner, I don't think we will ever see the big..."

"What the hell was that....."

A deafening sound from the direction of the mine broke into his reverie. Hurrying outside, he was shocked to see how dark it had become, not too dark that he couldn't see the clouds of dust and sand spiralling upwards from the entrance of the mine. Grasping a torch, he ran.

The noise had subsided when he reached the mine. Slowly he stepped inside.

He looked around cautiously. Some of the props had split and part of the rock face had collapsed... Where the fissure had been. He backed away. Fear striking at his heart. He wasn't going any deeper into the mine... not after yesterday.

"I'll leave it. Bring someone from town to take a look."

He turned to leave, playing the torchlight nervously around the floor.

"Oh... My... God." The words rasped in his throat.

There, reflected in the beam of light was the largest gold nugget he had ever laid eyes on, even in his wildest dreams. He couldn't believe his luck. He dropped to his knees, laughing and crying. All fear gone.

"Sam. I've done it. You were right... I've done it... My God... I'm rich! I'm rich Sam... Rich! Rich! Rich!"

He reached out eagerly with both hands. "It must weigh pounds." He grasped hold of it. Eyes burning feverishly with renewed life. He raised it upwards...

The sickening lurch of disappointment as it came easily off the ground was like a savage kick to his stomach.

"No .. No.. No.. NO.. NO.. NO!

Staring down at what lay in his hands was the bitter end.

"Pyrite... Fool's gold!" he cried. Tears of frustration ran down his face. The tension of the last few days finally taking it's toll. Rocking to and fro. Looking like the crazy man he feared he was becoming.

"It's no more than I deserve Sam." His speech a jumbled mixture of choking sobs.

"It's what I've become. An old fool scared of his own shadow."

"His tears were falling on to the object in his hands. A shudder of revulsion rippled through his body as he realised it was a skull. He threw it as far as he could, watching it make a graceful arc across the mine entrance. He listened, waiting to hear it hit the ground and shatter."

"Shatter like his dreams."

The look of anguish on his face froze, then turned to stupefied horror as the skull stopped in mid-air and began slowly moving back towards him, glowing menacingly.

"The blood drained from his face. His heart started hammering in his chest until he thought it would burst.

Disbelief at what he was seeing held him in a temporary grip of paralysing shock. Then he reacted."

Quickly scrambling to his feet, not daring to take his eyes off the horror in front of him, he tried to reach the entrance.

The skull moved... blocking his escape.

"My... God... I don't believe this is happening."

He backed away looking around frantically. Searching... Searching.

"His eyes fell on the pickaxe laying just a few feet away from him. Hurling his body with a speed he didn't know he possessed, he landed alongside it, gashing his leg wide open... he didn't feel the pain. Snatching at the pickaxe, he swung around to face the hideous thing. He poised ready to strike."

As the skull drew closer, he felt the strength ebbing from his body. He couldn't move. His arms dropped uselessly by his sides. The pickaxe fell from his lifeless fingers. Resistance left him.

"Dear God! ... I'm going to die."

"The skull slowly approached him.

His eyes bulged from their sockets, burning now with insanity.

His mouth dropped open, slack-jawed.

He felt the hot urine run down his legs and smelled the stench of his own excrement as he lost control of his bodily functions."

The skull grinned mockingly, evilly at him.

From some deep recess of his mind, he gathered his last hidden reserves and made a desperate effort to escape.

"A beam of light emitted from the skull, exploding in his chest. The force sent him staggering backwards. He hit the wall, clutching at air. Then he was burning... Burning as he had burned in his dreams.

"He saw the flesh on his arms burst and peel away.

His innards were burning... melting.

He screamed and the flames were in his mouth... And still he lived..."

"Oh God... Have mercy... God have mercy..."

He became an agonising, screaming human torch.

"Please... Sweet Jesus... let me die... **LET ME DIE**"

The laughter... The crazy maniacal laughter flooded his mind... Burning away the last remnant of sanity. The burnt out shell of his body fell to the ground.

The nightmare was over.

"The skull hung motionless. Hovering above the smouldering wreck that had once been a man. It tilted backwards, jaws wide open. The maniacal laughter filled the mine. Then it floated out into the open. As it did, the entrance of the mine collapsed, covering Pop Bailey's grisly remains.

The glow left it as it settled down on to the blocked entrance."

"The desert was silent now except for a gentle breeze sighing on the air. Even the night birds were silent as if sensing the birth of a catastrophe.

Moonlight danced on the silvery sands casting motionless shadows. One small shadow moved as the desert rat sat back on its haunches looking in the direction of the mine, whiskers twitching, watching intently. The glowing thing that had made the human scream was no longer glowing, but the animal knew it was still there.

It could sense its presence... It had always sensed its presence. A savage growl escaped from the back of its throat as it scampered away, throwing one last look over its shoulder."

"The skull lay waiting, as it had waited for two hundred and eighty years. But it was patient and stronger.

"Nemesis was awake."

THE LEARNING

"In thoughts from the vision of the night,
When deep sleep falleth on men, fear came
upon me, and trembling, which made all my
bones to shake."

Job iv, 13-14.

CHAPTER THREE: THE LEARNING

The furrow between Mike Mallory's brows deepened, he rubbed absentmindedly at his temple.

"God'struth! He had a headache. He was tired. He was ready for a holiday and he was damned if he knew why this graph was causing him so much consternation."

He raised his eyes from the graph and gazed through the large window watching the shimmering heat haze dancing on the surface of the desert. Movement caught the periphery of his vision.

"Problem out... Holiday in." he murmured with relief as he saw his colleague Simon Kane drive into the forecourt and park his open top car.

He studied the tall athletic looking young negro as he leaped effortlessly out of the vehicle. "The man has the grace of a cat," he murmured again to himself, with a twinge of envy.

A small lopsided grin appeared on his face. He liked this young man, even if he did sometimes make him feel like a stick-in-the-mud.

By the time Simon had entered the observatory, the grin had broadened into a welcoming smile.

"Good vacation?" he asked, handing over a cold beer.

"More than good, my far too serious friend." answered Simon.

"Anyway, I can persuade you to go to the coast instead of Caplin for your vacation."

Mike laughed. "No way. I have some good friends there and I have no plans to do anything more strenuous than enjoy their company and play a few rounds of golf for the next two weeks."

Simon had an instant twinkle in his eyes. "Man, I've been playing a similar game myself. Well, I scored a few birdies. Same thing is it not?"

Mike smiled broadly, pointing an accusing finger. "I have a sneaking suspicion that your birdies are a little different to mine. Eh?"

Simon gave an exaggerated shrug of his shoulders. "My birdies... May be... but my games are not so different. You aim to score with as few strokes as you possible can... Where as I aim..."

"Enough. Enough." laughed Mike. "Spare me the erotic details, please."

"The two men had worked together for several years. Mike at thirty five was the senior by ten years, and at five foot eleven was shorter then Simon by three inches. Sandy coloured hair and serious grey eyes were a total contrast to Simon's black humorous eyes, dark, almost ebony skin and irrepressible nature.

Between them, they manned the Seismology Station situated on the edge of the Great Salt Lake Desert, some hundred and forty miles from Caplin, Mike's favourite retreat.

The complex had everything they needed. TV, radio, tape and record player, an extensive library and a fully equipped gym, which boasted a small but serviceable pool. They also had Joe. Joe was the electrician, groundsman, odd job man and an amiable if terrible card player. Joe Daniels was in his fifties. A widower with no children. As far as he was concerned, Mike and Simon were his family. All the family he needed."

"Well, the sooner we get down to business, the sooner you can take off" said Simon. "So fill me in."

"Nothing much to report really," Mike answered. "The seismograph registered some movement north west of here five days ago on the eighth, it only lasted a few seconds and wasn't strong but for some reason it has niggled at me." He passed the graph to Simon. "Keep a watch on this area will you Simon, and let me know if anything further develops."

Simon dropped the graph. "Clumsy of me," he muttered, stooping to retrieve it. He glanced at Mile at look of puzzlement on his face.

"Yes, of course I will." he answered quietly.

Mike watched curiously as a glistening bead of perspiration ran from his friends brow. "Are you alright Simon?"

Simon nodded. "Yes, I'm fine. A little tired from travelling I guess."

"Well there's nothing much to do. Get your head down for a couple of hours when I've gone, Joe can keep an eye on things here. Maybe you did a little too much scoring, eh?" he added with a friendly concerned grin.

Simon's wide smile was back in an instant. "Nooooo way man."

They walked while talking and gradually made their way outside, picking Mike's holdall up from the foyer as they passed through.

"Oh, I almost forgot," Mike said. "You will have company next week. A person by the name of S J Millar will be arriving on Tuesday to

26

finish his studies. He has been training at Boston Centre, so I think he will find this place a little quiet after the city."

"Don't worry Mike. I'll make him welcome and if I decide we won't like him, I'll have rid of him before you come back."

Simon threw the holdall into the back of the car. "Now on your way man and enjoy your break. Give my regards to Al and Jeff, tell them I'll be through to see them shortly. Okay."

Mike got into the car. "Sure thing. See you Simon."

He drove off with a parting wave.

"Simon watched until the car was out of sight, then slowly walked into the coolness of the building. Helping himself to another beer, he stood looking at the graph now laying on the table. It may have niggled at his friend, but in him it had sounded alarm bells causing a mindless fear that he couldn't understand. The moment he had touched it, he had received bad vibes and heat. A powerful sensation of heat."

"Strange... I know I have a sixth sense... But jeeze."

A shudder passed through his body.

The ringing of the internal phone broke into his thoughts. He picked up the receiver still staring at the graph. "Hello, Simon here."

"Hi there," Joe's cheerful voice came through the speaker.

"Had a good time, Simon?"

"Great thanks Joe, shame it's over."

"Yeah, well that's the trouble with vacations, they don't last long enough. Listen, I have a message for you. A person by the name of Millar will be arriving tomorrow instead of Tuesday. Okay?"

"Thanks Joe. No problem."

"Hey Simon, sounds like you've got a bad case of the dismals. Tell you what, I'll not only make dinner tonight, I'll let you win at cards. How's that?"

Simon laughed. "Alright Joe, I'll keep you to that."

He replaced the receiver, the smile back on his face.

"Mike put the radio on and whistled softly to the music. It would take him a couple of hours leisurely driving to arrive at Caplin. To call Caplin a town was laughable, a hamlet was more descriptive. Less than five hundred souls resided there. A picturesque little place protected from the worst of the elements by the Ruby Mountains and Battle Mountain and Mike had come to love it and its friendly residents."

"Salt Lake City was by far the nearest to the station, but the city life never appealed to Mike. He didn't even miss it. He felt at home in Caplin, like he "Belonged". He'd made some good friends there.

27

Sheriff Al Jackson. As tough a lawman you'd ever meet, but so easygoing, it must have been his middle name. Jeff Ryan, Deputy sheriff. So much like Al, he could have been his son. In fact, that's exactly how Al treated Jeff. Like a son. Then there was Ralph and Mary Richardson."

"Since the tragic death of his parents in a car crash when he was thirteen, Mike had been very much a loner. A spinster aunt had brought him up. She had been good to him, putting him through college, making sure he lacked nothing. Unfortunately, she had been a very remote and withdrawn person - the gulf between them had been enormous. Just before she died, she had told him of the man she had loved deeply and lost during the war. It had been the only time, he had felt close to her. He had at least understood her before she died and for that he had been grateful. The Richardsons, like Al, were childless. Mike stayed with them each time he came to Caplin. Ralph and Mary treated him like a son, giving him some of the warmth his life had lacked so far, and for that he was also grateful."

Rising dust on the desert caught his attention.

"Looks like someone is in a damned awful hurry," he muttered. The track across the desert certainly wasn't intended for speed.

As he drew closer, he could see it was the police station wagon.

"Who the hell is driving... Crazy fool will turn over." Mike slowed down as the station wagon veered on to the road, causing a miniature sandstorm. "Christ! He hasn't even seen me."

He gave a long angry blast on the car horn. The station wagon slowed down and came to a halt. The two drivers left their vehicles.

"What the hell is wrong, Jeff?" Mike shouted at he recognised the deputy sheriff.

Jeff Ryan was grim faced as he apologised. "Sorry Mike." He pulled a cigarette from a crumpled pack and lit it, inhaling deeply before he spoke again.

"We dug Pop Bailey out of his mine this morning."

"Dear God! Was it a cave in?" Mike's mind going immediately to the graph.

Jeff shook his head and drew deeply on the cigarette again.

"The entrance had caved in alright, but that isn't what killed him. Pop was burned to death."

He threw the half smoked cigarette and ground it viciously into the road with the heel of his boot. "So was one of my men, Mike and I'm damned if I know how."

Mike stared at him in shocked silence. It took a lot to upset Jeff

28

Ryan, known affectionately to the locals as Iron Ryan, but the big man was visibly shaken.

"You driving into Caplin, Mike?"

Mike nodded.

"Then do me a favour will you? Let the rest of my men ride with you, the stench is pretty bad in there." He indicated the wagon with his thumb.

"We're okay, Jeff." A voice from the wagon called. "Let's just get on with it." Jeff shrugged his shoulders and climbed back into the driving seat. I'll follow" Mike called after him. "I'm coming to the office with you."

Mike drove behind the station wagon, crossing the state line from Utah into Nevada with scarcely a glance.

"The graph. The tremor had been in the same region as the mine." He cursed himself for not having realised. "Damn it, if I had alerted someone, two men might still be alive."

"Sheriff Al Jackson viewed the scene from his office window as both vehicles pulled to a standstill. He rose to his feet. Six foot two inches of solid muscle, with a face that looked as if it had been carved out of granite.

"Al Jackson had served his country during the war and had taken part in the liberation of the Jews from concentration camps. He had seen sights that had made him weep. Sights that had brought him and a lot of other war-toughened men to their knees in horror. He had returned home with a resolve that aggression must be kept down. So he had become a cop, most of his career spent in the tough areas of The Bronx. His job had wrecked him marriage. His ex-wife was somewhere in Europe now with another man. That had caused him some grief... but as a friend had told him... life goes on. A mild heart attack had eventually forced him to take life easier. So ten years ago, rather than retire from a job he loved, he had moved to Caplin as its Sheriff and was surprised how much he loved the peace and tranquillity after the madcap pace of the city. Now, with his fiftieth birthday just around the corner, he had an uneasy feeling that his peace was about to be shattered."

He walked out onto the veranda, thinking of the call he had received from Jeff on the radio. Whatever had happened out there had certainly ruffled Jeff's usually cool demeanour.

Nodding to Jeff, he turned to the two grey faced men who had accompanied him. "I want the bodies placing in the back room... You'll

29

both have to stay until I have all the details." Turning to Mike, he extended his hand in a quiet but friendly greeting. "Good to see you Mike, I gather you know some of what has happened."

Mike shook the large firm hand. "Yes, Jeff told me about Pop and one of your men, that's the reason why I have come straight to you." He then explained how he thought the graph reading may give some indication of what exactly had happened.

"Thanks for telling me Mike, but I doubt if a small tremor has any bearing on the incidents, especially the last one. We'll check it out of course. Come on in."

Al and Jeff helped carry the two victims in. Mike wrinkled his nose as they passed him. Being in zipped bags did little to hide the sickening stench of burnt flesh.

"I've sent for Mac," Al was speaking to Jeff. "He'll be here shortly. Now. Tell me again what happened."

While the two men were talking, Mike helped himself to a coffee from a percolator that constantly perked, or so it seemed to him each time he came to see Al. He enjoyed playing golf with Al. They could talk to each other and more important, they could be quiet in each other's company with equal ease. A friendship he valued greatly. He listened to the conversation.

"Apparently, Pop had been due in town last Tuesday. When he hadn't shown up by Friday and Al hadn't been able to raise him on the transmitter (This didn't surprise him), he sent Jeff and the deputies to check on him. "The stubborn old fool has more than likely got drunk, but you'd better check it out."

The pick-up had still been there and all of Pop's belongings. Seeing the mine entrance blocked, they had started to dig it out thinking the old man would be trapped inside. They had found what was left of him in the early hours of this morning.

Jeff had instructed Cal Stevens, one of the deputies, to collect Pop's personal effects from the shack. Fifteen minutes later, they had found him burnt to death. Cal was twenty seven, married with two children.

They had found Pop's belongings in a sack only a few feet away from Cal's charred body. Untouched by fire. No one had heard or seen anything. No apparent cause."

Al and Jeff walked towards the room where the remains of the two men had been placed. Mike, following them, found Jeff blocking his path.

"I don't think you should see, Mike... They're not a very palatable sight."

Mike turned to Al. "I was in medical school before seismology Al, and I still feel partly responsible."

Al shrugged his huge shoulders. "I understand Mike, but from Jeff has told me, nothing you could have done would have ma difference. I'd appreciate your opinion though."

They went into the room grimacing at the fouled air. The two lay side by side on the floor. Jeff unzipped one of them. There was an audible intake of breath from Al. What lay inside was scarcely recognisable as human.

Mike threw Jeff a questioning glance. "This is Cal... or what's left of him." Jeff said quietly. "Pop was even harder to identify because of the cave in."

"Incredible." Mike spoke slowly. "Looks like he burned from the inside outwards."

"What makes you say that Mike?" Al asked.

"Look... Some of the outer pieces of flesh are untouched but the inner tissue... Well, you can see what I mean." Mike stood up as he spoke. Medical school or not, he'd seen enough. Jeff zipped the bag again and they came out of the room.

Al sat down heavily at his desk. The stench had reminded him of the concentration camps. "Were there any other signs of fire near the mine or camp?"

"No," Jeff answered. "But the ignition on the truck had... melted... almost like it had been soldered. It'll have to be towed in."

Al's eyes narrowed, "Soldered, that's not possible."

Jeff shrugged, "No... not by accident anyway."

"How long was Cal out of sight?" Al asked after a tense silence.

"Fifteen... twenty minutes at the most and there wasn't another soul out there Al, I scouted the area thoroughly, we were the only ones around."

"Okay Jeff. Tell the men they can go, just remind them of the rules. I don't want this discussed outside the office. I'll get a Path report first, then you and me will go take another look around the mine."

Jeff shook he head. "We can go Al, but it will just be a waste of time. A pretty strong wind blew up as we were about to leave, that's what delayed us. If I missed anything, and I'm damn sure I didn't, it'll be well covered now."

Jeff had a word with the men, then came back and sat with Mike and Al, accepting the coffee Mike handed him with a grateful smile.

Mike glanced at a sack on the floor.

"Pop's belongings," Jeff said, once again answering Mike's unspoken estion. Jeff bent forward and dragged the sack towards him, he started taking the contents out. A clock, a diary, a faded photograph of a woman. "Does anyone know if Pop had any relatives?" he asked.

"None living that I know of." Al answered him as he was about to look through the diary. "This might tell us... What in God's name is that?" He stared at the object Jeff had placed on the desk.

"It looks like a gold skull." Jeff said, picking it up again.

"I don't think it is gold, but I'm no expert. Cal found it among the rubble where the mine had caved. Seemed right to put it with Pop's gear."

He put it down quickly wiping his hand on his shirt, a strange expression on his face. "Feels... Odd." he said with a nervous laugh.

"I could have sworn it moved in my hand." He looked at Al and Mike, then back at the skull. (For a moment there he had felt... No... No. Not possible. "Why should I feel..." He refused to voice the word to himself.)

Donald Macpherson, GP walked in at that moment, and broke the tension much to Jeff's relief.

"Morning Mac," Al said getting up from his chair. "Fraid I have a pretty foul job for you. Hope you haven't had breakfast yet."

His weak attempt to joke almost choked him.

Mac had a quick look at the remains and arranged for them to be taken to the hospital. "Give me a couple of hours Al. I should have something for you by then. Has Cal's wife been told yet?"

"No Mac. No one has been told. I'll go see Ann myself shortly, though God only knows what I'm going to tell her."

After Mac had left, Mike stood. "I'd better let the Richardsons know I've arrived. Would you like me to come with you to Cal's home first Al?"

"No thanks Mike, it's my job, I'll deal with it."

"Okay, I'll give you a ring later to see what Mac has come up with." Taking one last look at the object on the desk, he left.

The warmth of the sun greeted him as he walked outside, yet he shivered. That skull had given him the creeps. More than that, he had seen a flash of real fear on Jeff's face. Something he'd never seen before and that... made him uneasy... very uneasy.

Ralph and Mary greeted him warmly. Within a half hour, he was unpacked and seated in the garden with Ralph telling him of the mysterious tragedies, knowing he could trust him completely.

Ralph was greatly upset, he had known both men for years.

"How?" he asked. "How were they both burnt to death?"

Mike shook his head. "I don't know Ralph. I just don't know... Ralph, we can't tell Mary, not yet."

Ralph shook his head, watching his wife through the kitchen window.

"No... No point in upsetting her... until we have to, is there?" They remained in the garden talking until Mary announced lunch was ready.

Mike managed to keep a lively conversation going with amusing anecdotes of Joe and Simon throughout the meal, making light of the fact that neither he nor Ralph had an appetite.

Mary was in the kitchen when Mike rang the sheriff's office, Al answered.

"Well, you were right about how Cal burned, from the inside out, that is. Pop burned exactly the same way, but Mac has no explanation for either. He has read about something called spontaneous combustion which causes this kind of burning. Whether it is legally acceptable as a cause of death is not only debatable, it's too much of a coincidence in this case."

Mike waited quietly while Al paused for breath.

"No," Al continued. "I can't begin to imagine what happened to those men, I only know I intend to do my damnedest to find out."

"I agree Al, this whole business is... strange to say the least. I'm not a police officer, but I'd like to stay with you on this, I've got a bad feeling about it Al."

"Yeah... me too Mike. Like I said, I value your opinion."

"Thanks Al, if you need me, you know where I am. I'll be in touch anyway. See you later."

"Al replaced the receiver and carried on filling out a report as far as he could. When he had finished, he sat back in his chair thinking of Cal's wife. He had told her Cal was dead, that there had been and accident. She had demanded to know more, but even after speaking to Mac, he was still unable to answer her questions. How could anyone just burst into flames? How could two people burst into flames? It wasn't logical, and if there was one thing Al needed, it was logic."

His head ached. He would be on duty until Jeff took over at seven. Putting his feet up on the desk, he closed his eyes and relaxed.

The room was gradually filled with the rhythmic sound of the sheriff sleeping.

Pop's personal effects were in a tray on the desk. The air in the sheriff's office grew heavily humid, perspiration gleamed on Al Jackson's brow as he slept.

The skull stirred slowly as if being disturbed by a strong breeze.

33

There was no breeze."

It rose slowly from the tray, emitting a faint bluish glow. Turning full circle, it stopped opposite a wall covered almost entirely by a map. The glow grew brighter. It drifted across the room then hung motionless in front of the map. From conversations it had heard, it knew this was Caplin, Nevada.

Gradually moving across the length of the map. Suddenly jerking backwards as if agitated, glowing even brighter - The Great Salt Lake was in front of it. It trembled aggressively as if convulsing in temper. Quickly it moved on, the glow fading as it did so. It studied the map closely for several minutes until it found what it sought.

{Boston. Salem was in Boston. That is where I was invoked. That is where Rebecca Allen will be avenged. Somehow I will reach my destination. Fulfil my obligation and take my own revenge.}

Returning to the desk, it hovered for a while over the sleeping man. Studying. Probing.

Al grimaced in his sleep a low groan escaping from his open mouth. The skull probed deeper, witnessing the violent dream it was creating inside Al's mind.

It shook with silent, malicious mirth as Al, in his dream, was placed alive inside one of the grisly ovens he had seen during the war. It watched as the terrified man choked on the debris of human remains before the flames began to eat at his flesh.

Hate and contempt intensified the aura surrounding the skull.

{Mortals are despicably weak and so easy to fill with terror}

With that last thought, the skull settled once again onto the tray.

"Fred Colby was enjoying the warm sun. He'd had a few cans of beer and decided to go fishing. It was the first Saturday he'd had off work for months. The kids were at a birthday party. He wouldn't be pestered with them. The day was his to do as he pleased. He whistled happily as he walked down the main street, jauntily swinging his fishing rod over his shoulder. He was determined nothing would interfere with his day off."

A yell and a crash from the sheriff's office brought him out of his happy mood with a jolt. Running into the office, he shouted.

"You okay Al... Al where are you?"

Al was scrambling up off the floor. His chair overturned.

"Jesus Christ! That was some dream Fred!" He was visibly shaking.

"I dreamt I was burning. I could feel the bloody flames, I could feel them." He examined his hands and arms, then looked in the mirror at his face. "I could feel them Fred, I swear it."

Fred poured Al a coffee, adding a drop of brandy. Righting the cha
he insisted that he sit down. "You alright Al. Do you want me to g
Jeff?"

"No. No. I'm okay. Thanks for the coffee Fred."

He looked at the man's anxious face, realising that he had upset him.

"I am okay Fred, a stupid dream, that's all... Just seemed so real...
Know what I mean?"

"Fred nodded unconvinced. He didn't know what Al meant. All the
time he had known Al, he had never seen him so terrified. In fact, he'd
seen Al upset, he'd seen him angry. He had never seen him terrified. It
unnerved him. He left, deciding maybe he wouldn't go fishing after all.
Maybe he would just go check on the kids."

Al sat for a while, looking at his trembling hands. It was a long time
since he had dreamt of those ovens... why now?

Glancing at the skull, an unexpected flash of fear ran through him.

The hair on the back of his neck bristled. Angrily he picked up the
diary and went outside on to the veranda. He was allowing a bad dream
and an old fossil to give him the jitters.

He sat down on the wooden bench, lit a cigar and started flicking
through the diary, hoping to find something, anything that might throw
a light on the strange deaths. He felt like an intruder reading the old
man's most personal thoughts. The diary went back years, he skipped
most of it deciding the past would not be relevant to what had
happened out there last Monday. That's when Mac had placed the date
of Pop's death.

A photograph fluttered to the ground. Al retrieved it studying it as he
did so. A knowing smile creased his face. The photograph showed Sam
wearing a pair of Bugs Bunny ears and urinating into the gas tank of
Al's car.

"So it **was** those two juvenile old codgers who had done it!" The
writing on the back of the photograph was indistinct, but he could see
the date, Xmas 65.

"I always suspected it was those two reprobates. That was for locking
the two drunken old fools up for a few hours a couple of days before
Christmas."

Carefully, he replaced the photograph and turned the page, reading
quickly until he reached the last pages.

Any feelings of guilt he had, left him. He read them. Then read them
again.

'May 6th Sat. Had a bloody awful nightmare last night. Dreamt I was trapped in my coffin, being cremated alive. Then suddenly, I was in the mine burning, I could feel the pain. Odd thing is, I've always had a fear of being buried alive in my coffin and of being caught in a fire in the mine. Must be preying on my mind. Or maybe it's the mine itself. There's a strange atmosphere in there. Maybe I'm just getting fanciful in my old age.'

'May 7th Sun. Same dream. So real. I wake up expecting to find the flesh burnt off my body. I pissed the bed. Can't believe it. Truck won't start. Transmitter won't work. I'm shit scared.'

'May 8th Mon. Same nightmare. Not normal dreaming of burning every night. Must be going crazy. I swear there's something in the mine. Something dangerous, evil. Watching me. Pissed the bed again. Never did that, not even when I was drunk. Feel ill. Drained. I think I'm going to die.'

Al snapped the book closed, an angry expression on his face. He'd never known Pop to be scared of anything. Someone had terrorised the old timer before killing him. "But I'll get you," he vowed. (Pop dreamt of burning and he did burn to death. He had dreamt of burning.) He felt the hairs stand up on the back of his neck again.

"The transmitter... Jeff used it... it was working."

"Hold it Al," he said to himself. "You're letting this whole thing spook you."

He thought of Mike. Solid, down to earth Mike. He went into his office and phoned him, arranging to meet him in Charlie's that evening.

Charlie's Bar was the closest attempt at night life that Caplin had to offer. A one room affair with a large bar, a scattering of tables and chairs and a small area for dancing, for those so inclined.

Soft country music was provided by a pianist and guitarist.

"Someday," Charlie was insisting. "I'll invest in a juke box. That'll bring more of the kids in, maybe even encourage them to stay in Caplin. An awful lot of them take off for the city bright lights as soon as they are old enough."

The small group of men around the bar laughed. "You're just after more money in your till Charlie," one of them guffawed.

Charlie was insulted. "No I'm not. I'm thinking of Caplin. You should be. Caplin is going to have to move with the times or die a slow death."

"There ain't nothing wrong with Caplin," said another man quietly.

"We like it just the way it is. I hope nothing ever changes it."

Charlie moved away, bored with the conversation. The sheriff and Mike Mallory had walked in. He served them and watched them seat themselves in a quiet corner. "Too bad," he muttered to himself. "I might have been included in some decent conversation for a change."

When they were both seated, Al told Mike about the dream and showed him the diary. Mike read the last entries and closed the book with a puzzled look on his face.

"I fell asleep in the garden this afternoon Al, and I dreamt I was burning, Ralph had a similar dream also."

Al stared at him. "What the hell is going on. This is all too much to be coincidence."

Mike nodded his agreement. "Tell me. What did you think of that gold skull."

Al studied Mike's face before answering. "Frankly, it gave me the creeps, Jeff wasn't too happy with it either. I found him scrubbing his hands after handling it. What did you think of it?"

"Much the same as you and Jeff. I think it might be a good idea to have it examined."

Al shrugged his shoulders. "I'll see to it first thing in the morning, though I can't see what help it will be."

They sat for a couple of hours talking, neither of them making any sense of the deaths or dreams.

Just after ten, Mike drank off. "I have to go now Al, I promised Ralph I'd have a night-cap with him. By the way, I told him everything."

Al nodded and waived any need for apology or explanation away, he knew Ralph well enough to know that the man would keep his own council.

Mike was half way to the door when a disturbance at the bar brought him to a halt. A man who had been getting steadily drunk during the evening was thumping the bar demanding more drink.

Al groaned. "Every town has to have its drunk, Ed Burns is ours. Go home Mike, I can deal with this idiot."

Walking over to the bar, Al grabbed the man by his collar and effortlessly swung him across the room and out on to the street. Mike followed with a grin on his face. "Remind me never to get on the wrong side of you, Al," he said eyeing the drunk, who had decided any resistance would be a waste of time and seemed to be dangling limply from Al's powerful grip.

"I'm sure you won't Mike. I'll throw him in a cell for the night to sleep it off, then I think I will turn in as well, it's been a hell of a day." He walked away with a wave dragging the offender with him.

Reaching the office, he pulled Ed inside. Jeff looked up from the book he was reading, a frown on his face.

"Hell and damnation Ed, don't you ever learn?" Jeff's tone was good natured in spite of the frown. Ed gave a sheepish grin in return and would have fallen, but for Al's grip.

"Let the fool sober up here Jeff, we'll let him out in the morning." Giving Ed a friendly cautioning look, Al left.

Jeff looked in on Ed who was now sulking in a corner of the cell.

"I'm not going to sleep," he said, giving the deputy a baleful look.

"Please yourself." Jeff answered, amused at the change in him. "Just so long as you're quiet." He went back to reading his book. At midnight he put it down, rubbing his eyes. It was pretty heavy reading. "Nuclear Threshold". Not a subject he enjoyed but one he felt he should know something of. He stretched his long limbs, enjoying the sensation, looking forward to being relieved at one. "I'm going to check on the streets Ed," he called, getting out of the chair. No answer. He put his head around the cell door. Ed was asleep. The man was moaning as if in a bad dream.

Jeff chuckled. "Serves him right for drinking too much."

He went out locking the door behind him."

The skull rose slowly, high enough to see through the window. It watched until the deputy was out of sight. Turning, it moved into the back room where the remains of its victims had lain and stopped in front of a small window, checking again that there was no one in sight. It began to glow, muted at first, then stronger until it was a vivid turquoise. It directed a beam of light at the window. Seconds later, strands of liquefied glass flowed downward scorching the framework. The skull floated through the opening and moved towards the main street and the unsuspecting townsfolk. The drunk held no interest for the skull but the pulsating life of the town was like the inexorable pull of a magnet to the skull.

A surge of anticipation passed through it arousing its lust.

Staying in the shadows, the skull slowly drifted down the street, filled with a craving for strength and knowledge and eagerly went in search of both."

"The young man guided his girlfriend into a darkened alley. He had been plying her with drink all night. Drink he had persuaded his older brother to purchase for him. This time he hoped she would be willing. He held her close, kissing her gently at first, then with passion.

"No Pete. No." She moaned the words in unconvincing rejection.

"Oh, come on Sal. I need you. I love you." Undoing her blouse, he slipped a hand inside her bra. She moaned again. Working his way down her throat with his lips, he caught the now exposed breast in his mouth, flicking his tongue over the nipple until it became deliciously erect.

She trembled, pressing closer to him. Resistance replaced by the wild desire of youth.

Tugging at the zip of her shorts, he placed a hand inside feeling the muscles of her stomach quiver and he knew she was his.

Sliding to the ground, he dragged the restricting clothes from her body. Feverishly pulling off his own clothes so that he could feel her warm nakedness next to his skin.

"Oh God Sal, you're beautiful."

As he entered her, the girl moaned in ecstasy.

"Oh Pete. Pete. I can see light and my eyes are closed. Will the earth move for me too? Is everything I've read about it true?" She smiled in pure delight at the thought.

Vaguely she became aware of the light becoming brighter, of a warm tingling on her face. She sighed happily.

The warm glow became hot. It was burning her. She opened her eyes and saw the skull hovering, glowing menacingly above them.

Pete felt the tension rip through her body, she became rigid.

"Am I hurting y......."

He saw the look of happiness on her face change to sheer horror and turned his head to see the cause, hoping to God it wasn't her father. He froze in terror.

The skull, incensed at the life power that was emanating from the young couple, drew it into itself. Glowing with the surge of energy it was receiving. Its jaws were opened wide in a hideous parody of a smile. The smile grew wider as the youth, attempting to separate himself from the girl, found himself held captive in the vice-like grip of her now paralysed muscles. Red hot needles of pain passed into his groin. Panic gripped him. He slapped her face hard in an effort to free himself. The muscles of her throat suddenly relaxed. The scream was cut short by the twin lasers of white hot death aimed from the eyeless sockets of the skull. Incinerating them instantly. Fusing the two young lovers together in a permanent last embrace.

The skull hovered above the smouldering remains, savouring the strength it now felt.

{Humans are still quite primitive}. The thought amused it.

{But they are useful for providing the energy I need. Especially during their most... lustful moments. Soon I will have enough strength and knowledge to wreak my vengeance in full}

"The skull moved on. Clinging to the shadows of a house. An infant was crying loudly. It entered the house through an open window. A woman was seated on a settee, she too was crying. The skull probed her mind. She was wondering where her husband was at this time. Wondering if he was with that other woman.

Angry at such mundane thoughts, the skull shot a pale beam of light at her. The woman, startled at the sudden pain in her head, lay down and closed her eyes trying to put the unhappy thoughts out of her mind. The skull made its way upstairs unseen.

The infant stopped crying as the skull entered the bedroom.

It moved closer to the cot looking intently at the child's tear stained face. The child stared back curiously.

Cautiously, the skull probed the child's mind and was surprised to find that the babe not only knew of it's mother's distress, but also the cause.

{Mortals must lose their intelligence with age}, it thought with increasing contempt.

It sent out a small beam of light aimed at an object tied to the cot rails. The object moved and rattled. The child gurgled and held out it's chubby pink arms to the skull.

{You welcome me child? You welcome the embrace of Nemesis? For that, I may do you a favour this night child. I may preserve your intelligence for all eternity}.

The skull drew closer. Preparing to probe the child's mind deeper. Deep enough to destroy it.

The child's mood changed sensing danger, cowering back and whimpering, as the skull mercilessly approached it.

A sudden commotion downstairs... The man was back. They were shouting. Someone was running up the stairs. Filled with frustration, the skull fled through the open window out on to the street vehemently aiming a laser of light at a dog which disintegrated without a sound, leaving nothing but a smouldering heap of fur and bones.

Had the parents of the child not been so intent of verbally lashing each other, they might have noticed the extraordinary high temperature in the child's room... and the scorched rattle.

The skull moved on to the next house. A flickering of light showing through the window attracted its attention. It went eagerly towards it.

A man was slumped in a chair, mouth wide open, snoring loudly. The skull ignored the distasteful vision, it's interest caught by a small box in a corner of the room. {This must be television}.

People were moving on a screen. Carrying banners. They were protesting against nuclear tests. Calling for disarmament.

{What was a Nuclear Test. What do these strange words mean?}

The screen showed a nuclear test. The skull watched fascinated by the explosion and the deadly mushroom of cloud and fire that followed.

{This is what the man, Jeff was reading of. The humans actually possess this destructive power.}

It witnessed a bomb being dropped on a make believe city showing the mass destruction and... burning.

The skull could no longer contain its excitement. Glowing brighter and brighter. Gradually becoming a vivid turquoise.

The window exploded into a thousand blistering fragments, igniting the curtains and startling the man into wakefulness.

The skull was gone before the man could turn around.

Moving swiftly, the skull retraced it's path.

{Now I understand what I have absorbed from Jeff while he was reading.}

As it drew near the office, it could see Jeff in conversation with another man. The were stood on the veranda. Jeff walked away, the other man entered the building alone.

The skull waited a few moments, then slunk stealthily to the back window and slipped into the room.

"The relief deputy was on his knees examining the threads of now set glass adhered to the wall. He had seen the damaged window through the open door. He looked up as the skull entered and stared in mute horror at the thing hovering in front of him.

The burst of light hit him full in the face. He died before his almost headless body keeled over."

The skull floated over its sixth victim, into the main office and settled down on to the tray. It needed time to think of what it had learned tonight.

{It is possible I will not have to make the journey to Salem. Perhaps I shall have the ability to deal with all the hated mortals right from this very town using their own destructive nature as a means.

That would be a most befitting revenge.}

"Mike... Mike wake up... Wake up."

The words were reaching him through the searing inferno.

"Wake up Mike. Wake up."

41

Someone was shaking him by the shoulder.

"Oh God, I want to wake up... Let this be a dream... Oh God!..."

He sat up with a start. Ralph still gripping him by the shoulder.

"Are you okay, Mike?"

"Yes. Yes I'm alright now. What time is it?"

"It's six thirty." Ralph's voice sounded tense. "Al is on the phone, he needs to speak to you urgently."

Mike was instantly alert. "What's happened Ralph?"

Ralph gestured towards the door. "Al will explain it better."

The uneasy look on Ralph's face prompted Mike to move faster. Pulling a robe around him, he hurried to the phone.

"Hello Al... What's the problem?"

His face paled as he listened. "Three more deaths. Christ! I'll come over straight away."

He replaced the phone aware of Ralph watching his every move.

"What's going on Mike? I know you had the dream again. So did I. Mary too."

"I wish I knew Ralph... I'm going to get dressed."

Ralph was sat in a chair when Mike came down. He stared at him thoughtfully for a moment. (Was it his imagination... or had Ralph suddenly aged?).

He walked over to him placing a hand gently on his shoulder.

"You keep promising Mary that you'll take her to see her sister in San Diego Ralph. I really wish you would do it now."

"Maybe I'll do that Mike. And you. You be careful. Be very careful son."

Mike left.

He arrived at the Sheriff's office. Jeff, a couple of deputies and Mac were already there. The drunk was complaining loudly to be let out. Jeff walked over to the cell door, his face taut with anger. Mike didn't catch Jeff's words, but he heard Ed's voice plainly as the man retreated quickly into the back of the cell. "Okay, okay, no need to blow your top Jeff. I'll keep quiet. For a while anyway, but someone had better tell me what's going on."

Al led Mike into the back room and showed him the window, walking carefully around the area where the deputy had died.

"Mac had the bodies taken to the hospital. He's taking the dog himself. What's left of it."

Mike was puzzled. "What dog?"

Al sighed. He hadn't had much sleep. People were dying and he didn't know how, or who was responsible. For the first time in his life as a lawman, he felt out of his depth. He was angry, frustrated... and scared.

"Three people. A dog. A window and curtains. All burnt in the space of an hour or two."

Mike shook his head. "I just don't understand. What happened Al?"

"Jim Roley rang Jeff. He'd been ringing the station and got no response so he walked round. Ed had apparently woken up and wanted to go to the jon, when he got no response either, he started banging on the cell bars. By the time I got here, it was all hell and no notion. It was Roley's window and curtains that were set ablaze. He was lucky. That window must have been white hot."

"Didn't Ed see or hear anything?" Mike asked.

Al gave Mike a strange look and shook his head slowly. "No. He insists he was asleep. He had a nightmare about burning that's what woke him up. He says he had the same dream this afternoon when he fell asleep after finishing his shift. That's why he got drunk. Not that Ed needs an excuse for getting drunk."

Mike was acutely aware of the deathly hush in the room.

"Mac has rung the Californian Officials for a Medical Examiner. I think they will send the State Police in. Frankly, I'm not sure whether we need help from them or... or a psychiatrist." Al finally fell silent.

Mike distractedly ran a hand through his hair. "You should have rung me earlier Al."

"There was nothing you could do Mike. No sense in us both losing sleep, or didn't you get any. You don't look any better than I feel."

Mike shook his head, the look on his face telling Al everything.

"Where is the skull Al?"

"I've put it in my locker... Why?"

"Has it been there all night?" Mike persisted.

Al was beginning to look exasperated. "No, I put it there just before you came, it's been in the tray all night."

Mike examined the metal tray closely.

"Now look Mike." Al had a definite edge to his voice.

"I know that bloody thing give us the creeps but you can't seriously believe..."

"Al." Mike interrupted. "The tray is scorched."

Al gave the tray a cursory glance. "So there's a scorch mark. What does that prove? I could have left a cigar burning at sometime."

They faced each other. Tension and fear making them both angry.

"You don't leave cigars burning Al... Even if you did, there's no way you would leave them in the inventory tray."

43

He ran his fingers through his hair again, aware of the silent tension in the room. "I'm not going to argue Al. I've nothing tangible to argue with anymore than you have."

Mike deliberately eased off, they had enough on their hands without making matters worse by arguing.

"Come on Al, it's nearly eight, I'll buy you some breakfast."

"Yeah, you're right, Mike?" Al's voice sounded apologetic.

"A bit of fresh air and a bite to eat might help us both to think straight."

Al released Ed, cautioning him not to even think of leaving town. Ed had other thoughts. He had heard enough. He was getting out... but fast.

The skull curbed its anger at being locked away.

{For the moment I will permit the foolish mortals to think they have me under control. I must rest and... think.}

{I have learned a great deal through the night. Through television and the minds I have probed. Especially the one named Jeff. I now know that nuclear weaponry is the ultimate in death dealing warfare. I know that all the major powers have them and that these devices are even orbiting the earth in containers which the humans refer to as satellites.

So. The mortals are still violent, as they always were. Well I can make use of their violence. I will make use of their weapons. They will learn that I "Nemesis" am the supreme force.

Their puny armies will fall. Their cities will burn. They will learn that "Nemesis Goddess of Wrath, Retribution and Vengeance" is capable of turning their weapons against them.

Rebecca Allen will be avenged. I will be avenged. Then and only then will I be free to leave this accursed planet}"

S.J. MILLAR

Then thou scarest me with dreams,
and terrifiest me through visions."

Job vii, 14.

CHAPTER FOUR: S. J. MILLAR.

SUN MAY 14th SEISMOLOGY STATION.

Simon had completed a routine check on the instruments and was now relaxing quietly to the strains of his favourite music "Tchaikovsky's Swan Lake". He loved all this composer's music. He smiled as he remembered Mike's surprise on learning this. Closing his eyes, he allowed the music to drift over him filling his senses. The bleeper on the table would alert him to any activity on the seismographs.

The sudden ringing of the internal phone rudely shattered his peace.

Joe spoke the instant Simon picked up the receiver.

"Have you got the radio on Simon?"

The urgency in Joe's voice prompted Simon to turn the volume of his music down immediately. "No I haven't Joe. Is anything wrong?"

"Bad news I'm afraid." Joe continued. "They dug Pop Bailey out of his mine yesterday."

Simon took a deep breath. The weird sensation he had experienced the day before started again in the pit of his stomach. His skin crawled with pinpricks on apprehension. "What happened Joe? Did they give any details?"

"No, just that Pop hadn't showed up in Caplin when he was expected, so Ryan had taken a couple of men out to check on him. Simon, one of the men also died in an accident at the mine. No details on either incident, almost as if... they're deliberately keeping it quiet."

"I see." Simon answered quietly. "Thanks for telling me Joe, I'll give Mike a ring, maybe he will know more. I'll let you know if I find out what exactly happened."

He replaced the receiver, eyes automatically going to the graph.

The unease gripped him with a force.

"He thought of the sensation of heat he had felt when he had touched it. In the past, he had experienced premonitions. His mother had been a true psychic. She had tried to make him realise that he too had this special gift. That he should guard it, nurture it and learn how to use it wisely. Instead he had been afraid of it. Blocking it out of his mind.

Refusing to accept it. Now something was releasing that part of his psyche against his will and it scared him."

He rang the Richardsons, Mike was out. Ralph told him of the tragedies, his sombre voice emphasising the tension Simon could sense in him. He promised to ask Mike to ring him as soon as he came in.

Simon replaced the phone thoughtfully. The sense of impending danger alarming him. He picked up the phone again, this time to ring Al, then quickly changed his mind. He wasn't sure he could keep the alarm out of his voice and damn it... He didn't even know what was alarming him. (Maybe there's a perfectly logical explanation for these "accidents", Don't go jumping to conclusions Simon, be patient, wait for Mike to ring you.)

Closing his eyes, he went through the mental relaxation exercises his mother had insisted on teaching him years ago. Slowly his panic subsided. He lay back in a lounger and soon began to feel relaxed enough to drift into a light sleep.

The sudden ringing of the phone set his nerve endings tingling again. It was Mike.

Mike gave him the details, quickly and quietly.

When he finally fell silent Simon spoke, carefully trying to hide the tension in his voice. "This may not make any sense to you, but I have been receiving bad vibes ever since I touched that graph... Mike I think I should come to Caplin."

"No Simon, we cannot leave the station unmanned, but I want you to ring Boston and delay Millar's arrival."

"Too late Mike, Millar is arriving today."

"Blast!... Well there's nothing we can do about that, but all the more reason why you should stay where you are. As for making sense. That, it seems has deserted us at the moment. I'll keep you in touch Simon. Bye."

Around noon, Simon heard a car pull up and looked out of the window in time to see a woman emerging from a blue sedan. His eyebrows arched in surprise. "We're a little off the beaten track for visitors."

He reached the foyer just as she was mounting the steps.

"Hello there," he said pleasantly. "Are you lost?"

She looked up at him, smiling. "I don't think so. This is the Utah Seismology Station isn't it?"

"It certainly is." Simon answered, puzzlement raising the pitch of his voice slightly.

47

She held out her hand to him. "My name is Millar. Susan Jane Millar. I believe you are expecting me."

Simon extended his hand. The look of pure amazement causing a comical expression on his face.

The moment his hand made contact with hers... his mind reeled dizzily. The heat from her touch seared his hand. In seconds he knew she was in great danger. (Dear God. What is happening to me?)

It was the fleeting but crystal clear vision of a young Indian standing protectively close to her that shocked him most.

He released her hand quickly, glancing at his palm. When he raised his eyes to her, everything was normal.

"Are you alright?" she asked, alarm showing on her face.

He nodded, struggling to recover his composure. "Yes, yes... A little too much sun I think. Please forgive me. Do come in. You must be exhausted after travelling so far."

"I am a little tired and I'm longing for a shower."

Simon took her through to the living quarters, which thanks to Joe were looking quite respectable. "This is the lounge. I'll show you to your room where you can shower and change if you wish, and then join me in here for a drink. Unless of course you would like to rest?"

"Oh no," she protested with a smile. "I would love a drink. In fact a nice cold beer would be most welcome."

Simon returned the smile. "I know exactly what you mean."

"He was appraising her while talking, deciding she was probably in her late twenties. She stood about five foot six, less without the high heels he thought, slim but not thin and quite an attractive face. But her hair and eyes were without doubt the most beautiful he had ever seen. Her long hair was the colour of a glorious sunset. Red-gold with highlights that resembled flames (Why did I think of flames?) when the sun's rays caught it.

Her eyes... She had the greenest eyes... Like deep emerald pools. Eyes a man could drown in... Or die for."

"Well Mike," he thought. "S.J.Millar most certainly was not a man."

"Simon left her and returned to the lounge examining the palm of his hand as he walked. It was perfectly normal, yet the heat he had experienced should have left it blistered. Pouring himself a beer, he sat down thinking of the scene on the steps, wishing Mike was here. He desperately needed to talk."

"He thought of the heat when he touched the graph. Five people burned to death. The heat and sense of impending danger when he had touched Susan, but it was the vision that had the most impact. The young Indian who had stood so close to her as if to protect her...

But from what was he protecting her?

All this disturbed him greatly. Two things he knew instinctively.

That the Indian existed and he, Simon could trust him with his life."

Susan walked into the room looking fresher and cooler having changed into a loose cotton dress for comfort. "Hello," she said shyly.

Simon rose to his feet, realising he had not introduced himself.

"What must you think of me. I am Simon Kane, second in command to Mike Mallory, who unfortunately is on vacation. You will meet him in two weeks, or perhaps I will take you through to Caplin to meet him."

He poured her a drink and another for himself and they sat down.

"Did you receive my message saying I was arriving earlier?" she queried.

"Yes I did. I received it yesterday," he assured her.

"Oh... Then may I ask why you looked so shocked out there?"

Simon had already thought of a plausible answer, having anticipated the question. "Ah, I can explain that easily. The truth is, we were expecting a man, so you can imagine my surprise when you turned up on my doorstep."

She smiled. "I see. You had such a look of horror on your face, I thought there must be something terribly wrong. Tell me. Am I so horrifying?"

He gave her a warm smile. "On the contrary. You are the most delightful person to walk through these doors since I have been here."

She flushed with pleasure at the compliment.

"Come along, I will show you around and introduce you to Joe, I'm sure you and he will get along just fine. Incidentally, do you play cards Susan?"

"Not very well I'm afraid." She smiled again.

(She has a beautiful smile.) Simon laughed. "Now I'm sure you and he will get along fine."

He showed her the observatory, only briefly explaining the instruments as he knew she would have been training on similar. He then took her to the leisure areas and finally he introduced her to Joe.

Joe was delighted. "It's a real pleasure to have you here Susan. This place has always lacked a little feminine charm."

Susan laughed. "Maybe I should have phoned instead of sending a telegram, that way you would have known."

"And spoil a pleasant surprise like this? Not at all." he beamed.

Simon suspected with some amusement that she had planned a

certain element of surprise. (A little female stratagem. No matter.)

Joe turned to him. "That reminds me. I can't get transmission on either the television or radio. Nothing but static."

Simon frowned. (Coincidence... Perhaps... Perhaps not.)

"Nothing serious I hope." Susan asked, breaking into Simon's thoughts.

"No... probably nothing more than a sandstorm." Simon answered quickly. (Then why does this news make me nervous?) "It's happened before. Now I'm sure you must be quite hungry Susan."

"To be truthful, I'm ravenous." She rolled her eyes in emphasis. Joe pretended mock horror. "I can't allow that, I'll go make us all a snack and bring it to the conservatory."

"What are the cooking arrangements?" Susan asked as Simon led the way to the conservatory. "I imagine you have some sort of agreement between you."

"We have a good breakfast and evening meal with a snack at lunch time. And we all cook. It comes with the job," he added with a smile.

They entered the conservatory. It was a large pleasant airy room with a magnificent panoramic view of the desert.

Susan walked slowly towards the window which took up an entire wall. Simon followed, noticing a distinct change of mood in her.

"The room faces west Susan. You can watch a spectacular sunset from here." Simon informed her.

She nodded appreciatively, allowing her eyes to take in the expanse of the desert. "A person could disappear out there and never be seen again, couldn't they?" She murmured almost to herself.

(That was an odd remark.) Simon thought but remained silent.

She leaned against the window, silently staring outward.

"So, what made you choose this station Susan? I'm sure the company offered you several choices."

She pressed her forehead on to the window as if trying to see further.

"You are right," she eventually answered. "I had a choice of Seattle, Phoenix or... here. I'm not really sure why I chose Utah... Relatives of mine came to this area around 1693. No more was heard of them."

Her gaze remained on the desert, a faraway expression on her face. Her eyes appeared to be focused on some distant horizon only she could see.

"I don't know what possessed me to think that I could possibly trace them. I don't even know why I want to trace them, but I have this... This compelling urge to try."

Simon watched her closely. She seemed to be speaking more to

50

herself now than to him. The expression in her eyes had changed. As if there was some inner conflict distracting her."

She fell silent, still staring out of the window.

"Well, if I can assist you in any way, I will." Simon spoke quietly, so as not to break the trance-like state of mind that seemed to have possessed her.

"What do you know of your ancestors Susan? How many were there? Did they have the same surname as you?"

(You're hurling too many questions at her, being too eager Simon. Be patient. Be careful.)

"Yes, they had the same name. He was my father's great great grandfather. He was Martyn Millar, he brought his daughter Sarah here. Just the two of them."

She fell into the dreamlike silence again.

"Where did they travel from?" he prompted.

"They travelled from Salem, Massachusetts." Silence again.

"That was an extremely long and dangerous journey. There must have been a purpose behind it... Did they travel alone?"

She turned away from the window, a slight frown creasing her brow. The faraway look on her face was rapidly fading.

"Yes, I believe they did travel alone."

"Tell me," Simon persisted... "Why did they make such a journey?"

"I don't know." Her voice had an irritable edge to it now.

He ignored it. "There must have bee an urgent reason. A journey like that in those days would have taken months. Probably more than a year."

"I really don't know why they came here Mr Kane." She walked quickly away from the window, aggitation creasing her brow. The door opened and Joe breezed in.

"Here we are. Salad, fresh fruit, breadrolls and tea or coffee."

Susan gave a small nervous laugh, welcoming the interruption. "If this is a snack, what are the main meals like Joe?"

Joe gave her a pleased smile managing to ignore the tension he could feel in the room. "We eat well here Susan. I hope you're not one of those dieters."

She visibly relaxed, returning the smile, "You can rest assured Joe, I have a very healthy appetite."

While they ate, Joe kept a light conversation going, encouraging Susan to join in. Easing the tension.

She hadn't liked Simon's questions. She made no attempt to speak to him.

51

The meal finished, Simon rose to his feet. "I'm going back to the observatory, I have some work to complete. Would you care to join me Susan?"

"No... No thank you Simon."

(She answered a little too quickly) Joe thought.

"If you don't mind, I would like to rest. I feel quite exhausted."

Simon decided not to pressure her, he felt he had already pushed a little too hard. (I'll get a better response from her when she has rested.) They walked out together propelling the trolley in front of them. Joe followed in silence.

Susan gave them both a brief smile. "I'll only need to rest for a couple of hours, then I'll be refreshed." She made her way quickly to her room.

Joe waited until she was out of earshot before voicing his thoughts.

"She seemed awful tense when I came in Simon. You been giving her a hard time?"

Simon looked worried. "You know me better Joe. This trouble in Caplin is going to affect all of us. I can feel it. Maybe the lady more than anyone. I have to learn all I can about her."

"Joe watched Simon walk away, a thoughtful expression on his face. He took the trolley into the kitchen and started clearing it, thinking of all Simon had told him. He was right, he did know him better. He knew Mike and Simon better than anyone. That's how he knew Simon hadn't told him everything. More than that. Simon was afraid, and that unnerved him."

They had the main meal at eight. Simon made this with the hopeful intention of placing Susan in a mellow mood.

He had excelled himself. He knew how to create a variety of mouth watering garnished steak dishes. The kind a top chef would envy.

His father had been an imaginative cook and had taught Simon well. Lighted candles on the table and two good bottles of wine completed the setting. They had eaten in the conservatory, allowing Susan to watch the sunset.

She relaxed back in her chair with a small sigh of contentment.

"That was the most delicious meal I have tasted for quite some time." She smiled as she sipped her wine. "Thank you Simon, and you were right, the sunset was spectacular."

"I'm delighted you enjoyed both." Simon said quietly. He turned to Joe. "Susan is hoping to trace her long lost relatives here Joe."

"Oh really?" Joe leaned forward. "Do you know their last

52

whereabouts?"

"No, but that shouldn't be too hard to find out." She answered in a soft voice. The faraway look returning to her face. Joe was startled by the sudden change, but a warning look from Simon prompted him to continue speaking in a casual manner.

"Why do you say that Susan?" he asked.

She sat dreamily toying with the glass, her face expressionless....

"He was a witch hunter. People like that tend to leave their mark, don't they... He was a witch hunter... He put people to death by burning." The pitch of her voice had lowered to a scarcely audible whisper.....

"But then you knew that didn't you?" Her mood had changed again, addressing Simon so sharply, she startled both men. "That is why you were asking me all those questions."

There was no faraway look now. Her eyes were alert and demanding.

"No Susan, I didn't know. Please believe me. There are incidents occurring here that make it vital for me to know everything about you."

She rose to her feet, a deepening flush spreading over her face.

"Please don't be upset." Simon stood, taking her hands in his. "It is important that you trust me and tell me all you know of your ancestors and yourself."

"Why should I?" she demanded, trying to release her hands from his grip.

"I can't explain why to you, not yet. I need you to trust me Susan. As a stranger, I know I'm asking an awful lot. Please... please try."

She stared at him distractedly, then slowly sat down. Simon sat beside her still holding her hands.

"I'm sorry. I'm sure you are a person I can trust and God knows, I need to talk to someone I can trust."

She gently removed her hands from Simon's, gazing at him in silence for a while as if trying to gather her thoughts.

"Until a week ago, I was going to Phoenix. Two weeks ago I began having dreams. Odd dreams of Sarah Millar and two other people whose names I cannot remember, but they were connected with this place, or at least with the Salt Lake Desert. Then I had this incredible urge to come here. I had a difficult time in Boston convincing them that I needed to work at this station. Arrangements had already been made for me to travel to Phoenix. I couldn't even offer them a logical reason for my change of mind. They thought I was crazy." She took a sip of her wine. "I had never given my ancestors a thought until I started with the dreams. I've had no cause to. I scarcely know anything about Martyn and Sarah Millar. All I do know is that Martyn Millar was cursed by one of the people he had burned at the stake. That his daughter became a victim of this curse. He brought her here in the hope of saving her. Why I don't know. What possessed him to think that this place could possibly cure her, I don't know either." She gave the two men a beseeching look. "He must have loved her a great deal to travel such a distance in those days. He <u>cannot</u> have been all bad. There must have been a great deal of good in him. The journey alone must have been enough to kill them. Maybe it did. Maybe they both died out there."

She swept her arm towards the desert. "My fear is... I don't know if my dreams were a portent to bring me here or... or a warning to stay away. Since I have been here... even though it is such a short time... I feel it is the latter." She lapsed into an exhausted silence.

Simon was disturbed by what she had told them. He could see her bewilderment, her fear and felt a surge of sympathy and an even stronger desire to protect her. On no account he decided, would he allow her to see how much her words did disturb him. Until he knew exactly what was happening, he would somehow have to allay her fears.

She sat quietly watching him. Waiting for him to say something. Anything that would dispel her unease.

"Thank you for trusting me Susan. I am sure no relative of yours could possibly be bad. To even consider making such a journey must have taken a great deal of courage." He gave her a reassuring smile.

"They probably have nothing to do with circumstances here." He was relieved when she didn't question the circumstances he was referring to and pressed on before she could think to do so.

"As for your dreams, they are more than likely caused by tales you were told as a child. Tales told so long ago that you have forgotten. Not that I am suggesting you are old." he added with a disarming smile. She gave a weak smile in response.

"We can ring Mike," he carried on with a lightness he did not feel, "and ask him to check the reference library for evidence of your relatives ever having been here. Or... I can take you into Caplin and you can check for yourself and meet Mike at the same time."

He knew he was making rash promises, but carried on.

"While you are here, you may as well see if you can dig up your ancestors... In a literary sense that is."

He laughed and Simon's laugh was infectious. This time, the responding smile was a little wider.

54

"Now," he continued, "Let's change the subject, clear the table and have a game of cards."

"I'd like that." Susan said with a grateful smile.

She studied the two men as they prepared everything for the game, including fresh drinks. She was no fool. Although Simon had made her feel a little easier, she was convinced he was holding something back from her. The episode on the steps wasn't because he was expecting a man. No way could that have produced the look of horror she had seen on his face. She also suspected he was as unsure of the meaning of her dreams as she herself was. (But then you haven't told him everything, have you?) The inner voice made her feel cold. (How could she? How could she explain that she had dreamed she had terrible powers. And not only had she dreamed of burning people, but she had actually taken pleasure from it... In her dreams that is. Perhaps she **was** crazy.)

She pushed the upsetting thought from her mind. She was no longer sure of anything in her life... Except... (Yes she had been right to confide in Simon... Maybe she would tell him about the dreams... Maybe.)

She suddenly realised that the two men were watching her. She smiled. "I hear you are a good card player Joe."

Joe laughed, relieved that she was back with them. She seemed to have retreated into her own world again for a while.

"Alright Simon, what have you been saying to this lady."

"Nothing but the truth Joe." Simon answered.

(My attempts to lighten her mood appear to be working, on the surface at least. I just wish I knew all that was on her mind.)

Simon poured himself another glass of wine and lit a cigar. He was alone now. Susan and Joe had bid him goodnight a short while ago.

"So! Susan's ancestor had been a witch-hunter. The kind of person who was probably the most feared and reviled of that era. I wonder what the connection is between Susan and this situation in Caplin. That there is a connection I have no doubt. That she is in danger, I have no doubt. Why has she come here? She is afraid, I'm sure of that. I have to persuade Boston to recall her on any pretext. Moral... Three men, one woman... Anything. Once she is away from here she will be safe from danger. Perhaps we all will be. Without doubt she is the centre of a maelstrom. Somehow I have to get her away, then I will be free to strengthen my own abilities to comprehend what so far seems to be incomprehensible."

Simon undressed and lay on the bed. He needed to rest, he knew he would not sleep. He had tried the telephone on the way to his room and received only static. No phone. No radio. No TV.

They were now cut off from the town. From the outside world. He had failed to reach Boston and he knew it wasn't due to weather conditions. He was nervous. His senses were screaming danger.

At first light he would ask Joe to set up the transmitter.... Something they reserved for emergencies.

THE INDIAN

This is the happy warrior. "This is he...."

Herbert Read. (The Happy Warrior)

CHAPTER FIVE: THE INDIAN

CAPLIN SUNDAY MAY 14th

Mike and Al left the cafe, breakfast had consisted of toast and several black coffees. Al had dismissed the idea that the skull was responsible. Mike was convinced otherwise. Problem was, he had nothing concrete to convince Al with, only a gut feeling.

"I'm going back to Ralph's for a shower. See you at the office in about an hour Al."

"Okay Mike, I'll go prepare for the M.E. See you later. And Mike... keep your ideas to yourself... for the time being."

Al gave a tired wave as he walked off in the opposite direction.

Ralph met Mike in the doorway. "Simon rang five minutes ago. He has heard of the deaths of Sam and the police officer on the radio."

Mike groaned. "Damn it... I should have rung him."

"I had a word with him." Ralph assured Mike. "I told him what happened last night. I also told him you would ring him back."

"Thanks a lot Ralph. I'll have a quick shower first."

"By the way." Ralph called after Mike as he was climbing the stairs. "What you said about San Diego. We are going tonight."

Mike stopped in mid-stride. "I'm glad Ralph. More glad than you know."

"I don't suppose I can persuade you to come with us?" Ralph persisted.

Mike shook his head. "I really wish you could, but I have to stay, don't ask me why, but I know I have to stay."

"He felt better after the shower and lay on the bed, a towel wrapped around him. He was relieved that Ralph and Mary were leaving, he wanted them out of the way. He wanted them... safe. He frowned at the word. Safe... safe from... who... what?

"The warm sun was caressing him through the window, easing the tension from his body. His eyelids drooped.

....

He sat with his nose pressed against the car window watching the fields and trees flashing by in a whirl of colour. His parents were

58

singing as they always did when going on vacation.

"Sing out Mike," his father called over his shoulder as he lead them with his rich baritone voice. His mother turned her head towards him. He saw her reflection in the window and turned to face her, a happy smile lighting his face. She was laughing and singing at the same time. (How he loved her.)"

"He saw the gas tanker swerve across the road out of control seconds before it struck them. It all happened so fast. He didn't even have a chance to call out a warning."

"Somehow he was thrown clear. He couldn't understand how. His mother's agonised screams pierced his numbed brain. Staggering to his feet, he turned in horror towards the blazing car, choking on smoke and fumes... "Have to reach my parents."

The words were torn from him in terrorised sobs. He fought desperately to reach them. The flames entwined him. He was engulfed in the searing fire.

"Mom... Mom... MOM." No one heard his screams.

"Shiiiit!" Mike sat bolt upright on the bed. Fear making him shake with cold in spite of the warm sun.

"Damn... Damn... Damn." He pounded the edge of the bed with his fist. Painful memories of his parents' death tearing him apart again.

Anger took place of fear.

"What... is... happening? There has to be an explanation."

"You have a brain man. Use it."

Still shaking, he dressed and rang Simon. He sensed the disquiet in his friend as they spoke and was more than a little dismayed to hear that Millar was arriving today.

Replacing the receiver, he wandered into the garden deep in thought.

"What was happening in Caplin. How could it possibly be affecting Simon. There has to be a connection between the graph, the dreams and the deaths."

He paced up and down the garden muttering to himself.

"A common factor. The skull must have been in the mine when Pop died. It was near Cal when he died. It's in the town now. The victims were burned in the same manner. It has to be the link... the skull has to be..."

"Excuse me sir...."

"What..." Mike spun around frowning at the intrusion to his thoughts. He stared at the owner of the voice.

An Indian youth stood at the gate, both arms folded across his chest.

"Who the hell are you..." Mike bit back his words. "No cause for taking your aggravation out of a total stranger."

"May I speak to you sir?"

Mike made a conscious effort to hide the irritation he felt as he walked to the gate.

"The young man was tall with a proud face, eagle sharp discerning eyes and a strong jaw line. Characteristics that belonged to a much older person, yet Mike judged him to be about seventeen."

"You are Mr Mallory sir?"

"Yes I am. How can I help you?"

The youth gave a strange cognitive smile. "For the moment Mr Mallory, I think it may well be the other way around."

He smiled again at the puzzled frown.

"My Great Great Great Grandfather wishes to speak to you. You would be well advised to listen to him."

Mike stared at him in silent annoyance. (What the hell...)

"You and others are having dreams of burning." The youth carried on speaking, ignoring the growing impatience in Mike's eyes. "Your people are dying in a horrifying manner. Is this not true?"

The expression on Mike's face changed. He moved closer to the Indian.

"Yes it is true. What the devil do you kn...."

"Mr Mallory." The young Indian interrupted. "Time is not to be wasted. You are in need of enlightenment. Come... Now."

(That sounds more like a command than a request.) Mike thought to himself. "Where is your...."

"Grandfather will suffice." Mike was interrupted again. "We will dispense with formality. He is at the Indian Settlement on the outskirts of town." He paused adding significantly. "Time **is** vital Mr Mallory."

(There was something about this young man... something that...)

"I'll get my car." Mike said coming to a decision in seconds in spite of disliking the youth's abrupt attitude. He drew up alongside the youth, studying him as he seated himself in the car, glancing down at the strong looking bare feet.

"I ran here." he explained before Mike could make any comment.

Giving directions in the same short, curt manner, he settled back in the seat, arms again folded across his chest.

"My name's Mike. What's yours?" Mike asked, full of curiosity.

"Steve." came the short reply.

Mike gave him a sidelong glance.

The youth smiled. "Steve is my English name."

There was a strange quality about the smile. It reminded Mike of something... (What was it... The Mona Lisa... Yes, that was it.)

"Do you know why your grandfather wishes to speak to <u>me</u> Steve?"

"He is the one who will relate his words. I am the one who will translate."

The youth lapsed into silence again, staring unsmiling through the windscreen.

"You don't speak very much, do you?"

(In fact you are damned hard work.)

The young Indian gave him a strange look, one that caused Mike to wonder if he had spoken his thoughts aloud.

"I speak when necessary, I do not waste words."

"Then tell me, what do you know of these deaths Steve... or do you consider that a waste."

"Have patience, Mike Mallory." The voice was firm and authoritative.

Mike gave an irritable snort, but said nothing more.

"It took about twenty minutes to reach the Indian Settlement, which consisted of one large and several smaller wooden buildings, surrounded by a scattering of wigwams. A group of men were gathered outside the large building, talking excitedly."

Mike's relief at arriving there, quickly turned to dismay.

"A silence descended over the gathering, all eyes were upon him. These men didn't look too friendly, in fact they looked decidedly hostile towards him when he stepped out of the car. They prepared to bar his path as he followed the youth towards the entrance of the larger building. His impassive escort cast an unfathomable glance over the crowd. To Mike's relief and surprise, the men separated allowing them access with a look of fearful reverence on their faces."

Not for the first time, Mike wondered who this strange young man was. He looked over his shoulder as they neared the entrance. The hate he saw mirrored in their faces made him ponder the wisdom of being alone.

"They entered the large building. There were no seats but on either side of the doorway, were neat piles of woven mats. Steve took two of these, passing one to Mike. They walked further into the dimly lit sanctum. It took a few moments for Mike's eyes to adjust to the change in light. When they did, he saw an incredibly old Indian sat cross-legged in the middle of the floor, both eyes closed as if in sleep."

They approached him in silence, Steve motioning Mike to be seated, he also sat and whispered, "Now we must be patient."

"Mike looked surreptitiously at his surroundings. He found it difficult to see in the dim light, but could make out a Totem Pole surrounded by artefacts at the far end of the room. He was in no doubt that the artefacts were relics of a bygone age, when the Indians reigned over this country. He felt a twinge of guilt for the past and turned his head away from the reminders. His eyes met Steve's penetrating gaze. He had the uneasy feeling that this young man could read his thoughts."

(I must be getting paranoid) he thought, blaming it on the tense situation in town and trying hard to relax. He glanced at his watch. Twenty minutes had passed. He was uncomfortably aware of the young Indian's scrutiny of him and wished the old man would open his eyes. When finally he did, Steve offered his left hand to the old man motioning Mike to do likewise.

The old man placed his hands on theirs, moving them so that they were one above the other held captive in his own hands, murmuring low incantations. He then spoke to Steve in his own tongue. Steve answered in the same. Turing to Mike, Steve spoke in English.

"My Grandfather welcomes you and trusts you will listen with an open heart and mind. You must remain silent while he relates what he has to say. No interruptions. No questions. Do you understand?"

"Yes, I understand Steve." Mike answered quietly.

He felt stirred by a deep respect for this old man who must have seen a great many changes in the lives of the Indian population. Once again, Mike sensed that the younger man could read his thoughts as he smiled his approval of Mike's response.

Steve set a hurricane lamp closer to his Grandfather, creating an eerie glow around the ancient Indian.

The old man drew a roll of ancient looking parchments from the folds of his garments.

Mike's eyes widened. (An historians delight. They must be a couple of hundred years old at the very least.)

Steve passed a pair of metal rimmed spectacles to his Grandfather. They looked strangely out of place in this archaic setting.

"The story starts," Steve translated, "Two hundred and eighty years ago. It tells of a white man and his daughter. The girl is sick in the mind. They are shunned by all. They travel from town to town, never staying long. All Indians keep watch over them so it is known at all times where they are. They do not go near them and are forbidden to kill them. They are taboo. Bad medicine."

"All white people are afraid of them. Strange, unexplained happenings occur when they are near others. People have dreams of burning. People die of burning. Some blame the Indians for this. The Palefaces are unaware that these burnings happen to our people also. They would not have believed it if told."

"The man and girl travel alone. One white man is unafraid. He searches for them. The Indians name him The Follower. Always he is seeking the whereabouts of the man and girl. This lasted for many suns and moons. The man and girl are heading for the Great Salt Lake, but the man is now sick, more sick than the girl. He has the face of one who is haunted and lives in torment. He becomes lost and dies."

"They have passed by the Great Lake."

"The girl has been passive for five suns. She is now ready to join the spirit of her father. She walks far into the desert and dies alone in a small cave. Indians who witness this inform medicine man.

Medicine man takes a party of braves to the cave and enters. The insects have already started feeding on the dead girl's body, but have not touched her head. Nor will they.

Medicine man is aware of bad presence. He knows girl's body is not alone. He has cave sealed and declares this a bad place. No Indian must go near it again."

"The Indians find the Follower at the lake. This man can speak with the tongue of the Indian. He asks about the man and girl. He names them Millar. No Indian will speak of them, they are forbidden."

"The Follower speaks with medicine man. He informs him that the girl is dangerous to all people. Even though she is dead, she is still possessed by evil. He insists he can contain the danger with a neck ornament."

"Medicine man is foolish. He kills the Follower and takes the neck ornament so that he is one with great power."

"Now. The evil is awake and walks this land once more. Leaving death and destruction in its wake."

"Believe this white man for it is the written truth."

The old man rolled the parchments, removed the spectacles and closed his eyes. He looked exhausted after the narration.

Mike exhaled deeply. He felt he had been holding his breath since the name Millar had been mentioned.

Steve turned to Mike. "The cave where the girl died and Bailey's mine are one and the same. If you have listened with your heart and mind, you will understand all that my grandfather has revealed to you and you will know the truth."

Mike was stunned. (Either I have totally **lost** my reason... or the old man is telling me that the burnings, in both deaths and dreams are being caused by a girl who died two hundred and eighty years ago.)

"It was incredible... Yet... he believed it... He instinctively believed the old man's story. "Why?" he asked himself. But he knew why. He believed it because... what was happening in town was incredible... Because he knew he was very much in full command of his senses. And... again the powerful feeling in his gut. One he couldn't ignore. All these thoughts crowded into Mike's mind."

"What exactly are we fighting Steve. If the girl was possessed, what kind of entity possessed her?"

"I do not know this answer my friend, except that it is evil in its purest form."

"Where is the neck ornament your Grandfather spoke of?"

"I do not know the answer to this question either. My grandfather does know the answer but he will not reveal it to me until he is on his death bed. It is tradition."

"We must leave now and let my grandfather rest."

"Your Grandfather must be persuaded to break with tradition Steve. This neck ornament sounds pretty vital."

"Leave my Grandfather to me Mike Mallory."

Mike accepted the rebuke. "Tell me. Has the skull that was found at the mine got anything to do with this?"

Steve's face hardened. "Yes Mike. It most certainly has. It is the girl's skull. The part of her that was possessed by evil. I only heard a short while ago that it was found and taken into town. That is what made it imperative for my grandfather to speak with you."

Mike stared at the young man. "Why me Steve? Why not the sheriff?"

"Because my friend. You and the dark man are the chosen ones."

"Do not ask me questions about that, Mike Mallory, for I still cannot answer you."

"Mike studied the young face. He had always prided himself on being a sound judge of character. The first time he had met Simon, it had been a mutual meeting of minds. When he had met Al, he knew there would always be a staunch alliance between them, and with Joe he knew he would always be there when needed. Now the same old gut feeling was telling him that he could trust this young Indian with his life."

An odd sensation took him by surprise.

"Not could... but... WILL."

A shiver of apprehension passed through his body. Briefly, he saw a flicker of response in the young man's eyes. Then it was gone.

Mike spoke again, more to cover the unease he was feeling.

"I believe the skull has the power of movement... Some sort of kinetic energy. I think the sooner we have it under lock and key, the better."

"I agree with you Mike." Steve replied. "But that could prove easier to say than to do."

They stepped outside. Mike, blinking back the glare of sunlight was about to ask Steve what he meant, when he became aware of the throng of Indians closing in on them, still looking unfriendly towards him.

"Do not be afraid," Steve said. "They will not harm you. Come. I will walk with you to your car."

Once again the men fell back as Steve approached them, some murmuring a word that Mike couldn't quite catch. It sounded like "omcharge".

Mike walked alongside Steve, passing between the sea of hostile faces. (Whoever this young man is, he certainly commands great respect. Maybe "Omcharge" is his name or position within the Indian settlement.)

They reached the car and faced each other.

"What will you do now?" Steve asked.

"I'm going back to the seismology station tomorrow. I need to speak to my friend Simon Kane. It's... hard to explain... I have only spoken to him once on the phone... about what is happening I mean... I feel he knows more than I do. Simon is... Simon is psychic... although he refuses to acknowledge it... even to himself. When I last spoke to him on the phone, I suspected he was being forced into accepting the gift. Simon has to be the dark man you spoke of."

Steve gave a smile of assurance which quickly disappeared at Mike's next words.

"The name your grandfather gave me. "Millar". A person by the name of Millar is arriving at the seismology station today. A little too much of a coincidence, don't you think?"

Steve's eyes narrowed. "Yes it is. You must send this person away Mike. Now."

"I will see to it first thing tomorrow."

"You do not disappoint me. You are thinking straight. That is good. You need this man Simon. I know you feel as if a great responsibility has been placed upon your shoulders, and indeed it has, but do not be afraid. You are not alone."

Before Mike could question this statement, the young Indian spoke again.

65

"Tell me Mike Mallory. Will you remember all that has been revealed to you this day?"

"Yes I will." Mike answered with confidence. "I have an excellent memory."

Mike was convinced that he felt Steve's eyes reach deep into his soul.

"This may well be the truth, but you also have an excellent recorder tucked inside your shirt."

The young Indian touched it with his forefinger, the strange smile illuminating his face.

"Now go Mike Mallory. I feel we shall meet again soon."

Mike headed for town, his mind reeling. A dozen questions each fighting for priority in his mind. Questions he wished he had asked Steve before he left the Indian settlement. At least he now knew that his suspicions about the skull were right. All he had to do now... was convince Al.

He could see a lot of activity as he approached the town. He soon saw the reason. The place was swarming with state police.

Al was sat in his office. He looked pale and drained. He jumped to his feet as Mike entered. "Where the hell have you been for godsake? Jeff had to go to Salt Lake and you decide to go missing."

Mike glanced at his watch, surprised to see that it was almost one o'clock. Before he could answer Al shouted again.

"There's been three more deaths, and apparently I am chief suspect."

"What? Calm down Al, and tell me what has happened."

Al sat down, a look of exasperation on his face. "I'm sorry Mike. I've no right to pounce on you. This isn't your problem."

"You're wrong Al." Mike's answer was quietly serious. "This is everyone's problem. We're all in danger, every last one of us. I've found that much out today. Now tell me exactly what has happened."

Al lit a cigar before speaking. "I decided to have the skull examined as you suggested Mike. Not because I thought it had any connection with the deaths as you do, but because it is the human remains of someone. It's the usual procedure. So as Jeff's not here I took it to Mac. After examining it, he told me that it was about two hundred and fifty years old and female. A young female. He couldn't say how the female had died. He also told me that the tests were not conclusive, that it would need extensive tests if I wanted anything in writing."

Mike waited patiently while Al took a long draw on his cigar.

"From the hospital, I went to Brian Wilkins' home. Mac's suggestion. He felt it would be of interest to him. You remember Wilkins. He was a

66

school teacher and keen geologist."

"Mike nodded, noting the fact that Al spoke of Wilkins in the past tense, but remained silent.

"Brian showed a great interest in it, placing the age at closer three hundred years because of the pyrite that had formed on it. God! He was so excited because it was perfectly preserved and intact. At first glance he said, Pop might have thought he had found gold, but an old hand like Pop would soon have realised exactly what it was. A human skull coated in pyrite, fools' gold. 'Fools' gold,' he said is also known as firestone. Capable of withstanding or striking fire."

Al looked significantly at Mike. "I've known you a long time Mike. You're not normally given to wild ideas. I still don't agree with you, but I think maybe you are close to the right track. That there possibly could be a connection. I think someone is trying to scare us. I think Pop discovered a great deal of gold and someone killed him for it. Cal probably caught whoever it was at the shack and they killed him also."

Mike shook his head. (Too many unanswered questions.) He didn't say anything. He let Al carry on.

"From Brian's place, I went to old Professor Adams."

"Mike thought of Adams. He was one of the world's leading anthropologists, a brilliant man who included folklore and religious beliefs in his studies. A man whose views were highly respected. Adams was now retired. A recluse who had little time for people and even less contact with them.

Al grimaced, took a long drink of water and lit another cigar.

"I'm smoking too much."

"Yes." Mike agreed gently, knowing his friend was under stress.

"Only with a great deal of persistence did I manage to persuade Adams to open the door. Even the delivery boy has to leave his groceries outside. The old chap continued berating me for invading his privacy until I took the skull out of the bag and told him where it had been found. Huh, he stopped going on at me, pretty damn quick. Then he beckoned me in and told me to sit down."

Al carried on speaking a sombre expression on his face. Re-living the scene in his mind, while he related it to Mike.

"Where did you find this?" The old man demanded, startling Al.

"I just told you. It was found at Bailey's mine." Al informed the professor again.

The old man glared at him. "Why have you brought it to me?"

Al patiently explained to the professor, missing nothing out.

67

"I see," the professor answered.

He unlocked a small cabinet and took out a book, seating himself and again telling Al to do likewise.

The professor read quietly for a while occasionally examining the skull. finally he took off his spectacles and stared at Al.

"Do you have any idea what you have brought with you?" he demanded.

Al shook his head, disturbed by the tone of the Professor's voice.

"You have brought with you... the very Devil out of Greek Mythology!"

Al felt the fear dance down his spine as the Professor continued to stare at him.

"You have brought... "Nemesis!...""

"I... I don't understand." Al struggled to keep the fear out of his voice. "Who is Nemesis?"

The Professor ignored the question.

"Professor there is obviously some story behind this skull. One that's being used to scare people. Who else would know about it?"

Professor Addams stared at him as if he were speaking in a foreign language, again ignoring the question.

"You must leave this skull with me."

"No!" Al jumped up from his seat, the action restoring the authority to his voice. "I can't do that. I have to take it back. The state police don't know I have it with me."

"The state police. Pah! They will be as ignorant of the evil past of this thing as you are, sheriff."

Al was ready to go. He'd heard enough.

"You must leave it with me." insisted the Professor. "You do not know what you are dealing with."

"Look Professor. I'll bring it back tonight along with Mike Mallory. He seems to think on the same lines as you, then you can explain to the both of us what this is all about, and hopefully you will be able to help us."

He took the skull from the Professor's reluctant hands and placed it in the bag. (Odd... It felt warm... The Professor must have been holding it tightly.) He left with the Professor's warning ringing in his ears.

"Bring Mike Mallory back with you by all means, he sounds a damn sight more intelligent than you. Do not allow that thing out of your sight, not even for a moment. Guard it well sheriff. Guard your life. Or it may well take it from you."

Al's mind came back to the present with a shudder.

"I went out to the car Mike and placed the bag on the passenger seat. I sat for a while with my eyes closed, resting my head on the steering wheel. The Professor had scared the hell out of me. That's when I heard the scream. The most terrible bloodcurdling scream coming from inside the Professor's house. I could smell the burning flesh before I entered the house. The poor old guy lay on he floor, burned almost beyond recognition. I was still standing there when the state officer came up behind me. Do you know what he said to me Mike?"

Al gave a dry humourless laugh. "He said. 'You certainly leave a trail of death behind you sheriff.'" Only when I was brought back here did I find out that Mac and Brian had both died in the same way."

"The skull was still in the bag on the car seat Mike, I checked... but it was hot... it was damned hot."

Al finally fell silent.

Mike poured two brandies passing one to Al. "And you still think a person is responsible for these deaths Al?"

"Two people Mike. One of them does the killing using a flame thrower, the other does something to the skull... something to make it hot. I think maybe they found more than gold. They want to scare people away from this town."

"Al... You're clutching at straws... you're not even making sense and you know it. I only need fault you on one thing. It's not possible to burn a person from the inside outward with a flame thrower."

Al averted his eyes. He knew he was clutching at straws. He had nothing else to clutch at.

"Was the skull left alone at any time after visiting Mac and Brian?" Mike asked this question knowing that the answer was going to be yes.

Al reluctantly nodded. "Both times. When I came away from the hospital, I saw Cal's wife Ann. I put the bag in the car and went to have a word with her. I stood maybe ten minutes or so. When I left Brian, I put the bag back into the car and lit a cigar. You know I hate smoking in the car. I walked into the park, again only for ten minutes, that's when I hit on the idea of trying to talk with Professor Adams."

Mike studied Al's face. "The state police don't seriously suspect you do they?" he asked.

Al sighed. "I don't think so. The very nature of the deaths rules that out, but they asked me a hulluva lot of questions. Can't say as I blame them. What about you Mike. Where have you been? What have you found out?"

Mike told him of his visit to the Indian settlement with Steve, then played the tape.

"Thanks to you and the late Professor 'God rest his soul' I also know what the entity is... It is Nemesis the Avenger..."

Al groaned. "Jesus Mike. This is getting crazier by the minute. The skull probably is the remains of the girl, but who or what is Nemesis?"

"In Greek Mythology Al." Mike explained. "Nemesis is the goddess of vengeance. I think the skull is possessed by Nemesis."

Al shook his head. "Than Adams was right."

"What do you mean?" Mike asked.

"He said I didn't know what I was dealing with and he was right, I don't know what I am dealing with. I'm trying to find a couple of psychopathic murderers and you're talking about hobgoblins."

Before Mike could make an angry retort. Al spoke again.

"I know Mike... I know what you and the Indian are saying. You're saying that the skull is responsible for the deaths of all these people. Adams obviously thought it was capable of killing. I know that the situation is bizarre, but if the skull is capable of killing. **Why** didn't it kill me? I carried it around all morning."

"I don't know Al. Maybe it needed someone to transport it. Maybe it even suggested to your subconscious where to take it."

Al looked away. (I really don't want to hear this kind of talk, not anymore, not even from Mike.)

"Think Al. Think." Mike persisted seeing the expression on Al's face. "Why are we all dreaming about burning. Bailey dreamt of burning in his mine three nights running. On his own written admittance, a fear he had. You dream of burning in one of those ovens you saw in the war. I dream I am in the car with my parents and burn with them. With Ralph it's a works' explosion. He was in a works' explosion years ago. It's as if something knows our secret memories, our darkest fears, using them against us and it's only since that blasted skull came on the scene."

They sat quiet for a while, staring at each other.

"Look Mike. I'm not knocking anything you've said. Like you told me earlier. I've nothing to argue with. I tried to tell the chief of police what you thought. He looked at me as if I was demented and with three more unexplained deaths behind me, I decided not to push it."

Mike rose to his feet. "I know it's hard for you Al, but if you think about it long enough, you'll see that it is the truth... I'm seeing Ralph and Mary off shortly, they're going to San Diego. I'll meet you in Charlie's about eight, and Al... accept it... I need your support."

"Sorry Mike. I am trying. I'm a cop remember. I still have to look for the logical. It's instinct... and it's preferable."

Mike went straight to his room when he reached the Richardsons', and played the tape, wondering again how Steve had known he had it with him. The young man was an enigma.

He played the tape, listening carefully.

"I have to be sure I'm right."

When the recording had finished for the fourth time, he reached out to rewind it and listen once more. He drew his hand back sharply as Steve's voice came through the speaker again.

"I will seek the whereabouts of the neck ornament. I know we need it. We need each other Mike Mallory. You. I. And the dark one. For mankind's sake."

Mike stared at the recorder as if it had suddenly become a living thing.

"For mankind's' sake.... For mankind's' sake."

The words echoed around the room like a threat. The doubts and fears he felt deep inside, loomed in front of him, crowding his senses, suffocating his thinking powers.

"What do I know of this young man and his grandfather... Nothing. so why am I so convinced that they are genuine and not a couple of cranks?"

"Why do I have such a strong gut feeling about them... about what is happening?"

"I'm not like Simon... I'm not psychic."

"For mankind's' sake." Steve definitely did not speak those words to me. So how was it recorded?

"You must trust your instincts Mike Mallory. You must trust me."

Mike didn't know if the words he heard were in the room or in his head.

Suddenly he was afraid, more afraid then he had ever been in is life. Not of Steve but of the unknown. He lay down on the bed grateful for being alone. He would never allow anyone to see the stark fear he was feeling."

THE FOLLOWER

I have paid my price to live with myself
on the terms that I willed.

Rudyard Kipling. (The Refined Man)

CHAPTER SIX: THE FOLLOWER

SEISMOLOGY STATION MONDAY MAY 15th EARLY HOURS.

Simon could feel the warmth of the sun on his face. Opening his eyes, he leisurely took in his surroundings.

He was sitting opposite a lake, knowing instinctively that it was the Great Salt Lake, even though it was much larger than he had ever seen it. He was seated on one of a group of rocks, made smooth by years of exposure to the wind and sand.

The gentle ripples of the lake were reflecting the rays of the sun like a myriad of sparkling diamonds. He gazed serenely in fascinated contentment as rainbow colours flashed across the surface of the water.

"If this is a dream. Then let it last forever." he murmured with a smile.

Turning his head, he saw three people walking towards him, each wearing a long white garment. "Company, that's nice." he murmured again.

As they drew closer, he could see that the centre person was a man. A tall man with iron grey hair and an imposing bearded face that would be handsome at any age. On either side of him walked a girl. One with long golden hair. The other with long red gold hair.

"Lucky, lucky man." Simon's thoughts were lazily pleasant.

When the trio reached him, the man spoke.

"Hello Simon. May we join you?"

Simon smiled and extending his arm to the surrounding rocks said, "Please... be my guests."

When they were seated he asked, "How do you know my name?"

The man answered him. "We know everything about you Simon. Let me tell you about us."

"My name is Vincent Allen, and this," Extending his arm to the golden haired one, "Is my daughter Rebecca."

"Hello." Simon said politely. She smiled and inclined her head.

"And this young lady," Vincent Allen turned to the red-haired girl, "Is Sarah Millar."

"Hello again. I know you, don't I?"

A pair of beautiful emerald green eyes gazed seriously at him.

"No Simon, it is not I that you know." The girl with the red gold hair answered.

"Are you sure? Your hair, your eyes. I do know you. You are Susan."

"No Simon, I am Sarah."

Vincent Allen intervened. "Simon, I must speak with you. Listen carefully to what I have to say. A great many lives may depend upon it. Indeed your very world may depend upon it."

Allen spoke in such earnest that Simon immediately fell silent, giving the man his full attention.

"My daughter Rebecca was a scholastic genius far beyond her years and time. In the year 1692 she was burned as a witch by Martyn Millar. Sarah's father. She was eighteen years old. She wore around her neck, an ancient pendant given to her by a Greek philosopher who had a deep affection for her. He swore it would protect her from all evil. On it were carved the symbols of Alpha and Omega. The First and the Last, representing God's eternity. In the moments of her extreme agony in the flames, the child called out for vengeance."

Rebecca hung her head in shame at these words.

"Hey, I can understand that." Simon tried to ease the girl's obvious embarrassment.

"My daughter," Allen continued, ignoring Simon's comment, "Called upon Nemesis, Goddess of Wrath, Retribution and Vengeance, and from the realms of Greek mythology... Nemesis came."

"Rebecca called for Millar to suffer, for his own to be her Nemesis. So, at the precise moment of Rebecca's death, Nemesis attempted to enter Sarah Millar's mind and possess her body. At that same instant in time, the pendant burned on to Rebecca's body over her heart, erasing from it the fear and hatred she felt for Millar. Thus preventing Nemesis from possessing Sarah's body. Unfortunately it left her trapped inside Sarah's skull giving her only limited powers, but at the same time, sending poor Sarah insane."

Allen paused for breath and then continued.

"Millar took his daughter and fled. I was away from home at the time of this terrible deed. When I returned, friends told me of the events. There was nothing I could do for Rebecca. So, retrieving the pendant from a doctor, I went in search of Millar. I did not even allow myself the time to grieve for my beloved daughter."

"I followed Millar for over a year. Somehow he always evaded me. A holy man told me that they were making their way to the Great Salt

Lake in the hope that Sarah would recover there. She would never have recovered, although Nemesis would most certainly have become dormant. There is some quality about the area that affects her. Possibly the salt and possibly because it is regarded as a sacred place."

Simon was tempted to interrupt this strange tale, but was silenced by the serious expression on the faces of both girls.

Vincent Allen carried on speaking.

"Millar died and shortly afterwards, Sarah also died. This much I learned from the Indians I met at the lake. They were afraid to speak of the couple, but they brought to me a medicine man who gave me this information. I told him that the girl was a great danger to all people. Even though she had died, she was a great danger. I showed him the pendant. Explaining that with it, I could contain the evil that still possessed the girl, that I must know where the girl's body was."

Allen sighed. "The medicine man was convinced that he had already contained the danger. He had me slain and took the pendant for himself thinking it would give him great powers."

He looked deeply into Simon's eyes. "It now lies forgotten inside an ancient Totem pole. You need this pendant Simon. You need it to imprison Nemesis."

"Simon stared at Vincent Allen thoughtfully. (This was obviously an intelligent man in spite of the fantastic and incredibly absurd tale he had told. I also am intelligent. Yet I'm sat here listening to a dead man. On his own admittance... a dead man. What's more incredible... I believe him.)"

"Mr Allen, you are saying that Nemesis is still on this earth?"

"Yes." Allen countered Simon's statement without hesitation.

"She is still on this earth and getting stronger, but she has limited mobility. She needs a body and she can only possess a Millar."

At this point Rebecca joined in speaking for the first time. "Simon, you must confine the skull. It must be placed in a fireproof coffer, arranging the chain closely around it, making sure that the pendant touches the skull. You must then bury it here by the lake. It is the only way to restrain Nemesis."

"We could send her back to where she came from." Simon pointed out.

"I am afraid, we do not possess the knowledge to do this." Allen admitted.

"Remember, we are dealing with Greek mythology, not reality or the devil's work."

Sarah, who had been quietly listening, rose to her feet and stepped forward.

"You thought you knew me Simon. You thought I was Susan. Susan is a direct descendant of my father and myself. She is a Millar. If the skull learns of her presence here, it will stop at nothing to possess her. Nemesis conveyed dreams to provoke her into coming here. We conveyed dreams to warn her away. Unfortunately we failed. On no account must the skull come into contact with her."

She lapsed into silence, her earnest speech causing twin red spots of colour on her cheeks.

"Tell me." Simon spoke after digesting this information. "Why has Nemesis suddenly become active again. How has she survived all these years?"

"We are sure that the salt in the ground and the air retained Nemesis in dormancy." Allen answered. "Over the years, a protective layer of pyrite has formed upon the skull. Pyrite is fools' gold also know as firestone. Nemesis is akin to fire, she was borne to this earth by it. Fire is now her strength. As for why she is active again. That is obvious. She still has to fulfil the reason why she was called here. To avenge Rebecca. Being imprisoned has warped her reason. Her vengeance now goes beyond Rebecca. She seeks revenge on the human race. How she intends to do this, I do not know, but I fear her wrath and so should you."

Simon sighed. "This is certainly some story you have told me. Why me... Why has all this been brought to me?"

"You know why Simon." Allen watched him carefully as he spoke.

"You may choose to ignore your gift, but you cannot deny its existence. You have already experienced premonitions and visions as a direct result of what is happening. You know that Susan is in danger. She needs your protection. If Nemesis gains entry to Susan's body, her power will be awesome. Perhaps catastrophic, and I fear, you may be powerless to stop her revenge."

Vincent Allen continued studying Simon's face closely. Seeing the response he needed in Simon's eyes, he spoke again.

"You will not be alone. Your friend Michael Mallory will be with you." Allen smiled at the surprised reaction from Simon.

"Yes, we know of Michael also." He held his hand out to Simon.

"Accept these two rings, they will offer you some protection against Nemesis. You wear the First. Give the Last to Michael."

He dropped the two rings into Simon's outstretched palm. Simon stared at the rings, an unearthly glow radiated from them.

"There is one other with far greater knowledge and power than you.

He will lead you. You must obey him at all times without question. You know this man. His name is Onotage."

Simon sat upright with a start.

"Dear God, that was some weird dream."

He looked at the clock on his bedside cabinet, it read four thirty.

"I need a drink." he muttered to himself, swinging his legs over the edge of the bed.

"A clinking sound as he moved, brought him to a halt. Looking down, he saw two rings on the floor. He bent to retrieve them, studying them as he did so. Each had a different marking. He realised he was looking at Alpha on one and Omega on the other. The First and the Last."

Now he had a profound need of a drink.

"He walked unsteadily to the kitchen like a man in shock. Taking the half empty bottle of wine out of the fridge, he was about to pour himself a glass when a sudden precognitive feeling, caught him by surprise. Replacing the wine, he took out a bottle of spring water, poured himself a glass and took a deep swallow. It tasted fresh and clean."

"Simon Kane... Now you are thinking straight."

"Simon spun around at the sound of the voice. Through the window, he saw the same Indian he had seen stood alongside Susan in his vision. The Indian stood with his arms folded across his chest. Moonlight spilling down on him. It was the smile on his face that captured Simon's attention before the image gradually faded into the shadows."

It was the smile of one from whom he had no secrets.

"Odd. I don't feel afraid anymore." He spoke softly to himself.

"I know the (dream) was real. I know that I have spoken to Vincent Allen, Rebecca and Sarah. The rings are proof enough of that. Now I have not only seen the Indian again, but he has spoken to me."

Simon knew that this young man was Onotage. He felt calm as he made his way back to his room.

"The lull before the storm, perhaps." Simon mused.

He lay down and closed his eyes.

BESIEGED

"And life is colour, warmth and light,
and a striving evermore for these;
And he is dead who will not fight;
And who dies fighting has increase."

Julian Grenfell. (Into Battle)

CHAPTER SEVEN: BESIEGED

Mike met Al in Charlie's. After ordering a couple of beers, they sat at a vacant table a little away from the rest of the clientele.

"Ralph and Mary get off okay?" Al asked.

"Yes, no problem Al."

"Just as well," Al added flatly. "The state police will be enforcing a curfew. Starting tomorrow, no one will be allowed on the streets after ten. I have a feeling they will place a cordon around the town also. No one allowed to enter. No one allowed to leave."

He gave Mike an angry frustrated look.

"That's guaranteed to cause panic. Do you realise there is no radio or TV. We are practically... No, not practically. We **are** cut off from the rest of the country."

Al's voice rose sharply. "Damn it! This is **my** town Mike. What the hell is happening to it?"

"Take it easy Al." Mike cautioned him.

"I'm sorry Mike. I thought I could cope with anything this job could throw at me but..."

"You can Al." Mike interrupted. "You have to. Look around you. Look at the people in this room."

Al looked around. There were perhaps a dozen people, all men grouped around the bar. Unusual for Charlie's on a Sunday night. They were talking quietly and seriously amongst themselves. No laughter. No smiling faces. A few of them were looking straight at Al, an expectant expression on their faces, like children waiting to be told what to do.

"They're all afraid Al. You cannot afford to give in to panic for their sakes, not publicly anyway. If you crack, so will they."

Al brought his gaze back to Mike, looking a little ashamed.

"You're right. I don't know what's wrong with me. It's not like me to lose control of a situation."

"There's nothing wrong with you Al." Mike assured him. "Do you imagine that **I** haven't been tormented by doubts? I feel as if I have a tiger by the tail, just as you do. The difference is, you are taking the responsibility of it more than anyone else, because you are a police officer, and a damn good one at that."

Al visibly straightened. "Thanks for the vote of confidence Mike, I need it."

"I'm not trying to flatter you Al, I'm just speaking the truth and you know it."

"I know Mike. I know I'm a good cop, but even a good cop needs reassuring occasionally. This morning took a helluva lot out of me."

He looked around the room, seeing his own fear reflected in the faces of the townsfolk. He gave them an encouraging nod.

"I'm alright now," he said to Mike. The calm confidence returning to his voice.

Mike gave him a worried smile. "How's the old ticker?"

Al patted his chest with a light-hearted grin. "Still going strong, hospital gave it a check this afternoon. Take more than the bogeyman to stop it. I'm okay. So... let's get down to business. We'll go over the events from the beginning. One thing we do know for sure. Whatever it is we are up against... It has a lust for killing."

Mike smiled inwardly. Al had said "It". He was slowly coming round to his way of thinking, even if he wouldn't admit it openly.

"The Chief of Police says we have a psychopathic pyromaniac on the loose." Al added, when they had gone over everything they could think of.

Mike shrugged his shoulders. "He's right, we do have a psychopathic pyromaniac on our hands, but it definitely is not mortal. Tell me. What did Adams do with the book."

Al grimaced at the memory of the Professor. He felt that he and he alone was responsible for the death of the old recluse. "He put it back inside the cabinet, the state police haven't got it, so it should still be there."

"What did it look like?" Mike probed gently, noting the expression on Al's face.

"It was old." Al answered. "Very old. Bound in red cloth with gold writing on the front. I couldn't see the title."

Mike leaned forward. "I need to see this book Al. It may not tell me anything that I don't already know... on the other hand..." He left the sentence unfinished.

Al took a long drink of his beer before answering. "I have no real authority now Mike, it's all being taken out of my hands, but if you want this book. We'll get it tonight."

"Good man." Mike said. "And I don't really want to know this, but I have to. Where is the skull?"

"The chief saw me locking it away in my safe, he called me a superstitious old fool, and took it to the church hall along with everything else."

"Church hall." echoed Mike.

"Yes. They've commandeered it as temporary headquarters. Chief says my office is too small. Suits me Mike, I'm staying in my office tonight in case anything else happens... God forbid..."

"Amen to that." Mike agreed. "I'll get my things from the Richardsons and stay with you."

Al gave a sheepish grin. "I was hoping you would, Jeff won't be back until morning, can't say as I like the idea of being alone."

"You and me both. Al... You know... I don't **like** the answers I'm coming up with any more than you do... I don't like what's happening to us, it scares the shit out of me. But I'm right... I know I'm right. We have to get that skull back, it's important. We have to think of a way..."

The conversation between the two of them was disrupted by one of the men in the room approaching their table.

"Can I have a word with you Al?"

Frank Gibbons, chairman of the town's advisory committee, pulled up a chair, a grim expression on his face.

"Sure Frank. Go ahead."

"Me and the boys," gesturing towards the bar. "Think we should have a town meeting Al. We think someone should give us the facts on what is happening."

Al gave Mike a swift glance then nodded to Frank. "I agree Frank. I'll have a word with the chief of police tomorrow."

"Thanks Al. We've all got families here. So far this maniac has made his attacks on men, but we are all wondering how safe the women and children are. As for the dreams... My youngest woke up screaming this morning... She dreamt she was burning... She's just four years old. Seems everyone I know is dreaming of burning, one way or another. There's something crazy happening here... We want to know what it is and if anything is being done about it."

"I know this Frank." Al answered soberly. Not allowing the shock he felt at realising that the dreams were affecting even the very young, to show on his face.

"We are doing our level best to get to the bottom of it. Chief McCann will bring in all the help we need."

81

Frank thanked him and returned to the bar. Al's eyes met Mike's.

"Even the children are dreaming. What the f...ks going on?"

"He stared hard at Mike. (Surely to God Mike's not right... It's not possible... Is it?)

He put the thought to one side. "If the children don't escape the nightmares, then they won't escape..." He didn't finish the sentence, he couldn't. (Jesus! This gets worse by the minute.)

"What facts <u>can</u> they be given Mike?" Al changed the subject abruptly. "The only facts I have seem to have emerged straight out of a horror movie and Frank's wrong about it just being men who have been attacked. The two bodies burnt together were a young couple. Sally Goodman and Peter Riley... Both were eighteen years old."

They fell silent. Aware of the tension in the room. A stranger would have been forgiven for thinking the people of Caplin were hostile. Only someone who knew them would have recognised naked fear.

It was Al who eventually broke the silence. "Did you come in your car Mike?"

"No, I felt the need of some fresh air, I walked."

"Right." Al said decisively. "We'll have one more drink before I take you to the Richardson's for your things, and then... We will go purloin this book."

Al looked at his watch. "Ten o'clock Mike. Let's go. Don't want to leave it too late."

They stood, aware of all eyes focused on them as they did so.

"Al." A voice called after them.

Al turned around and met Charlie's steady gaze.

"I've heard there's a curfew starting tomorrow. Is it right?"

Al cursed under his breath. "How the hell did that get out?"

"Yes, Charlie, it's right. You may as well know that I doubt anyone will be allowed to leave or enter the town either."

A murmur ran through the room.

"There will be an official announcement tomorrow. I'll see that you have the opportunity to ask whatever questions you need to ask." He turned to leave and was stopped by Charlie's voice again.

"Are we under martial law, Al?"

Al looked around at the anxious faces. "You are not under martial law. What is being done is aimed at protecting you, nothing more."

"Protect us from what, Al?"

"I don't know Charlie... I just don't know... Come on Mike."

They walked in silence to the car. Al was relieved to be out of

82

Charlie's. He'd felt the weight of those frightened stares.

He drove down the deserted main road. "Look at this town. Sunday night and not a soul to be seen. You don't need a curfew with this kind of fear stalking the streets."

Mike stared through the windscreen. Al was right. The town looked deserted. There wasn't a soul to be seen.

"I'd like to know who let it out about the curfew."

"Whoever it was, did them a favour Al. You can't blame them for wanting to know the truth."

"Truth." Al gave a bitter laugh. "I wish I knew what that was."

"You do Al."

Al ignored the statement. "They've placed a guard on Professor Adam's house. We'll drive past first and check how many."

There was only one guard on duty, and a side window open.

"Probably to clear the air. It makes it easier for us." Al said expressionlessly.

After picking Mike's clothes up and checking that the house was secure, they made their way back to the professor's house. Al slowed the car enough for Mike to slip out unseen, then carried on and parked a little away from the gate.

"Everything ok officer?" Al asked as he got out of the car.

"Yes. Who wants to know?" The officer's voice had a suspicious tone.

"Yes sir," corrected Al. "This case may have been taken out of my hands, but I am still sheriff of this town."

"I'm sorry sir, I didn't recognise you." The officer saluted smartly as he spoke.

"That's alright son, no harm done. Are you alone on duty?"

"Yes sir."

Al took a notebook out of his pocket. "I'll make a note of that and have a word with your chief. We have plenty of manpower, there's no need for you to be alone."

"I'm fine sir. I can take care of myself."

Al studied the young face. Eager. Intelligent. Full of life. (So could my men son), he thought. (And they were a damn sight more experienced than you). Out loud he said, "We're up against a particularly vicious killer, officer. I want all duty rotas organised in pairs. I'll see your chief."

The officer was young. Twenty two at the most. Al honestly didn't like the idea of him being alone.

"Thank you sir. I think I would appreciate some company."

Al winked at the young man. "Consider it done."

He chatted with the officer for a while until a slight sound near the car told him that Mike was back.

"I'll not disrupt you any further. You're doing a good job son. Goodnight."

"Goodnight sir."

Al drove off with a friendly wave and a twinge of conscience. He disliked deceiving a fellow officer. The moment they were clear of the house, Al gave Mike the okay and he emerged from the back of the car.

"Did you get it?" Al asked, glancing at Mike's empty hands.

"Yes, exactly where you said it was. I didn't even have to force the lock, the key was still there. I've put it under the car rug on the back seat."

With the office door firmly closed behind them, they relaxed. Mike gave a wry smile. "First time I've ever been a housebreaker."

Al shrugged his shoulders, thinking of the young officer. "First time I've ever been a decoy for one."

"Mike placed the book carefully on the desk. It looked very old, and was probably quite valuable. He made a mental note to return it as soon as he possibly could."

"The ornate but faded title read... "Witch Hunters and Victims"... The book was a documented account of various barbaric acts carried out in the name of justice. It was written by a doctor of medicine and contained artists drawings re-creating the gory events which dated back to the year 1670, naming several witch-hunters. It was the last account that was of interest to them. Although under different circumstances Mike would have liked to read through the book."

"The last account was of one Martyn Millar, who apparently brought nineteen servants of Satan to justice. His final victim being an eighteen year old girl named Rebecca Allen in 1692. A drawing accompanied this. It showed a beautiful young girl, her long hair flowing on to her shoulders. (She looks more like a saint than a sinner) Mike thought.

It told of the girl calling on Nemesis to avenge her and the affect this had on the Millar family. How Millar had fled to Pennsylvania, leaving his wife and two sons there, he then disappeared with his deranged daughter. A girl so mentally deranged, she believed she was Nemesis."

"It's all here Al." Mike said excitedly. "Everything we have been told. Everything we have learned. No more conjecture. No more doubts. We are under attack from Nemesis, mythical Greek Goddess of Vengeance. Except that right now... She's not so mythical."

Al stared at Mike in dismay. "I was hoping you were wrong. I wish you were wrong."

"It's staring us in the face Al. Open your mind to it."

"Mike... Please... Correct me if I'm wrong... Mythical does mean fiction doesn't it?"

"Loosely yes Al, but most fiction is based on fact. The truth becomes lost with the passing of time." Mike took the tape out of his briefcase. "Listen to the end of this tape Al."

Al listened to the last message in silence. He didn't want this. He wanted logic. Solid concrete logic.

"Steve didn't say that to me Al. I don't know how he put those words on to the tape. I don't believe in magic, that's for children, but I do believe in the power of the mind. I believe Steve has developed the power of his mind beyond our imagination."

Al allowed all this to penetrate his whirling brain. He was being pressured into believing the impossible and he didn't like it. If it had been anyone else but Mike...

"For mankind's sake... What in God's name does he mean by that Mike?"

"I don't know, but I suspect the situation here in Caplin is far more serious than any of us realise."

Mike placed the book and tape inside his briefcase. "I'm giving Simon a ring. I have to go back to the station."

"Why! For godsake. You've spent most of the day trying to convince me that the impossible... is possible. Now you're going to go hightailing it back to the station. The skull is here. The Indian is here... The deaths are here. Surely if you believe all you have been saying, then this is where you should be."

"No Al... Simon is... Simon knows more than he has said over the phone... I'm sure of it. I need his help, we all do."

"Let me point something else out to you. You're an ex-soldier. Tell me... Do you know what the word Besiege means?"

This unexpected question threw Al, but the earnest expression on Mike's face made him answer. "Of course I do. It's war, or at least war tactics."

"That's right. It is a war manoeuvre. You surround and possibly infiltrate a chosen area. You make selected attacks within that area. You sever its communications. Its supply lines. You sap and undermine its strength. It is a threat. It is a preliminary move before a major attack... or a battle."

Al stared at Mike as if he had gone insane.

"What are you leading up to Mike?"

"We have had two attacks on the outskirts of town... Pop and Cal. We have had half a dozen physical attacks and God knows how many psychological attacks through the dreams. You've already told me there is no radio. No TV. Limited communications. And God knows, our strength and confidence is being undermined. I believe Caplin is a Besieged town."

"Al stared at Mike. For a while, he had thought he himself was losing his sanity. Now he wondered if maybe the dreams were having a far worse effect on Mike.

"Oh, come on Mike, you can't seriously believe that."

"I can and I do. This person Millar arriving here... It's too much of a coincidence. The old Indian gave us the name of the threat... Millar. This book gives us the name Nemesis and... Millar. I need to discuss all this with Simon... I can feel this strongly and Steve agrees with me."

"You are **deadly** serious, aren't you Mike?"

"I've never been more serious about anything in my life."

Al thought for a second. This was a man he trusted... Had great respect for, still... he had to say what was on his mind.

"I know we have an acute situation here, but I think you are adding two and two together and coming up with ninety. You're also placing an awful lot of faith in these Indians Mike. You didn't even know them until today. And one other thing." Al eyes Mike warily. "I wish you would see the doctor... Have a check up."

Mike wasn't upset. "I trust them Al. You must trust me. I haven't gone crazy, I don't need a doctor, and I'm not deserting you or the town. I'm doing what I think is the right thing to do."

He picked up the phone and dialled...

Al could hear the buzz of static from where he was sitting. Mike slowly replaced the phone, a strange expression on his face...

"The lines are dead Al. No TV. No radio. No phones..."

"No communications..... Zero"

A police officer walked into the office at that precise moment. He sensed the tension and stood looking at the two men.

"Well?" Al demanded sharply.

"Sorry sir," The officer came to attention. "The chief would like a few words sir."

"More trouble?" Al asked.

"No sir! The chief just wants to talk to you, if it is not inconvenient."

Mike picked up his briefcase. "I'll come with you Al. Could be they'll have some other means of communication. Failing that. I'll leave as soon as it is light... I have to reach Simon."

James McCann sat at the table that was serving as his desk. He looked at his watch. 11pm. He'd been in this town exactly twelve hours.

"What the hell is going on here?" he muttered to himself. "Three more people burned to death and I was **here**."

He ran his fingers through a shock of ginger hair. A habit which so far hadn't caused him any hair loss, in spite of his wife's persistent warnings to the contrary.

McCann had been on the force for more years than he cared to remember. And like Al, a war veteran before that. He didn't like the tension in this town. Fear gazed out of every pair of eyes he looked into. It walked the streets, and it wasn't helped by the unbelievable actions of Sheriff Al Jackson. He'd sent a man for the sheriff. It was time for a longer chat.

Mike and Al entered the church hall which now resembled a military establishment. About twenty officers were scattered around, some seated at tables going over paper work, one officer was typing with the proficiency of a dedicated secretary. A senior officer was versing a group of younger men on the case details. All this activity was in stark contrast to the childish drawings still pinned to the wall. A Happy Birthday banner was a reminder of the last children's party.

Al walked straight to McCann.

"You want to see me Chief."

McCann looked up from the paper work he was studying. Under the shock of ginger hair, were a pair of deeply penetrating blue eyes. The kind that saw everything and missed nothing.

'Almost but not quite as unnerving as Steve's' Mike thought as he stood alongside Al.

"Ah. Take a seat Al." The eyes rested on Mike.

"This is Mike Mallory from the Seismology station."

Al made the introductions. "Mike, this is Chief James McCann."

The two men shook hands. Each taking stock of the other.

"Sit down Mr Mallory." McCann's voice was as penetrating as his eyes. "Tell me. Do you go along with this hokus-pokus that Al has been trying to feed me... or are you the perpetrator of it?"

Mike stayed on his feet, a cautioning look of annoyance on his face.

"Chief McCann. I know we are dealing with something unnatural. Something beyond the normal range of thinking and I know beyond doubt that the words hokus-pokus are not the words to describe eight people burning to death or the nightmares that the people of this town

87

are experiencing."

Mike's eyes held the Chief's in a steady gaze.

"Hmm. I like a man who isn't afraid to speak his mind. Even when he is wrong. Sit down Mr Mallory... please, you're making my neck ache."

Mike, glowering at McCann took the offered seat.

"You strike me as an intelligent man." McCann carried on speaking. "So let us keep the conversation on an intelligent level. What we have here Mr Mallory... is a psychopath." He stared hard at both men, making sure his words were registering.

"Someone who knows how to induce spontaneous combustion either by adding some substance to a drink or by injection or maybe even hypnosis..."

"Has the medical examiner stated that any of this is possible?" Mike interrupted.

McCann's eyes narrowed, he disliked being interrupted.

"Not yet, but he is working on that theory and it is a damn sight more logical than insisting a skull is responsible. As for the dreams... mass hysteria brought on by fear and the likes of you two spouting demonic nonsense."

Mike leaned forward. Anger turning the grey eyes to slate.

"Chief McCann. The deaths and the dreams came first. The fear followed as a result of them and neither Al nor myself have discussed what we **know** with anyone."

"Good. Mr Mallory. That is exactly how I want it to stay, because I suggest there is an enormous gulf between what you **think** you know, and what I will **prove** to be fact."

Before McCann could pass any further comment, an officer approached the table. "Chief, I still can't get any response from either the radio or TV... only static."

Mike turned back to McCann. "Have you tried the phones?"

"Yes, I have tried the phones, it is one of the reasons why I sent for Al." McCann answered in a tight voice. "The lines are dead... just static again."

"You do realise." Mike spoke his words with deliberate precision. "That the town is completely cut off from any kind of communication... Don't you think this is unusual?"

"I think, Mr Mallory, that we probably have some adverse weather conditions in the des..."

"And I <u>know</u> McCann," Mike interrupted again. "That we would have been warned of any such conditions prior to them occurring. I especially would have been warned."

McCann glared at Mike, knowing that he spoke the truth. Deciding not to antagonise an already hostile situation, he merely shrugged. "I have a transmitter arriving shortly, hopefully I will find out what has happened to communications then."

Mike relaxed a little. "We have a transmitter at the station. I have to go back tomorrow. When your equipment arrives, will you allow me to use it? I need to contact my colleague urgently."

"Indeed I will Mr Mallory." McCann answered evenly. "But you will not be going anywhere tomorrow. No one will be allowed to leave this town until I have the person or persons responsible for these crimes under arrest."

Mike's temper flared again. "I have to go back to the station, damn it. I..."

"Mike is needed at the station chief, not here." Al intervened quickly. He didn't like the way this conversation was going. "I can vouch for his character and his whereabouts at the times of the deaths and for the fact that he has the people of Caplin at heart same as me."

"Okay, okay Al, don't get uptight. Frankly, if it wasn't for the fact that I know you, I'd say you weren't exactly in a position to vouch for anyone... Would you." Turning back to Mike, ignoring the flash of anger in Al's face, he gave a smile that didn't quite reach his eyes.

"Sit down Mr Mallory, I think perhaps all our nerves are a little taut at the moment. I won't keep you from your duty. Besides, as you also have a transmitter, you may be of more use to me there."

Mike raised quizzical eyebrows.

"The transmitter I am expecting is of limited range. If we don't get communications back immediately, I can transmit to you and you can relay it if necessary. Is that acceptable to you Mr Mallory?"

Mike was about to agree...

"Sorry to interrupt sir." An officer spoke to McCann. "May I speak to you alone."

McCann glanced at Al and Mike. "It's alright officer. Go ahead."

"Sir... There's been another death."

A shock wave travelled around the room as the three men stood in unison.

Mike looked around wildly at the tables. Searching for the skull, a tense expression on his face. He couldn't see it. (I hope to God they have it locked away somewhere.)

McCann beckoned Mike and Al to follow him as he and the officer quickly left the church hall. the officer explaining to them as they jumped into a waiting car.

"A gentleman by the name of Dorfson had heard some kind of disturbance in his backyard and gone to investigate. When he didn't return, and seeing the flicker of flames through the window, his wife had gone in search of him. At first she thought someone had deliberately started a fire and her husband had given chase to them. It was only when she attempted to douse the flames, that she realised it was the body of her husband."

"You know these people Al?" McCann asked.

"Of course I do." Al snapped. "His name is Erik Dorfson. Where is Mrs Dorfson now?"

"I left her in the care of a neighbour sir. I've sent for a doctor."

The three men carefully examined the still smouldering remains of Erik Dorfson as soon as they arrived at the house.

"Exactly like the others." Al was frustrated... angry.

Mike caught hold of McCann's arm. "Where is the skull, McCann?"

"The skull, Mr Mallory, is still on the table right behind where I was sitting. And kindly let go of my arm."

Mike tightened his grip on McCann's arm, a grim expression on his face.

"No it is not."

"It most certainly is Mr Mal..."

"I am telling you it was not on any table. I looked around for it deliberately. Had it been on a table... I would have seen it."

McCann's face flushed a deep red. Forcibly removing Mike's hand from his arm. "I am running out of patience with you Mallory. Right now I intend to have a word with Mrs Dorfson. I'll thank you to stay exactly where you are. I will speak to you later."

"Don't worry McCann." Mike's voice was cold with controlled anger. "I'm not going anywhere... Yet."

He sat down on the porch steps and lit a cigarette. Al went with McCann, giving Mike a worried look as he passed. Mike very rarely smoked. Unless deeply disturbed.

Mike smoked the cigarette while watching the police medics removing the remains of Erik Dorfson. (Another good man dead... How many more? I have to get through to Simon. **"Time is vital Mr Mallory"**.) He shook his head trying to clear the jumbled thoughts. (We should be doing something... we're wasting time. I'm wasting time... I'm going to Simon tonight... regardless of McCann and Al.)

Half an hour later, they came out of the house. McCann walked past Mike without a word. Al followed, touching Mike on the shoulder beckoning him to join them.

"Well?" Mike demanded once they were in the car. "What did Mrs Dorfson say?"

It was Al who answered him. "When Erik didn't come back into the house, Mrs Dorfson went looking for him. She saw a blue light moving at speed away from what she later discovered was the remains of her husband. It was the next door neighbour, Stan Roker who saw everything. He's a stargazer. He was in his bedroom, no lights on, using his telescope. He saw a blue light in Dorfson's garden. Dorfson was standing perfectly still. Roker couldn't see his face. The light hovered about eight feet in front of him. Dorfson never moved almost as if he were transfixed."

"These are Roker's words, not mine." Al added.

"The blue light moved closer to Dorfson. Dorfson still didn't move. A beam or flash like a laser projected from the blue light and hit Dorfson. Dorfson then... burst into flames."

"This all happened in the space of a couple of minutes."

"By the time Stan had recovered from what he had just witnessed and raced downstairs, Mrs Dorfson was in the garden and the light was gone." Al's face was expressionless.

(There's something else) Mike thought. (Something he's not telling me.)

The car came to a halt and the three men got out. Mike stood in front of McCann blocking his path.

"Do you believe me now?"

McCann gave Mike a withering look.

"Do you know what Dorfson was before he retired?" He didn't give Mike a chance to answer. "I'll tell you. He was a nuclear physicist. He was still working on a secret project. His wife doesn't know what it was. She does know that he received not only Government backing but Presidential backing. Now you can bet your bottom dollar that whatever it was has backfired and caused all these deaths. How else could you explain a "laser of light"."

Mike groaned. "How do **you** explain all... this starting at the mine before here. How do you explain the nightmares?"

McCann pushed past him walking angrily into the church hall.

"Dorfson was in the desert that day." he shouted over his shoulder.

Mike turned to face Al.

Al nodded. "It's true Mike. I'm sorry but McCann is coming up with logical answers."

Mike slammed a fist into the palm of his hand. "Al what's happening here isn't logical and you know it."

91

"Bring me some coffee." McCann barked at the nearest officer as he sat down.

"It's a coincidence." insisted Mike. "How do you explain Adams, Wilkins and Mac?"

"Now that is a good question Mallory."

Mike wanted to strike the smug smile off McCann's face.

"They were all educated men and all colleagues of Mr Dorfson, each one of them knew what Dorfson was working on, even Professor Adams."

"You're right." Mike looked at Al and McCann like a man who had just seen the light. "I should have realised. They were all educated. All knowledgeable. That's probably why it killed them... Something clever enough to penetrate the deepest recesses of a person's mind is clever enough to absorb whatever knowledge that mind holds."

McCann looked as if he were about to explode. He pointed to the table behind him. The skull lay in the centre of it. "The skull is there. It cannot move. It certainly cannot kill. If I have one more word out of you Mallory, I will have you locked up for disturbing the peace and obstructing the law."

Three coffees were placed on the table.

"There is a gentleman outside insisting on seeing you sir." The officer said cautiously.

"Who is it?" McCann snapped at the unfortunate man.

"His name is Karl Dorfson sir."

McCann turned enquiringly to Al.

"Karl is Erik's son. Let him in." Al said to the officer. The officer looked for clearance from McCann and received a curt nod.

The man who came towards them leaned heavily on a walking stick. A young officer quickly brought him a chair, but the man waived it away. He stopped directly in front of McCann.

"You are Chief of Police McCann."

"That is right. Please sit down Mr Dorfson and accept my sin..."

"You wish to know what my father was working on." Karl Dorfson interrupted. "I will show you."

He rolled up a trouser leg with difficulty, again waiving any assistance and revealed a limb, obviously being eaten away by disease. "This is what my father was working on... A cure for cancer. It did not involve death dealing lasers, nor could it create nightmares of burning. Nothing in my father's work could possibly roam around this town murdering at random. And Mr McCann. I was with my father in the desert that day. We were studying rock formation. I am a geologist. We were nowhere near Bailey's mine. My father was helping me. To accuse him... You will have to accuse me also."

McCann was startled as Dorfson threw a sheaf of papers on to the table.

"My father's work is fully documented in this file and there is a letter here confirming approval of and support for his work from President Nixon. So, Mr McCann, do not attempt to lay any blame on my father or myself for the horror that is taking place in this town, or I will personally ensure that you do not work again."

He turned and left after asking Al to return the papers as soon as possible.

The deafening silence was broken only by a few embarrassed coughs.

Al cleared his throat. "I'm going to catch a few hours sleep. You coming Mike?"

"I'm going to the seismology station Al, I'm going to Simon."

"Mike it's too late, another few hours and it will be sunup, stay here until then."

Mike looked at his watch, surprised to see that it was one thirty in the morning. "God! I feel like I haven't slept for a week. Okay Al. I'll be back tomorrow to use your transmitter McCann." He received no answer.

"Goodnight."

Still no answer. Mike reached across to the table where the skull lay.

"Leave it where it is," barked McCann. "I intend to have it examined."

"Come on Mike," urged Al. "There's nothing you can do."

Mike and Al were up just after six, both having slept badly because of the dreams.

Al had just nicely got the coffee perking when Jeff walked in. He didn't look any better than Mike or Al. He slumped down in a chair and lit a cigarette.

"Al, there is an absolute loss of communication in this town. The radio, TV and phones are all out and everyone is having nightmares about burning. Including me."

"I know Jeff." Al brought him up to date with the deaths of Mac, Wilkins, Adams and the previous nights incident.

"My God Al... What's happening?... I shouldn't have gone... I should never have left you."

"No recriminations Jeff. Who in Gods name could have predicted all this. Everything has happened so fast but all further leave is cancelled from now until we have this problem under control."

He turned to Mike. "I don't know what is happening or what to believe Mike. I've tried to remember seeing the skull before we went out of the church hall and I can't. I only know I have to do my utmost to protect the people in this town from what could be happening. I just don't know what to tell them."

Mike took a drink of the hot coffee, savouring the taste while he thought. He wanted to shout, "Open your mind Al. Tell them the truth." He bit the words back. "Tell the men to keep their families off the streets at night. Keep their windows and doors securely locked and be on their guard for a blue light. Should they see this, on no account are they to go near it. As for what I have found out... use your own judgement. You know these people better than me, if you think they can accept it... tell them everything regardless of what or who you believe... or what McCann says."

"They have a right to decide for themselves whether or not it is the truth Al."

Mike picked up his briefcase and holdall. "I'm going to see McCann, then I'm going to the station. I'll be in touch somehow..."

"Al... Jeff. Take care."

As they shook hands, Al warned him. "You take care Mike, don't push it with McCann. He's a tough man and a good police officer. He won't hesitate to lock you up if he thinks he should."

Mike grinned. "I reckon I came close to that last night. I'll be careful."

Mike walked to the church hall, his car was still in the garage. He could sense the change in the town. The few people he passed looked tired, nervous, strained. above all else... They looked afraid.

"Mr Mallory." A voice called out. A young man caught up with him.

"You remember me Mr Mallory?"

"Yes I do." Mike said. "You're Todd Walker. How's that pretty young wife of yours?"

"She's pregnant Mr Mallory. I tried to take her away from here about an hour ago, but the police stopped me. There's something wrong here. I'm afraid for Netta and the baby. What can I do?"

Mike could see the anxiety on the young face. He had a soft spot for the lad, being orphaned at a tender age as he himself had been.

"Where were you going to take her Todd?"

"To Sacramento. Netta's parents moved there a couple of months ago."

94

Mike rested a reassuring hand on the young man's shoulder.

"Okay son, come with me, I'll see what I can do."

They entered the church hall together.

"Morning." Mike said to McCann.

"Morning Mallory, we have the transmitter, you can contact the station."

Mike nodded his thanks, noticing a distinct change of attitude in the man. "Thanks, I'll use it in a moment, first I'd like a word with you about Todd here."

"I know about Todd. I told you Mallory, no one is leaving this town until I have arrested whoever is responsible for these murders."

"Damn it McCann." Mike spoke softly, not wishing to cause a scene. "He's twenty years old, his wife is eighteen and pregnant. They have no family here now. Give him a pass and let them get the hell out of here."

The tension between them was building up again.

"You are a stubborn and troublesome man Mallory."

The words barely made it through McCann's clenched teeth.

Mike nodded. "Yes... and you haven't slept well have you McCann?"

McCann's shoulders drooped, he lowered his gaze and with a sigh, he wrote two permits out and gave them to Todd.

"This one will enable you to buy gas, the other will enable you and your wife to leave town. Now get out of here before I change my mind."

"Thank you sir. Thank you Mr Mallory. Todd ran out as he spoke.

The two men faced each other once more.

"Thank you for that McCann, I appreciate it."

McCann waved a weary arm. "I spoke to your colleague Simon Kane ten minutes ago. He sound pretty desperate to talk to you. Why are you really going back, I know you are supposed to be on vacation?"

"You know what I believe McCann. What is the point of my trying to explain a series of events you won't accept. Something you won't even listen to."

McCann studied Mike, a sombre expression on his face.

"Every man in this room who slept, had dreams of burning including me, which I admit is .. strange. Two men. Two good men have swore to me that you were right about the skull being missing last night...."

"I'm not saying I've been converted to your way of thinking Mallory. Frankly I think you're way off the mark to put it politely. I don't accept unnatural forces, but I do concede to the fact that something odd is happening here. I am prepared to listen to all you have to say."

95

"Mike had to admire McCann's perseverance. The man was unnerved, at a loss, yet he still clung to logic like it was a lifeline. Exactly like Al."

He told him all he had found out, in detail. Showed him the book, and allowed him to listen to the tape.

"You must give the skull to me." Mike urged.

McCann shook his head. "I cannot believe any of this is possible, not the way you think. I won't give you the skull, but I will have it examined today. If necessary, I'll send it to the University of Science in California."

Seeing the expression on Mike's face, he added. "If it will make you happier, I will lock it in the safe and place a guard on it. According to what you have just told me, it only seems to move when unobserved."

Mike saw no point in arguing. "Where is it now?"

McCann opened a drawer, took out the skull and stood it on the table.

"Do me a favour McCann... Place a double guard on it."

McCann gave a cynical smile. "You don't give in do you? Dave, put Mr Mallory's call through."

Mike put his holdall down on the floor and took the offered handset.

"Hello Mike." Simon's voice came clearly through the speaker.

"Chief McCann tells me you are coming back here today. Over."

"Yes Simon. I'm ready to leave. I'll be there about nine. Over."

"Good. I'm glad to hear that. I badly need to speak to you but first there is something you should know. Millar is a woman."

"Susan Jane Millar. She is a direct descendant of Martyn and Sarah Millar. This information probably doesn't mean anything to you and I cannot explain over the transmitter..."

Mike's swift intake of breath stopped Simon in mid speech.

"Mike... are you okay. Over."

"Yes Simon, I'm okay. Your information does mean a great deal to me. What surprises me is that you know about the Millars. Over."

"Yes... well there's quite a story behind that. I'll explain when you arrive here. Over."

All attention was on Mike, especially McCann's. A disturbed expression rapidly spread across his face...

None were more attentive than the skull. No one noticed the agitated tremor.

"[So the girl did heed the dreams I sent to her. She is here and this man will take me to her.]

Furtively it left the table and slid into Mike's partially open holdall."

"I think the sooner we can talk... The better Simon. Over."

"I agree. I won't keep you on the air any longer. Bye Mike. Over and out."

Mike passed the handset over to the operator with a barely heard thank you.

"I'll walk with you to the door." McCann said picking Mike's holdall up.

"I know you don't accept the deaths and dreams are caused by unknown forces," Mike said. "All the same, I urge you to keep an open mind for your own sake and the sake of the people in this town. As for the skull... in view of what Simon has just told me, perhaps it will be safer in your hands for the time being."

McCann remained silent until they were outside the building.

"I am... a logical man Mallory... It is how I have risen to be chief of police... I'm not sure... what it is I am trying to say... I told you we all had dreams of burning last night."

Mike nodded in encouragement.

"I asked each man separately. They all had similar dreams. Burning in a house or car. Accident type of nightmares... Odd thing was, some of these dreams have actually happened. Some were a deep seated phobia, phobias that these men haven't discussed with anyone."

"My dream was... different."

"What do you mean?" Mike asked. He was unnerved by McCann's obvious difficulty with his words, the expression on his face causing him to fear the answer.

"I wasn't going to mention this, but after listening to the... to the conversation between you and Mr Kane... I'm confused... I know you haven't been in contact with Kane, I know this because all communications have been monitored since I arrived here. That's how I knew straight away that the phones were out. Yet you and Kane both have the same... information... I no longer know... I'm unsure...." McCann was stumbling with his words.

"My dream Mallory... was of.... Armegeddon."

"McCann stayed outside after Mike had left. An officer brought yet another coffee. He sat on a bench and lit a cigar. His mind in turmoil. His logic turned upside down.

"God! I feel as if I have been here a lifetime."

He wished he could shake off the brooding depression that had settled on him like a grey blanket."

"He stood to go inside and was thrown to the ground by the violent explosion.

His men came running out of the church hall.

"It's the gas station." one of them shouted.

The flames were already licking the air as several of the men ran towards the station. The parked gas tanker discharging it's volatile load, erupted like a firebomb....

"Mike had been travelling fifteen minutes when he heard the first explosion. Braking hard, he heard the second explosion as he jumped from the car. He could see the cloud of thick black smoke hung like a sinister shadow over the town and he knew it was the gas station."

"Christ!" He thought of the gas tanker he had passed, outlet valves open, filling the underground vault with the highly inflammable fuel.

"No TV... No radio... No telephones... And now no fuel for transport."

"I have to go back."

"He threw himself into the car and started turning, pulling at the wheel like a mad man. A voice deep inside him was saying "No! There is nothing you can do. You will be of more help to the people in Caplin if you go to Simon."

He rested his forehead on the steering wheel, knowing that the explosions would be the work of Nemesis. Torn between his conscience and the inner voice... the latter won.

He pointed the car in the direction of the seismology station and drove on, hoping against hope that he was doing the right thing.

"The preliminaries of war were over........ the Battle had begun."

THE POSSESSION

"If never more his face I see
In pure light pouring into me,
And if I may not feel again
The splendour of this quickening pain,
Nor break in glory as I pray -
I thank thee Lord, for this good day."

Myra Reeves. (Revelation Remembered)

CHAPTER EIGHT: THE POSSESSION

SEISMOLOGY STATION UTAH - MONDAY MAY 15th

Less than forty-eight hours had passed since driving into Caplin, looking forward to two weeks relaxing vacation. Mike gave a bitter laugh. The sinister events in that short time was unbelievable. He put his foot down hard on the accelerator, in a hurry now to reach the station and Simon. He desperately hoped that no one had been hurt by the explosions, but he knew that the chances of that were pretty slim.

Simon had seen Mike's car approaching the station and was in the parking lot waiting.
"Can't tell you how good it is to see you." he said gripping Mike's hand. "We need to talk urgently."
"I know Simon, but first ask Joe to try contact Caplin." He told Simon about the explosions. "I suspect it was the gas station and a fuel tanker."
Simon took the holdall from him. "I'll have Joe get on it right away Mike."
As they approached the steps, the foyer door opened. Susan stood framed in the doorway.
Mike came to an abrupt halt, his heart missing several beats.
(What's wrong with you Mike Mallory), he wondered. (There's nothing wrong with you), he answered himself soundlessly. (You're only looking at the most beautiful woman you have ever laid eyes on.)
"Mike this is Susan Millar." Simon's voice penetrated through the pleasant shock waves that this woman was arousing in him.
Susan held her hand out, smiling at him. "I didn't expect to meet you quite to soon Mr Mallory."
"Mike. Please." he said taking her hand quickly. (This is the woman I'm supposed to get **rid** of.)
"They stood gazing at each other. A stunned expression on both their faces.
Simon's discerning gaze travelled from one face to the other, a slightly amused glint in his eyes.
(Well, well.) He thought. (I think I could be witnessing love at first

sight.) His gaze went back to Mike's face then downwards to their hands still firmly clasped together. (I always knew that when it happened for you my friend, it would happen fast.)

They became aware of Simon's silent scrutiny. Allowing their hands to separate in embarrassment.

Simon laughed gently. "Let's go inside."

"Have you had breakfast Mike?" Simon enquired.

"No," Mike answered trying to remember when he had last eaten.

"I'll make it." Susan volunteered giving Mike another dazzling smile as she headed for the kitchen.

"Susan. Will you ask Joe to contact Caplin please?" Simon called after Susan's hurriedly retreating back. "Tell him it is urgent."

"I will yes. Is there a problem? I thought I heard you mention an explosion just as I came out."

"Yes, there's been an accident of some kind." Simon answered guardedly. "We won't know until we have been in touch with the town."

"I see." Susan gazed anxiously at Simon and Mike trying to read the expression on the faces of the two men. She gave up with a small shrug. "I'll do that now."

When she was out of hearing distance, Simon gave Mike a knowing but concerned smile.

"Looks like you have captured the lady's heart Mike. Though God only knows how. You look like a deaths head."

Mike murmured agreement, rubbing his hand over his chin surprised at the growth of stubble. "Maybe she likes the rugged type."

He gave Simon a tired smile, lack of sleep showing in the lines and shadows around his eyes. "Unfortunately it seems we have to send her away Simon... she has to go as soon as possible. Come on, let's go to my room, I'll have a quick shower and we can talk while I change."

Simon placed the holdall on the floor and started to unzip it.

"Anything you want out of here Mike?"

"No, I packed in a hurry, everything will be creased. I'll get some fresh clothes from my wardrobe."

A ray of sunlight through the window caught Simon's hand.

"That's an unusual ring Simon. Did you buy it during your vacation?"

Simon studied the ring on his finger. "No," he said slowly, an odd expression on his face. "There is quite a story to tell and it's attached to the ring. Have your shower Mike. I'll be back in a moment."

The skull rose from the holdall as Simon left the room and took in its surroundings. It had come very close to being discovered. As for the human Simon, he would never know how close he had come to being incinerated.

{I must take great care not to be discovered. I will present myself when I am ready.}

The skull could hear Mike in the shower.

{I have to move quickly before the man Simon returns.}

It glided smoothly through the open door and out into the corridor.

{Where was the girl?} Thinking of her created an evil glow of anticipation deep in the eye cavities of the skull.

{Careful now. So close to possessing a Millar. So close to total freedom and power.}

Staying close to the ground and wall, it sped swiftly down the corridor.

{Voices, I can hear voices.}

The man Simon was speaking to the girl. The sound of his voice carried clearly down the corridor. The skull followed the sound.

"Give me a half hour, then we will have breakfast in the conservatory and I will answer all your questions."

"Alright Simon, but I expect you to be completely honest with me."

"I will Susan, I promise."

The skull hid beneath a small table until Simon had passed. As it watched the man, a warning tremor of alarm caused it to glow involuntarily. {There is a latent aura of danger surrounding that being... He is one to be dealt with speedily... First the girl.}

The skull slowly approached the door of the kitchen. It could see her preparing a meal. She had her back to the door. The skull entered and quietly hid among the fronds of a large potted plant where it could safely study her. There was something vaguely familiar about her. The skull willed her to turn around. She did so, putting her hand nervously to her hair and looking wildly around the kitchen.

{Easy, easy. Mustn't frighten her, she senses my presence. Good, that shows perception.}

The skull waited until she had calmed before continuing with the observation.

{She is the very image of Sarah Millar. Same hair, same eyes, but has greater intelligence, as far as intelligence exists in humans.} the skull thought derisively. {The little fool is wondering how the people of Caplin are. Burning girl. They are burning.}

The agitation was showing on Susan's face again. The skull cooled its anger. It ceased studying Susan and thought instead of Sarah Millar.

{Sarah had been scolding a hapless maid and had struck the girl with a hairbrush. The maid had insolently raised her hand to strike back at Sarah. At this, Sarah had flown into a fury. This, plus the speed at which I had been obliged to take possession of Sarah's body must have been the cause of the disastrous union between the two of us. The result was, being a virtual prisoner inside the skull of an imbecile, and being trapped for two hundred and eighty years in a miserable dark cave.... "Send you away, would they?... I think not." <u>I will have my revenge.</u>}

The skull brought its thoughts back to the present.

{I will not allow that to happen again. This time I will succeed. I will bide my time until the girl is in a relaxed and happy frame of mind. Then... and only then will I possess her. I will avenge Rebecca as I must, but I will wreak my own vengeance on these inferior mortals.}

A man came into the kitchen. The girl greeted him volubly, obviously glad of the intrusion.

The skull studied the man's intellect.

{An electrical expert, and an affinity to the girl and the men Simon and Mike. He may also be of use to me.}

The skull was well aware of the fact that Mike and Simon knew of the existence of Nemesis. It had been amused by probing the minds of Mike and Al while Mike was learning and coming to terms with the truth and Al denying it's existence.

{Simon... he was different. This man is highly dangerous. He has far too much knowledge, but I will take care of that. He will be most fortunate if he can remember his own name by morning. These men will stay alive, only as long as I require them. Then...}

The skull followed at a discreet distance behind Susan and the man Joe. They took the breakfast trolley into the conservatory. The room had large double doors, both of which were open. The skull glimpsed the Salt Lake Desert through the enormous window and shuddered.

It waited until Susan and Joe were helping themselves to food, then reluctantly slipped unseen through the doors and hid behind a lounger.

Mike and Simon entered the room shortly afterwards, both looked strained.

Mike nervously twisted the ring on his finger and wondered again at Simon's sketchy explanation of it. He was worried about Simon, it was unlike him to be vague or hesitant. More than that... the transference from the solid, positive character he knew was Simon, to the unsure, confused person he had suddenly become, was happening too fast, it was.... unnatural. Simon's personality had suffered a drastic change in less than thirty minutes.

"Would someone please tell me what is wrong?" Susan's voice

interrupted Mike's line of thought. "I can see the tension and I can feel it." her voice was tremulous. "You," she spoke to Simon, "Have asked me to trust you. You said you would explain to me..."

"You are quite right." Mike brought her outburst to an abrupt halt.

"Simon and I have decided to acquaint you and Joe with the plain facts... though you may find them... unbelievable to say the least." He gave her a reassuring smile. "So at the risk of giving you both indigestion," he said, trying to lighten the tense atmosphere. "We will discuss it over breakfast."

The skull listened with bored amusement, watching Simon struggling to remember. Witnessing Mike's concern for his friend.

{How touching.}

Relishing the expressions on Susan's face as they changed from incredulous to fear, one hand clutching occasionally at her throat.

Joe silently attentive. Looking from one face to the other. Mentally vowing that he would die for any one of them if he had to.

{Die for them... Hah.} If the skull had dared to risk laughter, the room would have resounded to the hideous sound of it.

{What was that?... Mike had mentioned an Indian... What Indian?... Damnation!}

The skull cursed itself for not paying full attention.

{Who was this Indian?} Frantically the skull raked its memory. {I do not recall an Indian. Not one with powers. It could not possibly be the savage who called himself a Medicine man.} The skull cursed itself again for not probing Simon's mind deeper before beginning to erase his memory. It turned its attention to Mike's subconscious.

Mike ran a hand across his forehead, the beginnings of a headache causing a furrow between his brows. Slowly the pain moved until it formed a circle, like a steel band around his head, growing ever tighter. He stood gingerly, rubbing his temples.

"My head aches with all this talk, I think we have discussed the situation as far as we can. If no one objects, I'd like to bring it to a close and take a walk in the garden... get some fresh air."

Simon was obviously relieved. "You are quite right Mike. I think I will run a check on the instruments."

Susan glanced at Joe who had started clearing the breakfast dishes away.

"Would you like a hand Joe?" The tone of her voice suggested that this was a half hearted offer.

"No thanks Susan, I can manage just fine."

She turned to Mike. "I'd like to join you, if you don't mind that is."

"I'd be delighted." Mike answered truthfully. It would give him the opportunity to know her better in private and be a pleasant diversion from the horrors of their conversation, even if only for a short time.

Simon watched as Mike led Susan to the door. Mixed emotions flitted across his face. {She spells danger for you Mike... For all of us.} He turned and walked slowly to the observatory.

They walked around the garden that Joe had cultivated with loving care. Mike found out that Susan had been born in Harrisburg, Pennsylvania in 1943 and had spent all of her life there until leaving to attend the Boston University when she was seventeen. As a promising geologist, she had won a place at the Seismology Centre in Boston.

"I have no brothers or sisters. My father is a lecturer on Botany. And both my parents now spend most of their time abroad. They are somewhere in the rain forest at this moment. The rest you know." She smiled at him as they sat on a rustic bench in an area of the garden Joe had named Tranquillity. A small pool with a miniature waterfall was the centre piece. Flowering cacti bloomed alongside bougainvillaea.

"What are those plants around the pool, they look quite dead."

Mike smiled. "Those are Joe's pride and joy. They are moonflowers. They only bloom at night. This is why he named this area Tranquillity."

She sighed. "That is a good name, I like Joe. I like all of you. For a while, I thought I had made a grave mistake in coming here. Now I know I made the right decision."

A slight but very attractive blush had appeared on her cheeks. Mike felt like a rat listening to her talk... She still had to go.

"Tell me a little about yourself Mike."

Mike intended giving her a brief outline of his life and was surprised when he found his entire life story tumbling from his lips. She was so easy to confide in... Too easy.

(She hasn't mentioned a man in her life.) Mike thought.

"I see by your hand you are not married Susan."

"No," she replied quietly... "Are you married Mike?"

"No I'm not, then I'm not a very social kind of person, but you... I would have thought a pretty girl like you would have been snapped up long ago."

Susan laughed. Not harshly. An attractive, slightly embarrassed laugh.

"That sounds like a very old line, but I'm not laughing at you Mike, in fact coming from you I think it is a very nice compliment. I'm not married because I have never met anyone I felt I could spend the rest of

105

my life with... Until now." she added softly.

Mike's heart did a complete somersault. When he had first seen her framed in the doorway, he had fallen instantly in love. He looked at her now. {Was it possible she felt the same... No, too soon... Much too soon.}

He didn't trust himself to question her statement.

"Let's walk again." he said, not daring to think much beyond the moment.

They walked in silence for a while, then she suddenly came to a halt.

"Would you rather be alone Mike? I'll go indoors if you wish."

"No..." His words came out sharper than he intended. "No of course not Susan... I'm not much company, I know... I have such a lot on my mind."

He looked deeply into her beautiful eyes, then quickly turned away.

"I don't want you to go indoors Susan."

She gave him an unfathomable look. "Mike. I'm not a bold person." Apprehension created an edge to her voice. "I have never spoken to any man like that before. Maybe it's this crazy situation that is prompting me."

She was looking earnestly at him. "If I've spoken out of line, I'm..."

"No." Mike cut short her apology.

She gazed up into his face. "Have you ever known by instinct that something or... someone was right for you?"

Mike nodded, not trusting himself to speak.

"That is what I could feel the moment I saw you Mike. I think even if you had been married, I would have still felt the same."

The expression on his face softened. "I've never believed in love at first sight... until today Susan."

He placed his hands on her shoulders, resisting the urge to hold her close. "I think this is what has happened and it scares me, it scares me because I am afraid of what is in front of us. I am afraid for Simon. I am afraid for you. Susan... You have to..."

She cupped his face in her hands stopping his words. Her fingers feeling cool, yet sensual on his skin. Arousing his dormant senses to a powerful frenzy.

"Mike, can't you see? That is the reason why you should embrace our love, not fear it. Somethings are meant to be. I truly believe that. Call it Kismet if you like. I think we were meant to be."

"Mike. I love you and love will make us stronger."

"He didn't speak. He pulled her into his arms and kissed her with a burning passion that shook both of them to the very core."

106

When they finally separated, he held her at arms length.

"Susan. You have to leave here... Today."

Her look of happiness disappeared. She opened her mouth to protest.

Mike gently placed a hand over it. "Susan... I'm being blunt... probably too blunt... I don't mean to sound... Susan... I love you. For all our sakes, you must leave... Now."

She stared at him in dumbfounded silence.

"It's true I came here with the intentions of getting rid of you. This is no longer the case... When we have dealt with this... with this Nemesis... I intend asking you to marry me Susan Millar. Would you consider it?"

"Oh yes Mike. Yes. I think... No... I know you are the person I have waited all my life for. But surely I should stay and help, you may need me. It not only concerns me... It surrounds me... It is me... I can feel it. I have known this ever since I came..."

He kissed her again, gently this time, silencing her torrent of words, keeping a tight rein on his passion for her. He would not risk spoiling the fact that something beautiful had finally entered his life. When the time was right, he would give himself to her totally. Until then, he was committed to help Simon tackle the formidable task he knew was in front of them.

"No Susan. You will help us more by doing as I ask. You need only go to Salt Lake City. I'll come for you... I promise." Neither of them were aware of the Indian observing every move. He smiled in approval of what he had witnessed.

'This is good. The woman needs protection and love is a strong protector. She will be safe in Salt Lake.' His gaze went to the station. A frown creased his smooth forehead. There was evil in there. Evil he knew he had to face. The sooner the woman departs... The better. Quietly he slipped away unseen. Mike and Susan walked back to the station hand in hand.

"I will do as you ask Mike... though I am not sure you are right."

"I am right... trust me, I'll come for you as soon as I can... I love you Susan Millar."

Simon looked from Susan's radiant face to Mike's happy but more serious face.

"Well," he said, allowing a smile to relieve the tension he was feeling. "Life isn't quite as bleak as it seems. Are congratulations in order?"

Mike nodded wondering what his friend would think of them at a time like this. He didn't have to wonder for long.

"I think you're timing's way off, but cupid never did go in for perfect timing, did he? What the hell... as long as you're both happy."

"Do I get to be best man?"

"I would never forgive you if you weren't!" Mike said shaking the hand that Simon offered him.

Susan stood on tiptoe to kiss him. "Neither would I," she whispered.

The skull witnessed this scene and knew that the time was now. Gently it sent a command to her subconscious.

"I'm going to my room now Mike, I won't be long."

"Alright Susan," he answered lightly, kissing her forehead. She left, humming a tune.

The skull followed taking great care not to be seen.

"She entered her room and sat down on the bed. Her heart was singing but she couldn't for the life of her remember why she had wanted to come to her room. What did it matter, today was the happiest day of her life. No. Today was the first day of her life. Today she had met, fallen in love with and agreed to marry the most wonderful man she would ever meet. Perhaps now she could tell them of the burning dreams. Not yet... She didn't want to think of them now. She lay back humming to herself again, thinking of Mike... his kiss. Forgetting for a while, the horrors of what she had been told. She could hear sweet words inside her head.

"Close your eyes my darling and I will come to you."

She closed her eyes, waiting for the promised love.

.... **And passed into oblivion....**...................

Nemesis sat upright and looked down at the body she had possessed. She rose gracefully from the bed and walked over to the full length mirror. Removing all garments, she examined the body.

(Mmm, I have possessed better in other times, but the eyes and the hair are quite pleasing, as is the soft skin.)

She began to dance in slow sensual movements, watching herself through the mirror. Seductively she ran her hands over her body, relishing the soft curves and finishing at the nape of her neck. Slowly she piled the glorious hair on top of her head, admiring the way it caught the rays of the sun. "Almost like flames."

Throwing her head back, she laughed in delight. "Yes Susan Millar, your body is quite pleasing to the eye. It will be a great pity having to destroy it when I have no further use of it. Now I suppose I shall have to re-clothe it."

She walked lightly across the room enjoying the movement, the freedom. She threw the wardrobe doors open pulling dresses, skirts, blouses and shoes out and tossing them on to the floor.

"The girl had absolutely no taste in dress."

She wrinkled her nose in disgust at the pile of clothes on the floor, kicking a walking shoe under the bed."

"She stood naked in front of the mirror again. Her eyes flashed like twin sparkling gems. Light radiated from her body. In seconds she was clad in a voluminous caftan style garment in a shade of green that more than complimented the colour of her eyes and hair.

"Let the fools try to send **me** away."

She remained gazing into the mirror, admiring the stunning reflection.

"Her skin seemed to take on a lustre creating a vision of creamy white velvet.

She was beautiful... She was Evil... She was mobile.

It was time for the world to meet "Nemesis".

THE AVENGER

"I believed the one to fear on earth
was the Devil and his dark Abyss.
But no. Fear the fiery wrath
of the Avenging Goddess Nemesis.

M.C

CHAPTER NINE: THE AVENGER

SEISMOLOGY STATION -MONDAY MAY 15th

Simon and Mike were in the conservatory. The book and the tape lay on a table in front of them.

"Susan has taken this better than I expected her to," Simon remarked. "Though I suspect it's because of you. I'm delighted that you two have found love, but I hope it doesn't distract you from the critical situation we and the people of Caplin are facing."

"Distract me! There's no way it could distract me. If anything, it strengthens my resolve to beat this thing." Mike said emphatically.

"Susan knows that this entire situation centres on her... I have persuaded her to leave, she is driving to Salt Lake this afternoon. So let her enjoy the euphoric state she is in at the moment, it will relax her. Right now I am more concerned with the fact that we haven't got through to McCann yet."

"You think it **was** the gas station that exploded?" Simon asked.

"Almost certainly. The tanker also... First the deaths. Then the dreams. communications completely severed. Now mobility brought to a halt. There isn't another gas station between here and Salt Lake City. Caplin is a besieged town Simon."

"That's a pretty strong statement Mike. What you are speaking of is war."

"Yes I know." Mike frowned, he had given this a great deal of thought... It was crazy .. so crazy it scared him to think of it let alone put it into words.

"I think this is exactly what is happening Simon. The initial stages of war. The kind of war no one could ever have imagined."

"Question is... what are we to do?"

"I agree with you Mike, I just needed to hear it from you without any prompting from me."

Mike was relieved. "Thank God you believe me... no one else does. So what do we do Simon?"

"First we must contact Steve. I think he is one and the same as the Indian of my visions."

111

He placed his fingers on his temples, a deep furrow creasing his brow.

"We must also retrieve the... pendant."

He stared at the ring on his finger as if hoping for inspiration.

"Vincent Allen told me something about it. If only I could remember... Odd, I've always had a good memory... I have to remember Mike. I feel it is vital."

A shadow fell across them. "You had better come." Joe said. Anxiety clouding his usually smiling face. "Chief McCann is on the transmitter... He said to tell you... The skull is missing."

"What!" Mike and Simon both shouted at once.

"McCann was obviously under stress. "The skull has gone and if we hadn't got these fires under control, the town would be gone."

Mike was at the transmitter. "Has anyone been hurt... over."

"Four of my men. Three men who were manning the gas station and the driver of the tanker. All are dead. Some of the townsfolk are injured, I'm not sure how many yet... over."

"I'm sorry McCann... I wish there was something I could have done. Is Al okay?...over."

"Al's fine but if you are right about the skull being able to move... Mike, it was on the table right where you dropped your holdall... over."

Mike paled. "My hold..." He turned to Simon, but Simon was already on his way to Mike's room.

"Listen McCann, I'm going to try get a message to the authorities. I don't think they will accept what I have to tell them, but I have to try... McCann I need your support in this... over."

Silence... then. "Okay... You've got it. Ask to speak to General Mitchell, code name Triton. That will get you through. Tell him I have given you the code name. He will listen to you... Then hang us both if you are wrong... over."

Mike smiled in spite of the gravity behind the words...

"Will do. Good luck with the fires McCann... over and out."

Simon came back, a shirt gripped tightly in his hands. He held it out. "Was this done... before you packed it?"

A large scorch mark had ruined the garment.

"No." Mike answered.

Simon shook his head at Mike's questioning look. "If the skull was in your holdall, it certainly isn't now."

"It is imperative that you find the skull."

The two men whirled around at the sound of the voice.

112

The young Indian stood in the doorway. His presence dominating the small room.

Joe took a threatening step forward.

"Relax Joe." Mike caught Joe's arm as he spoke.

"Steve. Am I glad to see you."

"We meet again Mike Mallory."

He turned his impressive face to Simon and inclined his head.

"You and I have met under different circumstances."

"Yes," Simon agreed. "But your name isn't Steve... You are... you are..."

Again the furrow creased his brow. His memory was failing him rapidly.

"You are... Ana... Onotage."

The Indian's eyes narrowed.

(I should have expected and prepared for this manner of attack.)

"Yes Onotage is my name Simon. The skull must be found. It must not come into contact with the girl."

"Is anything wrong gentlemen?"

She walked into the room. A stunning smile on her beautiful face. They stared at her, sensing the change.

Mike went to her side. "Yes Susan, the skull we have told you about is missing."

"Really! Well I am sure it is of no importance."

She smiled again at them. "Goodness, the three of you look so intense. Come along, we will sit down, have a drink and I will convince you of just how unimportant this skull is."

She turned her back on them and walked towards the conservatory.

Simon turned to the others. The Indian had gone.

Mike gave Simon a grim look. "Go with her," he said quietly. "I'll make the call to the Pentagon."

Simon glanced dubiously at the transmitter. "Will it transmit that far?"

"That's no problem. The radio ham, the one Joe used to talk to in Chicago can patch me through. The problem will be getting them to listen to me."

"Okay Mike, do your best. Come with me Joe."

As the two men left, Mike sat at the transmitter and making a mental effort to put Susan out of his mind, he made the contact.

"Hello Chicago. Utah here. Can you patch me through to the Pentagon... over."

"You joking fella." came the astounded reply.

"No joke. Can you do it?... over."

"Yes but this had better be for real man, or I could be in big trouble... over."

"I will take full responsibility." Mike assured him. "This is a matter of extreme urgency... over."

Seconds later a booming voice came over the speaker.

"Who the hell are you mister? I'll have your transmitter traced and closed down. over."

"There will not be any need to trace it sir." Mike replied, unintimidated by the voice. "This is the seismology station of Utah, Mike Mallory speaking. I wish to speak with General Mitchell. Code name Triton... over."

Total silence... Mike was beginning to think they had gone off the air. Then suddenly...

"I'm putting you through now Mallory... over."

Mike heard a strange clicking noise, then an authoritative voice spoke.

"Who the f... are you? And how do you know my code name?...over."

Mike didn't waste words, he gave the General a brief but full account, finally adding... "McCann needs help and he is asking you for it sir.....over."

Silence again except for the radio waves crackling in Mike's ear.

The transmitter burst into life again.

"Only two names have prompted me to listen to what otherwise sounds like the ravings of a madman. "Triton" and "McCann"... I will send a detachment of armed men to investigate. If this turns out to be some kind of sick joke Mallory, I will have you found and shot. My word on it. End of transmission."

"For a few moments Mike allowed himself to think of Susan. He had finally met someone he knew he could spend the rest of his life with. Fear constricted in his throat. She wasn't Susan anymore. What if they had to kill her? He closed his eyes and pushed the thought out of his mind."

He went to join the others.

The atmosphere in the room was electric and oppressive. Susan's cool relaxed composure was a stark contrast.

"Where have you been Mike. You are neglecting me."

Although his nerves were strung out. Mike surprised himself by matching her coolness. "I'm sure Simon and Joe have given you their full attention Susan."

"Of course they have, Simon has made me the most delicious drink.

Sweet white wine and honey... Almost like nectar."

She smiled at him over the rim of her glass.

"Nemesis was enjoying this cat and mouse game immensely.

(It is an age since I have been in a position to toy with human fears.) She smiled at her thoughts. (Now that I have full powers and a human form, I am in no hurry. I will take great pleasure in tormenting them for a while before I destroy them. After all, I have suffered greatly, imprisoned on this earth because of these inferior beings.)"

She could feel the elation rising inside her. The delicious anticipation.

Mike watched her intently. Her eyes were changing colour. They were slowly becoming a vivid turquoise.

Nemesis saw the observation. Quickly repressing her thoughts, her eyes reverted back to emerald.

Simon couldn't stand the tension any longer, rising from his chair he spoke to Mike. "Would you like a drink Mike?"

"Yes I would thank you Simon. I'll have the same as you," noting the clear liquid in his colleague's glass.

Simon nodded and left the room.

"Mike noticed a slight droop to his shoulders. He felt the anger rise inside him for what this being was doing to him, to everyone. Now she had taken someone very special from him. One way or another... They would overpower her... They had to."

Simon was both startled and relieved to find the Indian waiting for him in the kitchen. "Did she see you when we were at the transmitter?"

The young Indian shook his head. "She will not see me until I am ready to show myself to her."

The strange smile played on his lips for a moment, then was quickly replaced by gravity. "You must humour her, on no account force her hand. Warn Mike and Joe of this. Her arrogance could buy us the time we need. Time to find the pendant and the skull. We have misused Time so far... we cannot afford to misuse it further."

Simon placed his fingers on his temple, he felt... inadequate.

Something was stirring deep in his mind... out of reach.

"I will do my utmost... Tell me... Is Susan..."

"Susan is unharmed," the voice was emphatic. "The essence of her being is in suspended animation, but take care, her body must not be harmed. If we win the battle with this fiend. And we **must** win. Then whatever state the body is in, is what Susan will return to."

Simon gazed unseeing through the window. "Onotage... that is your name isn't it?"

"Yes Simon"

"Will we have to .. kill Susan in order to destroy Nemesis?"

"Have faith Simon. I **will** find the pendant. You **must** find the skull. We need both in order to imprison Nemesis. As for Susan. Killing her is the last thing on my mind, she is an innocent victim. I will do everything in my power to preserve her life. You have my solemn promise."

"I will find the skull, if I have to tear this place apart." Simon answered with determination.

Walking back to the conservatory, he regained a little of his confidence, but he was deeply troubled, (I feel I should know the whereabouts of the pendant.) The hand holding the glass shook, spilling some of the liquid.

He stood for a moment remembering his mother's advice in times of stress. Taking several deep breaths, he entered the deathly silent room, forcing a smile.

"Well come on folks." He smiled into each face. "Unwind, relax a little, we're getting too uptight. I suggest we have a game of cards. Get the deck out Joe."

Mike shot him a swift glance, realising that something had brought about a change in Simon, whatever it was, he would give his full support.

"Good idea," he said getting out of his seat and bringing the card table over to the centre of the room. "Susan, let me refill your glass."

Nemesis was momentarily confused... {What trickery is this?} She focused her mind on Simon probing deeply... Nothing... She could perceive nothing but mists. Dense, swirling twisting mists.

{This is definitely a man to be considered. A man to be vigilant of even though I am destroying his memory.}"

She rose slowly to her feet and walked towards Simon.

The table lifted upwards... spinning out of her path, as if a pair of unseen hands had thrown it, scattering cards to the furthest corners of the room. The drink in Simon's hand crashed to the floor.

She stood in front of him... gazing hypnotically into his eyes... Now she perceived the image of a woman. A woman as dark as Simon himself but with eyes like spacial Black Holes. She could feel herself being drawn into their infinite depths. The alien feeling of fear hit her. Dizzily she backed away, arms outstretched in a defensive gesture.

"You are not like the others. You are different but you are no match for me." She spat the words at Simon.

Mike and Joe were like statues during the confrontation, not daring

116

even to breathe.

"Come!... To the top of the building... All of you," she commanded.

Mike walked towards her. "Susan... Please..."

He felt the force hit him as she turned her now turquoise eyes on him. Five feet away from her, yet the force struck him like a physical blow sending him reeling backwards crashing over a chair.

Joe ran to assist him. "Are you alright Mike... Jesus!... She's scorched your sweater."

"Yes, I think so." Mike answered shakily as Joe helped him to his feet.

"I am... Not... Susan. I **am** Nemesis... Remember this."

She led them to the rooftop stairway, turning only once to make certain they were following. So sure of her power over them.

She stood at a parapet facing Caplin. Both hands resting on the wall. A look of pure malice in her beautiful eyes.

A sense of foreboding deep inside Simon made him feel sick. He spoke quietly to Nemesis. "We are well aware of your powers Nemesis. Talk to us. I know you are trapped here, surely with your power and our assistance we can find a way to set you free. Free to go back to where you came from."

She turned on him... Fury enhancing the colour of her eyes.

"I have been trapped here for two hundred and eighty of your years. Why! Because an imbecile who thought she knew all there was to know about Greek mythology called upon me for vengeance and only vengeance can set me free... Make no mistake... I will not take revenge for her alone. I will have my revenge for being held prisoner in your miserable world."

"You cannot seriously intend to hurt innocent people because of one misguided girl."

Simon spoke with a calmness he did not feel. Hoping desperately to persuade her to calm herself and listen to him.

The grotesquely twisted smile that appeared on her face, chilled his blood.

"She turned her glittering eyes towards the town."

"Simon watched in helpless fascination as a whirlwind developed in front of them. He tore his gaze away from the spectacle and saw Nemesis for what she really was.

Hair whipped back from her face. Eyes almost electric blue now. She lifted her arm and pointed towards the town. The whirlwind slowly moved... heading towards Caplin.

"She is insane. Totally and dangerously insane." Only Simon heard

his own murmured words. Desperately he turned to Mike and Joe...
(Where was Mike!)

Joe threw him an answering look casting his eyes in the direction of
the stairs.

She turned abruptly, her terrible gaze looking more like Medusa than
Nemesis.

Simon placed himself between Nemesis and Joe.

"Why are you killing innocent people?" he shouted. No longer caring
if she should turn on him.

"Killing..." She laughed hideously. "I'm not killing them... Not yet."

She stepped to one side. Her eyes capturing Joe, riveting him to the
spot.

"Where is he?" She demanded.

"He stayed downstairs." Joe answered defiantly. He had seen and
heard enough of this creature's arrogance. "He stayed downstairs. You
hit him... Remember? He twisted his ankle."

Nemesis probed his mind and let out a peal of maniacal laughter.

"You dare to harbour rage against Me," another peal of laughter. Joe
took a step towards her, both fists clenched.

She ceased laughing immediately. "Do not tempt me fool." The voice
was softly threatening. "Come! Let us go find your... injured friend."

She walked calmly in between the two men and started down the
stairs.

Mike was in the kitchen placing a bandage on his ankle.

She studied him intently for a moment.

He concentrated hard on the bandage, keeping his eyes averted from
her.

"I shall retire to my room. I have had enough of your boring company
for a while mortals. Do not attempt any form of trickery, it would be
futile and most inadvisable." She gave a penetrating look to each man,
ensuring that her words had the desired impact. Turning on her heel,
she left them to their thoughts.

Simon checked the doorway making sure she had gone before any of
them spoke. It was Mike who broke the silence.

"I sent a message to McCann warning him of what was heading for
them. They have less than two hours to evacuate the people judging by
the speed it was travelling at when it left."

"What!" Simon was astonished. "How on earth did you manage
that?"

Mike gave a wry smile. "We know she can read our minds. I told Joe
that I had hurt my ankle as an excuse for not being with you on the

roof. I figured she had something in mind. I could see and hear what was happening from the garden door near the transmitter..."

"Some being we are up against eh .. Simon?...What chance have we really got... What chance has Susan got?"

"Susan is unharmed Mike. Onotage has assured me of that. He was in the kitchen when I went for your drink. He told me not to aggravate her... Huh, I couldn't have aggravated her more if I'd put a gun to her head."

"It wasn't your fault, you know that." Mike assured him.

"When she got close to you Simon, she read or saw something in you that scared the hell out of her. What was it, what were you thinking of?"

Simon sat down, a frown creasing his brow.

"You're right, something did scare her... What?"

Mike and Joe looked expectantly at Simon.

He shook his head. "I don't know Mike, I stood outside of the room for a few moments while I got a grip of my nerves. I did a couple of the deep breathing exercises my mother taught me."

"Your mother is dead, isn't she Simon?"

"Yes she is. She died four years ago."

"She had psychic powers didn't she? She must have been in your thoughts. Is it possible. Is that what frightened Nemesis?"

"I think you could be right Mike. Nemesis can read our minds, she must know our every thought. Right now we have to think and fast. Apart from scaring her for a moment, she weakened out there, I could feel it, but why... What caused that?"

He faced the two men, looking from one to the other.

"Damn it! I have the answers locked in here somewhere." He jabbed viciously at his temple with his finger. "Something did happen to her out there... What was it!"

Joe shrugged his shoulders. "I don't know Simon. I mean what is out there beside sun, sand and wind. Nothing... but I do know what you mean. She knew my anger, that was in my face, but she couldn't read that I suspected Mike hadn't hurt himself .. and it was there."

"That's right." Mike said quickly. "She couldn't read my mind at all. She doesn't know that I have warned the town, otherwise she would surely have taken some action."

Joe rubbed a hand over his mouth. Getting up from the stool he opened the fridge door staring gloomily inside it.

"Anyone want a drink?"

Both silently waived the offer.

119

Joe took a deep swallow of water, wiping his mouth with a grimace.

He walked slowly over to the large potted plant, studying the yellowing leaves thoughtfully. "You could do with a drink couldn't you old girl." he said softly as he poured some of the water into the container. He spoke to his plants as if they were human. More so if he was feeling low. He turned to Mike and Simon wishing he could say or do something that would help.

"I think I'll make some coffee, get the taste of salt out of my mouth. Are you sure neither of you want a drink?"

Simon stared at Joe, a look of triumph on his face. He clapped both his hands of Joe's shoulders.

"That's it Joe... That's it."

Joe was puzzled. "What Simon... What are you talking about."

"Salt... It's salt that weakens her." Simon laughed, slapping his thigh with his hand.

Mike was instantly alert. "That is why Millar tried to take his daughter to the Salt Lake. Brian Wilkins told me years ago that there was large salt deposits in and around the area, through to where Bailey's mine is..."

"Where the skull was first found." Simon finished the sentence off nodding vigorously to Mike. "But how in God's name did she escape from it."

"Brian was able to determine the age of the skull by the formation of pyrite on it." Mike said. "Wouldn't that have protected it from the salt?... Great Scott!.... Firestone! Adams said that was another name for pyrite... she'd certainly be akin to it. She has a definite yen for fire."

"Damn and blast my memory." Simon shouted. "That's exactly what Vincent Allen told me. How could I forget. Salt is the reason why the skull has to be buried near the lake. Somehow we have to entice her back into the skull."

"Christ! What's wrong with me? If I can forget that... What else have I forgotten."

He paced the kitchen floor like a demented caged animal. "I have to remember."

Joe caught hold of his arm bringing him to a quick standstill.

"This thing we're fighting... This Nemesis .. it seems she is capable of just about everything. Surely she can induce a kind of... of amnesia also. You know you have a good memory Simon, both me and Mike know it. Stop blaming yourself. This is just the kind of panic reaction I'm sure that bitch would love."

Simon gave a brief smile of surprise.

120

"You're right Joe... That's something else I should have known... We have to keep her out of our minds somehow... I am going to my room. It's time I did something positive about my memory. If you are right Mike and it was my mother Nemesis was afraid of, then perhaps she can help us. I'm going to try and contact her. But first we must find the skull."

"I've searched her room." Mike told him. "I didn't have much time, but I don't think it is in there. You go do what you have to do Simon, Joe and myself will look for the skull. Come on Joe... Joe! What are you doing?"

Joe was busy filling three muslin bags with salt.

Simon placed a hand of Joe's shoulder. "Good thinking Joe. It's just as well you two are foresighted enough to be taking action."

With a grim expression on his face, he turned to go to his room, a muslin bag dangling loosely from his fingers.

Mike called after him, "Simon... We're in this together... All of us, not just you. We will find the skull."

CAPLIN. SAME DAY.

"McCann reacted swiftly to Mike's warning of the approaching whirlwind. He and Al had called a town meeting that morning once the fires were more or less under control. In an emergency, the klaxon would be sounded, everyone would gather at the edge of town and do as instructed. It had been put to the test quicker than they expected. The klaxon had been sounded and the residents of Caplin had responded immediately to the alarm. Still it took more than half an hour of precious time to gather the people together."

"Right," McCann shouted. "What fuel we have is in these three trucks. I want the elderly and infirm in them now. The rest of you pick up the children and start walking that way." He pointed north of the town.

"The whirlwind is moving in from the east, I want as much distance between us and the town as quickly as possible. Now move it!" He had to admire these people. Frightened, confused but they sprung into action without question or argument.

Al stood alongside him. "Do you think we'll make it?"

McCann nodded. "We'll make it. We only need a few miles. Mike thinks the whirlwind will stay over the town... It's a show of power Al."

"His own words shocked him. A complete reversal of his way of

121

thinking... Of his logic in less than twenty four hours. After his dream and the unexplained explosions, he hadn't hesitated in believing Mike when he rang with the warning of the coming whirlwind."

Al broke into his thoughts. "Did Mike manage to contact the general?"

"Yes thank God, I just wish my transmitter was strong enough to reach him, but he did listen to Mike enough to promise a detachment of men."

Al stood in the middle of the main street, a mixture of anger, resentment and fear flitting across his face.

"Why the hell didn't I listen to Mike earlier? We might have been able to prevent all this. That she-devil has reduced my town to a ghost town." He spat the words out passionately.

McCann. Jeff. Al and a relief deputy were the only living creatures left in town. Every man, woman, child and animal had been evacuated. The four of them stood in the main street with only the rustling sound of discarded rubbish and occasional banging doors to break the silence.

"No Al, you are wrong. These are just buildings. Your town is out there." McCann pointed to the desert. "Waiting for you..."

"Hell and damnation!... Let's get out of here."

"Al turned eastwards suddenly aware of the rushing wind in his ears. The sky was dark and threatening. The column of the twisting whirling vortex could be plainly seen. A sight that chilled Al to the bone. The noise was becoming deafening as the whirlwind gathered speed heading straight for the town.

"Jesus." Al responded. "Let's get the hell out of here."

Movement down the street caught his eye. He started running, a stream of profanities lost in the wind.

"McCann, startled at first, saw the little girl clutching a kitten seconds after Al. The wind was already buffeting the small body.

Al reached her, scooped her up in his arms and turned to run back, all it seemed in one transition.

McCann, Jeff and the deputy were running towards him.

McCann's warning cry was swept away by the noise of the violent screaming wind as the wooden shop sign left it's moorings and hit Al in the middle of his back, bringing him to his knees, still clutching the child."

"Jeff was the first to reach him, pulling him to his feet and taking the terrified child from him. McCann and the deputy caught hold of Al supporting him between them. Half carrying. Half dragging him. Jeff, seeing the station wagon still parked outside the sheriff's office headed for it , battling to stay upright.

Quickly placing the child inside (still hugging the kitten to her body), hoping to God it wouldn't turn over, he ran to help the others. Between them they hauled Al into the back seat."

"The noise was now ear-splitting. The whirlwind was almost upon them. Ominously dark and threatening, like an accusing finger of wrath pointing to the town."

"There just might be enough fuel left to get us out of here." Jeff had to shout as loud as his lungs allowed to be heard.

"Keep your fingers crossed," he bellowed at McCann.

"Pausing only to strap the child in, he put his foot down, climbing gears faster than he had ever done in his life.

Tyres and engine screaming, he skidded down the street, swerving and mounting the kerb as debris careered across his path. The small post office in front of them imploded. First scattering bricks and money, then drawing them upwards before spewing them onto the town."

"Something solid hit the windscreen shattering it into a million fragments, showering him and the child with needle sharp tiny shards. He could feel the force of the wind lifting the vehicle as he struggled for control. Still he kept his foot down, grim determination etched deeply into his face."

"The road in front of him was blocked. McCann was shouting to him, the wind stealing his words. He caught one word "playground".

The veins in his neck stood out like thick cords as he savagely pulled at the wheel, almost turning the vehicle over. A section of the school collapsed like a child's lego building. He drove towards it."

"The iron railings around the playground had been uprooted from their cement bases. Solid blocks of concrete and rails with vicious looking spikes reared up at them. Jeff's speed never faltered, he tore across them feeling the metal ripping into the tyres, tearing at the wheel frame. He didn't dare stop, another few seconds and the vortex would be on them. He headed for the gap he had seen as the school collapsed... it was still there.... Thank God."

Only when they were clear of danger, did he ease off the pedal." He glanced down at the little girl. Frightened clear blue eyes stared back at him.

"You okay honey?" he asked gently.

She nodded, solemnly hugging the struggling kitten ever closer. She looked alright, no sign of blood although she was surrounded by glass.

"How's Al?" he called to his passengers.

"If I can survive your blasted driving, I can survive anything."

Jeff gave a wide grin at Al through the cracked driving mirror.

"A little tetchy today aren't we?"

McCann laughed out loud, the others joined him. Relived at escaping the noise and fury of the whirlwind.

"That was a skilful piece of driving Jeff. I'll ride shot-gun for you anytime." McCann said patting Jeff's shoulder.

Jeff saw three men running towards them. "I think this is your daddy sweetheart," he said, recognising Frank Gibbons in the lead.

Jeff slowed the limping vehicle to a stop and eased himself out, surprised at the ache in his muscles.

"Okay Frank," he could see the strain on the man's face.

"She's here. She's safe."

Frank stopped as he caught sight of the child in the passenger seat. "Katy."

He walked swiftly to the door, taking the child out, holding her close to him, both eyes shut tight.

"Don't cry Daddy, I'm fine. Mr Al came for me and Bluey, but Mr Al got hurt."

Frank's eyes sprang open. "You hurt bad Al?"

"No Frank, only bruised I think. Where is everyone?"

"Just beyond that hill Al. We thought it would offer more protection."

Al nodded appreciatively. "Good thinking Frank. Is everyone accounted for?"

"Yes, we've done a check, that's how we realised Katy was missing." Frank hugged the child again.

"McCann." Jeff shouted pointing towards the hill.

An army vehicle had driven into view. McCann stood waiting, arms folded until the driver drew abreast of them. A young officer stepped down from the truck.

"Which one of you gentlemen is Chief of Police James McCann?" His eyes settled on McCann.

"I am."

The officer saluted, then extended his hand. "Lieutenant John Brady at your disposal sir. General Mitchell sends his compliments... and a message." The officer looked uncomfortable.

"Go ahead Lieutenant." McCann prompted.

"Sir, I have been instructed to deliver this message word for word... The message reads. "McCann. What the f...k is going on and who is the demented b.....d on the transmitter." End of message."

"Sorry sir."

McCann gave a quick smile before placing a hand on Brady's shoulder. "Don't apologise son, I understand the man and the message perfectly."

McCann turned and watched the whirlwind, now directly over the town.

"Sir," Brady spoke, concern in his voice. "We have been tracking this twister ever since it came into view. It's been on course for the town without veering, but none of the weather stations I have contacted know anything about it."

McCann continued watching the whirlwind tearing the town apart. He face an expressionless mask.

"Sir, I think we should move these people now. It may change course."

The residents of Caplin had gathered near the parked vehicles. They were witnessing the destruction of their town. Some were weeping openly. Most watched in total silence.

"It won't change course lieutenant. It won't even leave the town." McCann answered quietly.

"You can't be sure of that," Brady persisted. "These devils are bloody well unpredictable if you'll excuse my saying so."

McCann held his arm up to still Brady's words.

All eyes were riveted on the whirlwind. It was diminishing. Fading. Gradually becoming less visible until suddenly... it was gone.

A shocked silence filled the air.

Brady stood open-mouthed. "That's... Incredible..."

McCann nodded. "Come along lieutenant, I'll ride with you and fill you in on what is happening here. After what you have just witnessed, you should find it easier to accept than I did when I first came to Caplin. I then want you to make a full report to General Mitchell, I'll back you up of course. You <u>can</u> contact the General?"

"Communication has been intermittent sir, the closer we got to Caplin, the harder it became."

"Well do your best Lieutenant... it could be vital."

McCann took command with the ease of a man who expects to be obeyed. "Jeff will you organise the soldiers and my men for checking the buildings in town, we have to get these people under cover before nightfall. I'll take Al with me. Have you a doctor with you lieutenant?"

"Yes sir."

"Good. I want him to take a look at Al, he took a hefty knock saving that child."

"Yes sir, I'll have the medic ride with us. You have been lucky only having one casualty. I'm curious as to how you knew about the whirlwind in advance."

"Like I said lieutenant. I'll explain everything on the way back to town. By the way. How did you get here so fast?"

"We were already in the area on manoeuvres, that's how come we got the assignment."

"The return to town was better than McCann expected. The church was reasonably safe, as was the chapel. Most of the hospital was still intact, even some of the houses were habitable."

Lieutenant Brady watched as the townsfolk cheerfully set up temporary dwellings. He was sceptical of what McCann and Al had told him, but General Mitchell had a high opinion of McCann so... until proven otherwise...

"You must be proud of them sir." he spoke out loud to Al.

"I am. Proud of them... And afraid for them."

Brady studied the sheriff's profile. He had been given an outstanding report on the sheriff also. A war veteran. A courageous intelligent man. A man to be trusted."

"So am I." McCann broke in on Brady's thoughts. "I feel like I am a part of them and I've only known them for a short while. Don't worry Al. We're not on our own. We have help now."

"Lieutenant," one of the soldiers called. "There is a man by the name of Mallory on the transmitter."

McCann jumped in. "Okay if I take the call lieutenant?"

"Certainly sir. It's probably you he wants anyway."

"You need salt McCann." Mike's voice came over the transmitter. "Plenty of salt. Spread it around the town. Insist on people carrying it around with them. I don't know how much protection it will offer, but it will help. Over."

"Okay Mike. Anything else. Over"

"Yes. You must convince General Mitchell that Nemesis **does** exist. She is not only powerful... but potently dangerous. I think she intends to destroy more than Caplin. We need a lot more than a detachment of soldiers. Be prepared for the worst. Over and out."

Brady had thought he would have to drive out of Caplin in order to contact the Pentagon. To his surprise, the General came through loud and clear. He made a personal report to General Mitchell.

"Alright lieutenant. You are there. What is your opinion. Over."

"McCann and Jackson are both sound men. It's Mallory I'm not too sure about." He related the instructions Mike had given about needing

126

salt.

"Alright lieutenant. Leave it with me. I'll be in touch. Over and out."

Brady was puzzled McCann had told him they couldn't reach the General on their transmitter. Yet it had the same range as the one he and his men had brought with them. He shrugged his shoulders.

"This whole situation is bizarre." he muttered.

SEISMOLOGY STATION SAME DAY.

"Simon walked slowly to his room, worried and uneasy at his forgetfulness, yet common sense told him that Joe was right, this was indeed the work of Nemesis. After a quick shower, he lay naked on the bed. Closing his eyes, he gradually forced the jumble of confusing fears and thoughts, out of his troubled mind.

His body began to relax completely. Allowing his inner self to release command of his mental and physical energy."

"He drifted in time and space. Fleeting images of people he knew flashed before him. Whispered voices. Long forgotten memories stirring in the recesses of his mind. Then blissfully. Nothing. Only darkness and a feeling of being at one with peace.

He was aware of the much need courage and vitality pouring into him. Filling his body and soul until he thought he would burst.

His mother's face appeared mistily before him and he knew she was helping him."

"My Son." Her voice floated across timeless aeons.

"You have a trial of strength facing you. Your opponent is a powerful and merciless Avenger. She clouded your mind for a while, creating forgetfulness of all you have learned, but you will remember everything.

You are aware of her probing your thoughts. You must be on your guard against this. Cloak your mind. Think only of the rings. Think of Alpha and Omega. Instruct your friends to do likewise. For all her power, she cannot go beyond this thought.

Listen carefully to my words Simon. She has learned of nuclear weapons and I fear she will attempt to use this knowledge. Her revenge knows no boundaries. It is imperative that you stop her. One thing is in your favour. She has been wrongly informed."

"What do you mean Mother?"

"I cannot say more than I have my son." Her face was fading from his vision.

127

"Mother... Mama... Don't go... We need your help."

"Have faith Simon. I can do nothing that may change the chosen path of your life. But know this my son, you have a staunch ally with more power than you realise..."

She was gone... She was gone and he was no wiser... Yet another face appeared before him. Long red-gold hair framing the exquisite eyes.

"Susan!"

"No Simon. It is I... Sarah." The emerald green eyes smiled sympathetically.

"Simon, the skull is inanimate now and is destroying the life that hides it. You must place it in a salt filled casket. Keep it safe. It is vital."

The vision was fading.

"Sarah... Sarah... Don't go... I'm afraid of Nemesis... I'm afraid of losing this fight."

She too was gone, but her voice drifted back to him.

"Only a fool is unafraid Simon. You are not a fool."

"Simon opened his eyes and sat upright. His mind clear once more. He remembered everything as his mother had promised."

(So! Nemesis knew of nuclear weapons. How... was unimportant but in what way was she wrongly informed. The skull. Destroying the life that hides it. Where?)

"Simon's thoughts came to a standstill. Vital questions without answers. He had once read that the answers to all questions were in the labyrinth of the mind. He sincerely hoped this was true."

He dressed and went in search of Mike and Joe. He found them in the observatory. Dejected expressions on both faces.

"Where is she?" he asked.

"Still in Susan's room." Mike answered. "We have looked everywhere for the skull Simon." Mike spread his arms in a helpless gesture.

"I just don't know where else to look... How do **you** feel now?"

"I feel fine Mike. More important... I remember everything."

He told them of the powerful ally. "This," he smiled, "Can only be Onotage." He told them of his visions and the puzzling words. Joe jumped to his feet excitement showing on his face. "I can't help you with the nuclear part, but I sure as hell know where the skull is now. Come on."

He led the way to the kitchen, running, slipping on small carpets. Simon and Mike close at his heels. He burst through the kitchen door.

"Look," he said triumphantly, pointing to the large potted plant in the alcove. The yellowing leaves were drooping. Joe touched one gently.

The leaf fluttered slowly to the floor. Carefully he picked it up, placing it beside the container. He felt guilty.

"That's only happened today. I have to admit it's puzzled me. You know how I feel about my plants, I haven't given it much attention with all that is happening."

The plant was obviously dying.

"Destroying the life that hides it." Mike said hopefully. He turned the plant around. The disturbed soil was plain to see. Probing gently, he slowly pulled out the skull.

"Hell! I never thought I would be so glad to see this thing again." He held the repulsive object at arm's length. Staring at it as if it was the Devil himself. The sunlight caught it in its rays producing an eerie sheen from the pyrite coating. Mike shuddered.

"In here." Joe held out a large bag of salt. "We haven't got a casket, but I'm sure this will do for the time being."

"Now." Mike spoke grimly. "I have to contact the Pentagon again. Warn them that she may try use nuclear weapons."

Simon looked dubious. "Do you think they will listen Mike?"

"I don't know. I'll contact McCann first, find out if everyone is okay. If they don't listen to me, maybe they will listen to him, he cannot possibly have any doubts now. I'll patch him through to the Pentagon if necessary."

"Mike was relieved to hear from McCann that apart from Al's injury, there had been no other casualties, thanks to his warning. He learned that the solders were there, which meant that the General had not only listened to him, but had been as good as his word. It also meant the General could possibly contact McCann himself."

Once more he asked Chicago to patch him through to the Pentagon.

"Mallory. I don't know who you are or what you are." General Mitchell sounded dangerously impatient.

"I have already sent a detachment of men to Caplin. I am now sending another detachment by helicopter. This time I am sending them to you. Over."

"Good." Mike responded. "If that is intended as a threat, believe me sir, it is a godsend. Maybe you should try contacting McCann yourself, I think perhaps you will find his logical outlook has changed a little. Over and out."

Mike looked up from the transmitter. Joe stood alongside him, an odd expression on his face.

"For God's sake Joe... What... is... wrong?" The words came out slowly.

129

"Simon's gone!"

"Gone!... What do you mean. Where has he gone?"

"I don't know Mike. He seemed to go into a trance. Then said the Indian needed him. He took my bike and... left."

THE PENTAGON. SAME DAY.

General Mitchell replaced the receiver. The red scrambler :ON: light was flashing, he ignored it.

"Well." He said to the man sat opposite him.

The man picked up the dossier in front of him. The name Michael Mallory printed in large letters across the front. He pushed his rimless spectacles back onto the bridge of his rather large nose, shaking his head in silence.

"Come on Saul. You are the best goddamned psychiatrist we have. I want an answer. What is your opinion?" General Mitchell pounded the desk with his fist.

The man looked at the general over the rim of his specs, nervously cleared his throat and answered.

"Based on the dossier. The tape recording of his first conversation with you and the conversation I have just heard now, it is my opinion that Mr Michael Mallory is a very intelligent, positively sane but extremely frightened man."

The silence weighed heavily in the small room for a while, then the general spoke again.

"I was afraid you would say that Saul. I have had a gut feeling all along that Mallory is genuine." Silence again.

"So, if I am to assume that this... Nemesis creature exists, then I have to assume that she is capable of and intends to turn nuclear weapons on this country... I have to act."

"You surely do not have the authority to place the forces on alert without the President's consent." The psychiatrist's tone was acidly sarcastic.

"No, I do not." General Mitchell ignored the sarcasm. "But I do have the authority to contact Naval Command and have them place the U.S.S. "Medway" on alert."

"Medway! She is in Japanese waters isn't she?"

General Mitchell gave a cynical smile. "I have told you before Saul, you do **not** know everything that goes on in this building. You only think you do. The U.S.S. Medway is in the Pacific, just off Coos Bay. A perfect position in fact. She carries Phantom aircraft, the best fighters in the world. I'll have her placed on alert, then I will contact the President and persuade him to listen to me."

"And how do you intend to do that?" The psychiatrist's tone was deliberately belligerent now.

"I believe that something strange is happening, and so do you, but convincing the President on such flimsy evidence could prove rather difficult."

"You sir," The cynical smile around the general's mouth again belied the softness of his voice. "You sir are a close friend and confidante of the President. You... are coming with me."

The psychiatrist leapt to his feet. "I am sorry, but it is out of the question, I cannot place my reputation in such jeopardy."

"Saul. You already have, and there is no backing out of it." General Mitchell gently tapped a finger on the recorder alongside him. A warning expression on his face.

Saul Kramer looked as if he was about to explode, then with an unhappy look of resignation on his face, he reluctantly nodded.

General Mitchell picked up the phone. "Get me Naval Command." He came off the phone with a grim but satisfied smile.

"Now... The President."

"You believe all of this General Mitchell?" The president spoke his words with precise care.

"Yes Mr President, I do. I believe McCann, I believe Mallory, and I believe the situation requires an immediate investigation."

Kramer was painfully aware of the ticking of the clock as the President's eyes came to rest on him.

"And you Saul. Do you believe it?"

"Yes I do believe it Mr President. It is the most incredible tale I have ever heard... but I do believe that something of extraordinary proportions is happening in Caplin."

"Then gentlemen, I have no alternative but to believe it too. If I refuse to believe it then I am perhaps placing this country in mortal danger..."

"General Mitchell, you will go to Caplin yourself and take command of the situation. You will report directly to me. Whatever the problem is, I want it contained. You understand. On no account must any of this be made known to the public. If it is true, then it would cause serious panic. If it proves to be a .. fallacy... Then it would cause serious damage to the credibility of myself and of the U.S.A.. We would be... a laughing stock to say the very least. It must remain top secret until I say different... Good day gentlemen."

General Mitchell contacted McCann.

"Mac, I have discussed the situation with Saul Kramer and the President. We have come to a decision. As for Mallory, if he contacts you again, tell him I believe him. I will see you shortly. Yes, I am taking command myself. I will fly to Salt Lake City, from there I have a helicopter laid on. Over and out."

THE INDIAN SETTLEMENT. SAME DAY.

"Tension in the village was running high. The elders were in council. Onotage and his grandfather were leading the gathering.

Onotage looked worriedly around the old faces. All the younger men were elated. They had seen the whirlwind. They had seen it bypass them and hit the white man's town. They knew that the Power walked the earth once again. Instead of being afraid, they welcomed it. They saw it as a sign. A sign of freedom from the white man. They were convinced that only the white man would suffer, and that they, the Indians would gain their lands back. They were drunk with euphoria. Not even their respect for Onotage and his grandfather could quell the fever of excitement rising in the blood of the young men."

"The old Indian could not be persuaded to give the location of the Pendant unless all the elders were in agreement. Onotage was disturbed and astounded when he realised that some of the elders actually believed the young men could be right. He could see it in their faces. Hear it in their murmurings. The old dreams being resurrected."

He stood and entered the circle of elders. The babble of voices hushed.

"You know who I am." He addressed them in a firm voice.

"You know who my forefather was... Hiawatha... The greatest Indian of all time... The creator of the Five Nations. I speak with his wisdom... With his knowledge. Do not listen to the wild dreams of the young and foolish. The Power will not stop at the white man. Have you forgotten that Indians died also when the Power walked this earth the first time?"

One of the elders stood and faced the council.

"We have the symbol of the Power. It will protect us as it protected our ancestors before us."

"It did not protect our ancestors."

Onotage glared at the faces that surrounded him, the glow of the small fire cast an elongated shadow of his body, creating a larger than life effect.

"It did not protect them. It will not protect you. It will be the cause of your destruction. She has to destroy the Pendant. It is the one thing that can inert her powers. Force her into dormancy again. I must have the Pendant now."

He turned to his grandfather. "It is your duty to make the right decision."

"He didn't voice his thoughts in front of the council, but the old man saw them in his eyes. Onotage would make the decision for him. He would claim his right to Chieftain and the old man would be obliged to reveal the whereabouts of the Pendant."

"Onotage walked out of the building. He would give them fifteen minutes then... He didn't want to think of what he must do. He did **not** wish to disgrace the old man... but he would if he had to."

"Onotage sat cross-legged beneath the stars. Closing his eyes, he called on the ancients for the strength and wisdom he needed. He thought of Simon. Simon knew where the Pendant was, Onotage was sure of this. Nemesis was robbing him of his knowledge, he had seen this when he had last spoken to him. Onotage projected his thoughts to Simon."

"I need your help Simon... I need your mind wholly."

Simon's face floated before him. "I am in full command of my mind again Onotage. I know where the Pendant is. Look inside the old..."

"The blow to the back of Onotage's head rendered him unconscious. His last fleeting vision was of the shock on Simon's face."

"Onotage opened his eyes to darkness... (No stars). He shook his head trying to clear the fogginess. (Still no stars.) (Where am I... What has happened).

The pain in his head reminded him. He tried to put a hand to his head, and realised he was bound hand and foot. He shook his head again in disbelief, clearing his vision and saw that he lay inside the council lodge. Empty now of the elders.

Struggling to sit upright, he looked around the now semi-darkened room. His eyes came to rest on the still form of his grandfather laying beneath the Totem Pole."

"Grandfather."

"He is dead."

The voice from behind startled him. Straining to turn his head, he gazed into the blind eyes of Eagle Star, his grandfather's closest friend.

"They did not kill him... His heart was old and tired. Too old and tired to deal with the anger of the younger men. It stopped beating."

"They killed him Eagle Star." Onotage cried passionately.

"They killed him with their stupidity. Listen to them."

The sound of the young Indians dancing the almost forgotten Ghost Dance could be heard outside.

"They are trying to resurrect an age that is dead and buried. You must help me. Set me free."

"If I do this," the old man pondered. "They will kill me."

"If you do not... We will all die Eagle Star..."

"You are right Onotage... Your grandfather had decided to reveal the whereabouts of the Pendant to you. They attacked you. He died soon after."

The old man shuffled towards him, dropping to his knees when his feet came into contact with Onotage. From the sleeve of his garment, he produced an ornate handled knife honed to razor sharpness.

"You will have to guide my hand with your voice lest I cut you. It is many years since this weapon drew blood. Let it stay that way."

Onotage knew the old man was speaking metaphorically, his reference to blood... was to the blood of battle... not to his blood.

When his bonds were cut, Onotage led the old man to the Totem Pole at his request.

"If I am to die this night, then it will be beside my old friend." Onotage placed his hand on the old man's shoulder. "I was unable to help my grandfather. I swear you will not die."

The old man smiled, patting the firm hand on his shoulder.

"Tell me Eagle Star, how long was I unconscious?"

"Not very long. You are young and strong and being who you are, they dare not hit you too hard."

"Moving cautiously to the doorway, he studied the skies deciding he had been unconscious for no more than an hour. He then took in the scene before him.

It was like a glimpse of the past. The young men were in full war paint, dancing around a fire, the pulsing beat of the drums sending them into a frenzy."

Drawing back from the door, he shook his fist in anger. "I have to find the Pendant."

"The whooping suddenly grew louder. He looked out again, striking the ground with his fist in frustration. Several Indians were dragging a wildly struggling figure towards the fire. Whoever it was, they were putting up a tremendous fight. Fury surged through him as he recognised Simon. If he went out now, they would both be lost. He ran back to Eagle Star."

"You said my grandfather was going to tell me where the Pendant is hidden. Did he say anything at all?"

The old man turned his sightless eyes to Onotage.

"Your grandfather's last and only words were... "Lay me beneath the Totem Pole."

"Onotage stepped back staring up at the still impressive Ancient Symbol of the past. His past. This totem was Hiawatha's legacy. Each carved image represented one of the Five Nations.

Onotage felt his blood quicken. Ancient memories stirring in his mind. He forced them away. Concentrating instead, on Simon.

"Look inside the old..."

"The Totem Pole. It has to be in there."

Gently but swiftly, he scooped his grandfather's body into his arms. Eagle Star placed a hand on his shoulder and stood upright with him.

"I have sensed turmoil in you for many years my son. May the wisdom of your ancestor be with you in what you are about to do."

Onotage placed them both on the far side of the room. Standing beneath the Totem Pole, he mustered every ounce of strength in his body and pushed. The strain showed on his face. The Totem Pole was moving...

"Have... to... keep pushing."

Now it was beginning to rock...

"One... more... pusssssh."

Over it came .. Onotage falling with the momentum.

"It hit the ground with a force that split the old timber asunder, bringing the front of the wooden building down with it, allowing the glow from the fire to enter.

There reflected in the flames... Lay the Pendant."

"Onotage grasped the Pendant and walked towards the Indians, holding it aloft. The Indians who had surged forward now fell back, some dropping to their knees, fear on their faces."

"Release that man." Onotage commanded.

Simon staggered towards him. "Thank God you're safe."

His eyes fell on the Pendant, a wry smile creasing his face.

"Now... maybe we can kick that hellcat's ass."

"Onotage flashed a returning smile. Without doubt, Simon was definitely in command of his mind again. He turned then to the now silent Indians, surveying them with a disparaging expression that made him look much older than his seventeen years. The look brought fear to their hearts. He started to address them in their own language, but the drone of approaching helicopters drowned his words."

"Huh! Trust the cavalry to arrive too late." Simon muttered.

The joke died on his lips as a piercing flash of blue light sprang from the desert, striking one of the helicopters. The machine erupted in a violent explosion of flames, lighting up the darkened skies. The Indians scattered as burning fuel and white hot pieces of metal descended on them, killing several men."

Throwing themselves to the ground, Onotage and Simon glanced at each other... The unspoken word flashing between them...

"Nemesis."

"We must return to the station." Onotage shouted above the mayhem. He turned once more to the regrouping Indians.

"Tend your wounded and dead. Clean your faces." His voice had the sting of a whiplash.

"I am charging all of you younger men with the safety of the elders, the women and the children. If just one of you should be foolish enough to disobey me... I will know and I will deal with him. Take great care of my grandfather's body and of Eagle Star."

He turned his back on the subdued Indians....

"Come Simon... The Battle has begun."

THE BATTLE

"I know that I shall meet my fate,
Somewhere in the clouds above;
Those that I fight I do not hate,
Those that I guard I do not love."

W.B. Yeats. (An Irish airman forsees his Death)

CHAPTER TEN: THE BATTLE

MON NIGHT MAY 15th

Simon followed Onotage. His admiration for the young Indian growing almost as fast as his curiosity. "I left the bike not far from here."

"Good." replied Onotage. "Speed is vital and judging by the speed you must have driven here, I gather you know how to handle this machine."

Simon gave a short laugh. "Yes I can handle it, motorbikes are no mystery to me... but you are. Tell me. Who are you? What are you? Why do I feel so... akin to you?"

Onotage gave him a piercing smile. "So many questions I am surprised you do not already know the answers. I am a man with a gift like yourself. Did your mother never tell you that her spiritual guide was an Indian?"

"Yes she did."

"Onotage smiled again. "Your mother's guide was the greatest of all Indians... Hiawatha." He spoke the name with a fierce pride.

"Of whom I am a direct descendant. You inherited your mother's powers and my forefather's guidance, though until now you have chosen to ignore them. They are the bond between you and myself."

"I am a part of your Destiny Simon Kane."

Simon's heart missed a couple of beats.

"It is also the reason why my grandfather and I are held in great esteem at the lodge. Until emotions ran higher than intelligence that is."

The anger rose in his voice. "My grandfather is dead because of this."

They reached the bike.

"Come." Onotage commanded. "We have no more time for words. We have a battle to fight... And Win."

Mounting the bike, Simon pointed it in the direction of the station.

"I am a part of your Destiny Simon Kane."

"The words spun around in Simon's head. He didn't ask their meaning. He didn't want to know... Not yet."

138

"He looked towards the lodge. At the burning fires dotted here and there from the wrecked helicopter. There had been no survivors.

The smell of burning fuel filling the air along with the shouts of the Indians endeavouring to extinguish the fires, gave the words of Onotage greater impact."

"The Battle **had** already begun."

The station resembled an armed forces camp. Twice they were challenged. The second time Mike intervened.

"Thank God you are here. Susan has gone. She is heading for the town."

"Have you informed McCann?" Onotage was quick to ask.

"Yes. There is a detachment of soldiers there with them, but I think the Major here should take his men to the town also. They are better armed."

"I disagree Mike." said Onotage. "I do not think arms are going to have much affect on her, assuming it was her who brought the helicopter down."

"My God yes. Did you see it? Those poor devils didn't have a chance. She seemed to glow from head to toe. Held out both her arms... It was like... like pure fire power pouring out of her. We couldn't stop her."

Mike thumped the wall in frustration. "There's only one solution isn't there. She can only possess a Millar. There are no other Millars. Not here anyway. The only logical answer is to... kill Susan." He threw a challenging look at Onotage. "That's the truth of it... isn't it?"

Onotage placed his hands on Mike's shoulders, looking sternly into his eyes. "It is not the only way. I have made a vow to rid the earth of Nemesis and save the life of Susan. Only as a last resort will we consider such an action. And Mike. It will not be my action." He didn't add that it could well be impossible to kill Susan while Nemesis possessed her body. That Nemesis herself would most certainly kill Susan once she had no further use of her.

"You have proven yourself worthy Mike. Do not lose faith now. I need you to think positive. Susan needs you to think positive. Now introduce me to the Major please. I need to speak with him."

"Simon, I want you to relax and concentrate on Vincent Allen, his daughter and Sarah Millar. They have come to you before and given their help. We need their help again. I want Sarah Millar to materialise and offer herself in place of Susan."

Mike jumped at these words, his face alive with excitement.

"Is this possible? Can it be done? Will she do it?"

"Mike... Mike... I do not know if it can be done... I only know it is worth trying. Now calm down and come with me. Leave Simon to relax."

"Major Ian Price was in deep conversation with his lieutenant. He was a tall, wiry straight backed man with eyes such a pale blue, when the light caught them, they looked almost colourless.

Until recently he had been in action in Vietnam. Badly wounded and shipped home. He had surprised his superiors by being back on his feet and reporting for duty again in less than four months.

This was the duty he had received. He had just witnessed sixteen of his men wiped out in their own country. He was an angry and confused man."

Mike approached the two men. The Major turned his pale gaze on him. "Yes Mr Mallory. What can I do for you now?"

He tolerated this civilian, only because he had been instructed to do so.

"Major Price." Mike ignored the impatient tone in the Major's voice. "This is Onotage, the young man I have spoken to you about. He would like a word with you."

"The Major's depreciating gaze slowly travelled to Onotage. He ignored the offered handshake. "I presume you are a part of this far fetched, totally incredible yarn I am expected to believe... No," he held a hand up. "You do not have to answer that question, I can see by your expression that you are. I have orders from General Mitchell to listen to and assist Mr Mallory, Mr Kane, Chief McCann and yourself in any way that I can... but I will add that while I have every respect for General Mitchell and will of course obey him. It is in my opinion, that this country is under attack from a foreign source... possibly Japan or Russia. That was a highly technical laser attack that brought one of my helicopters down, killing sixteen of my men, and I intend to seek out and destroy the persons responsible."

Mike sighed, he had already heard this from the Major as soon as he had set foot in the station.

Onotage merely shrugged, "Major, I understand your feelings..."

"Fine." Major Price interrupted. "Then there is nothing more to be said on the matter. Now, how may I assist you."

The dangerous glint that had appeared in Onotage's eyes slowly subsided. "I require a helicopter to transport Mr Mallory, Mr Kane and myself to Battle Mountain..."

Mike's mouth opened and closed in shock as the astonished Major echoed the words.

"Battle Mountain!... What on earth for?"

"I am convinced that is where she will go." Onotage answered calmly. "That is where she will prepare to take her revenge in full."

Major Price gave him a sneering smile. "You actually believe this Nemesis exists, don't you?"

"She exists Major. You have witnessed her first serious attack."

"Are you not afraid she will attack the helicopter and kill you as she supposedly killed my men?"

"Onotage ignored the heavy sarcasm in the Major's words.

"She exists Major. She killed your men just as surely as she has killed people in the town, just as surely as she created a whirlwind. Yours were not the only casualties in this attack. The helicopter came down over my lodge. Simon and myself were very lucky... Some of my people were not so fortunate. As for attacking us... That is a risk I am prepared to take... I will inform you when we are ready to go."

The Major gave him a withering look. "I will decide what risks will be taken with my men and transport. We are going to the town. That is where they are needed. If it is possible to drop you near Battle Mountain, I will... but I will not endanger my men to do so. I hope I have made myself clear."

"Crystal clear Major. When will General Mitchell arrive?"

Price stared arrogantly into Onotage's eyes for a moment... A nervous tic appeared in the corner of his mouth... he lowered his gaze.

"I suppose while you are out chasing will o' the wisps on Battle Mountain, you will be out of my hair and as I do not want demonic alarmist near my men..."

"Will you take us Major?" Onotage demanded.

The tic was visible again.

"Yes...."

Cutting short another tirade of words, Onotage abruptly turned away.

"That... Major Price is all I need to know. Come Mike. We have preparations to make."

As they walked away, the Major called after them.

"By the way Mr... Whatever your name is... I will tell **you** when **we** are ready to go."

Mike spun around to go back, fury on his face. Onotage caught his arm and silently shook his head.

"Mr Mallory." An officer caught up with them. "I am Lieutenant Skellern. Please don't think too badly of Major Price. He recently returned home from Vietnam. He saw a lot of good men die over there. Young men. He saw a lot of women and children killed or horribly maimed. He believes in facts and war is a very unpleasant fact. You have your beliefs... and he has his. He said he would get you to Battle Mountain... and that is exactly what he will do gentlemen." With a smart salute, the lieutenant left them.

"I don't suppose we can blame him." Mike said still struggling to control his temper. "But he's one hell of an arrogant b.....d. I don't know how you managed to stay calm... I wanted to... hit him." (I seem to be losing my temper a lot lately. Small wonder.) He dismissed the thought.

"Mike... anger is a negative emotion, useless. As long as he keeps his word... his arrogant opinions are of no consequence."

"Why do you think she will go to Battle Mountain?" Mike asked as he and Onotage were packing climbing equipment.

"Nemesis has been locked inside Sarah Millar's skull for nearly three hundred years. She wants revenge for this... but first... she wants to show her power. She wants to see human fear."

"Why Onotage... why is she so vengeful? I don't know a great deal about Greek gods, I remember reading that some had a wicked sense of humour, but this being is pure... malice. But that still doesn't explain Battle Mountain."

"She has become so warped Mike, that she will stop at nothing in order to satiate her lust for fear. She has a sense of the dramatics. The very name "Battle Mountain" not only will, but has impressed her. What more aptly named place could she choose to make her final impact on us... She will wait until the whole world knows of her existence. Then she will engage in a battle to bring about the downfall of mankind."

Mike stared at him. "You think she will try to destroy the entire human race... Why?"

"She has become a misanthropic. She has a hatred of mankind."

"How can you be so sure of all this Onotage?"

Onotage frowned. "I cannot reach into her mind... but I do receive impulses from her... I can feel her hatred of humans... It is when she is in this highly charged state of mind that I receive these impulses. The words "Battle Mountain" have entered my sub-conscious several times." He paused for a while. The silence giving his next words more impetus.

"We have to stop her Mike before more armed forces arrive. Don't you find it strange that the only communications allowed to carry through are the ones to bring armed forces here. This will only provide her with a means to display her power... and our vulnerability."

"Do you really think she intends to destroy the world?" Mike asked quietly.

Onotage's young features suddenly appeared much older. "Yes I do Mike. Remember the words of Simon's mother. "She has learned of nuclear weapons." I think she intends to turn them against us."

"Simon's mother also said that Nemesis had been wrongly informed and this was in our favour." Mike pointed out.

"Yes... I have given those words a great deal of thought. This information has to be something the media thinks is fact... But in truth.... I have an idea about this. I am hoping General Mitchell will be in a position to clarify it when he arrives here."

They went to Mike's room and retrieved the skull from the inside of the TV. Joe's brain wave for a safe hiding place.

Mike opened a drawer and carefully took out a metal chest.

"This was my late aunt's most treasured possession. It survived the horror of Pearl Harbour, so I know it is fireproof. It belonged to my aunt's fiancee. He didn't survive unfortunately... I think they both would approve of us using it. Under the circumstances."

"Onotage took the chest in his hands, gently running sensitive fingers over every groove, every dent.

"This chest has a good feel to it Mike. Vibrations of love, courage and strength radiate from it. That is good." He half filled the chest with salt, removed the pendant from around his neck and placed it, and the skull into the still solid and once ornate chest. The scars of the holocaust still evident on the metal. He closed the lid gently but firmly."

"What do you want me to do Mike?" Joe stood in the doorway.

"I feel like a third leg. I need to help."

Mike left the answer to Onotage.

"You're a good man Joe and you will help. I want you to go with the Major to town. I think you may be receptive enough for me to contact should it become necessary to warn McCann of impending danger. You must drink only spring water and keep your mind as clear as possible. Think only of me."

Onotage removed a thong necklet from around his neck and gave it to Joe.

"This talisman will help you. Wear it with pride and dignity Joe, it was my grandfather's."

Joe solemnly placed the necklet around his own neck, clutching tightly for a moment at the amber amulet attached to it, wondering how on earth he would keep a clear mind when everything around them seemed to be falling apart. He was about to speak, but the smile on the young Indian's face stopped him.

"We have not fallen Joe." Joe remained silent.

The three of them sat talking for a while, then gradually lapsed into silence, each with his own thoughts.

"Onotage thinking of the adversity in front of them. Impatient to be active, aware at all times that each tick of the clock brought mankind closer to imminent danger."

He closed his mind to the immense problem allowing his thoughts to dwell on his grandfather.

His grandfather's death saddened him greatly, yet he had known that his death was inevitable, hadn't he told Onotage many times during his talks with him.

He had never known his parents, they had drowned at sea in a tragic shipping accident. Onotage had been found floating in a wicker basket lashed to a life belt.

"It was a miracle." The newspapers had announced at the time.

"It was inevitable." His grandfather had told the young Onotage when he had reached thirteen years.

"Your parents were young and foolish. They attempted to change the course of your life by taking you to England. They refused to believe it would not be permitted."

His grandfather's words had terrified him. What kind of power was it that ruled his life to the point of destroying a ship that carried his parents. Eighty six men, women and children had perished in the disaster.

"He had seen photographs of his parents. His mother was young beautiful but wilful... according to his grandfather. His father had been a tall, handsome man, totally besotted by his wife. It had been her wish to leave the country with their infant son."

Onotage had hoped and prayed deeply that none of the victims suffered.

"You cannot alter destiny," his grandfather had told him gravely. "You are here for a reason Onotage. Do not question this. I am here to guide you. You must listen to me. Listen well. I will be with my forefathers at the hour of your greatest need."

His grandfather had been right. His grandfather had always been right. Now his spirit rested with his forefathers and he, Onotage was alone. The voice of his grandfather came into his thoughts.

"You are not entirely alone Onotage."

His gaze went to the troubled faces of his companions.

"Joe, while not a religious man, was not an unbeliever, either. He knew there was very little he could do to help his friends. He fervently prayed that someone up "there" liked him if Onotage needed his help."

"Mike's thoughts were with Susan. Until settling in this area, he had spent his life being something of a loner. He had never had the confidence or led the social life to meet and become attached to a woman. Never expected to fall in love, and now... He looked at his watch. It was just after midnight."

(Dear God. I've fallen in love with someone we may have to...). He wouldn't allow himself to think any further. Sixteen hours... That's all it was. Sixteen very precious hours since he had first laid eyes on her. "Please God... Susan..." he whispered softly.

Simon walked into the room. Mike's eyes met his, stopping him in mid-stride.

"Sarah understands Mike. She is prepared to try."

"Thank God." Mike closed his eyes. Some of the tension leaving his face.

"Vincent and Rebecca will help her."

"They send you a message Onotage. One I don't understand. They say you are correct, Battle Mountain is The Arena". Simon looked questioningly at Onotage.

"That is where she is going now Simon."

The drone of helicopters made any further conversation impossible. Onotage leapt to his feet. "The General," he shouted, racing for the door, the others close on his heels.

TUESDAY MAY 16th 00-15 hrs.

Once outside, they joined the Major who was shielding his eyes from the sandstorm created by the whirling blades of three helicopters.

General Mitchell jumped lightly to the ground followed by more soldiers. He stood for a moment surveying his surroundings. His eyes stayed on four civilians standing with Major Price. The young Indian captured his attention. Even though he stood with a group, his youthful face caught in the light streaming through the windows of the building. His stance told the General that this was a man who stood alone.

Major Price saluted smartly as the General approached them. General Mitchell returned the courtesy. "Major." His keen gaze remained on the four civilians.

145

Mike stepped forward extending his hand. "General, I am Mike Mallory."

Mike found himself being studied, assessed and evaluated by General Mitchell's penetrating steel grey eyes.

"So! Mallory. We meet at last."

He gripped Mike's hand in a firm handshake. "I feel I already know you."

"I'm sure you do sir." Mike answered, fully aware that his entire life had probably been scrutinised by this man.

"This is my partner Simon Kane."

Simon was treated to the same deeply penetrating stare.

"Pleased to meet you Kane."

The General was instantly aware that this tall impressive looking negro was analysing him, just as surely as he was being analysed.

He could not resist a smile as he shook hands with Joe Daniels. This man was on the defensive. He did not like the way his friends had been scrutinised. (Unquestionable loyalty. A rare and admirable quality.)

"This is Onotage."

Mike stepped backwards as the two men joined hands and watched the startled expression flit across the General's face.

"I am very pleased to meet you sir." Onotage spoke swiftly and decisively, fully aware of the effect he was having on the man.

"I would be grateful for a word with you in private as soon as possible... it is vital."

"Now, now young man," Major Price interrupted. "General Mitchell has only just arrived. His first priority will be to assess the positioning of the men."

General Mitchell answered with scarcely a glance at Major Price.

"The positioning of the men is something I am sure I can leave to your sound judgement Major. I will see this young man now."

"Is there somewhere we can speak?" His last words were directed at Mike.

"Certainly. Follow me sir." He led them to the conservatory, Simon accompanying them.

"I'll make sure you are not disturbed." Mike said, preparing to close the doors.

"Don't go away Mallory. I want to see the three of you together."

Mike nodded. "Simon and I will wait here."

As the doors closed, the General faced Onotage, openly studying him again.

"I have reached my position in life, primarily because I am a very

146

shrewd and sound judge of character. Granted, I asked the opinion of a psychiatrist in Mallory's case, but I had already decided that the man was genuine and that a problem of extraordinary proportions existed here. Daniels' loyalty to you all is unquestionable. As for Kane. He is a man with whom I would trust my life without hesitation..."

"Yes." Onotage prompted.

"In you I sense courage. A dignity and wisdom that belies your years. I also sense... Turmoil."

Onotage stared at the General but said nothing.

"You are an enigma... as much to yourself as to others. Even **you** do not know why you are here. For all this... I would trust you with everything I hold dear to me... And my intuition tells me... That is exactly what I will be doing."

If the General's words had shaken Onotage... he was careful not to show it. "I am relieved to hear you say this sir, because the question I am about to ask is probably top secret. I have reason to believe that Nemesis intends to use nuclear weapons against us. The public have been led to believe that Russia and America have such weapons orbiting the earth... Is this fact... Or fiction ?"

General Mitchell was startled by the direct question.

(This young man was right. The question, or rather the answer, was top secret.)

He took just two seconds to come to a decision.

"There are no such weapons orbiting the earth. It is true there are satellites from both countries, but none contain weapons, nuclear or otherwise."

"Thank you for your trust General. Your answer at least eliminates one possible source of her obtaining control over nuclear arms. Now, if you wish to call in Mike and Simon, we will give you an account of what is happening here and answer any questions as briefly and informatively as possible. On no account sir, must they be made aware of the information you have just given me."

The General rolled his eyes. "Heaven forbid anyone being made aware of that information. I could be shot for what I have revealed to you."

Mike and Simon entered the room and the three of them related the events of the last four days. When they had finished General Mitchell asked just one question.

"When do you wish to leave for Battle Mountain?"

Onotage smiled. He liked and trusted this man. Only two other men had ever seen so deeply into his troubled soul. His grandfather and

Eagle Star.

"As soon as possible," he answered.

The General nodded. "My helicopter is ready and waiting. The pilot is one of the most skilled in the business. He will drop you on the mountain wherever you wish, or wherever he can in safety. One word of warning... I know you do not wish the armed forces to take any action against this being... but while you must deal with this situation in your way... I must deal with it in a manner that will be acceptable to the President. I am taking the troops to Caplin with the intention of evacuation. But I must add that the protection of the people of Caplin and any other area that comes under threat of physical violence, has to be my priority."

Onotage accepted this honest statement. "I understand sir. I hope we can avert any further threats to life by immobilising Nemesis quickly. Now... With your permission... We will leave."

General Mitchell shook hands with each of them. "God go with you. Come back safe."

"The helicopter ride was hair-raising to Mike. The pilot stayed close to the ground. A precautionary measure to avoid being attacked. Mike groaned as the machine was blown and buffeted by a ground wind that became stronger as they drew closer to the mountain. With each gust Mike could see the ground spin dizzily away or seemingly rise dangerously upwards."

"Dear God. I don't know what we are heading for, but the sooner I get out of this whirligig, the better." His voice sounded thick, even to his own ears.

"Almost there my friend," Simon said encouragingly. "Don't look at the ground Mike," he added remembering his friend's fear of heights. A fear that had caused Onotage to insist he should stay with the General.

Mike had been adamant. "I either go with you. Or by God, I will follow you. Anyway, I'm one of the "Chosen Ones" remember?"

Onotage had merely said. "Yes Mike. You are."

Remembering his voice still chilled Mike. (I wonder what I was chosen for... and by whom. Odd, I've never questioned this.) He was relieved when the pilot landed on a small plateau part way up the mountain.

"This is as far as I can safely take you men," he shouted above the roar of the blades.

The three men scrambled out into the darkness.

The pilot handed a small expensive looking two way radio to Onotage.

"This is the General's. He knows that there is a break in communications with the exception of the transmitters. What he doesn't know is the radius of the break. Lieutenant Brady managed to get a message through... You may be able to... Who knows. Good luck."

"The three men watched the helicopter veer away from them and head back to the station. They watched until it was no more than a speck on the horizon. Onotage faced Mike and Simon.

"We are on our own now. Do not be alarmed. This is the only way to fight her... believe me. I want you to concentrate more than ever on the rings you are wearing. On Alpha and Omega. As a safeguard, I will only inform you of any action to be taken as and when necessary. You must be prepared to act swiftly on my word."

"Do you think she knows we are here?" Mike asked.

"She know. She awaits us up there somewhere." Onotage looked upwards to the peak of the mountain.

Simon glanced at his watch. The time was 01-15. "Then let's not keep the lady waiting," he said. "Let's go." He led the way. A calm and determined expression settling on his dark features.

"General Mitchell relaxed back in his seat as the helicopter sped towards Caplin. There had been no further attacks. The helicopter taking the three men to the mountain had made a safe journey both ways. He had first rebuked Major Price severely for his belligerent attitude towards Mike, Simon and Onotage. Then brought him up to date with the course of action to be taken in event of an attack, including placing Medway on full alert. He had an admiration for the Major. The man had taken the upbraiding without a murmur, but then he was a good man, both on and off the battlefield. A man he was more than willing to have alongside him. He did not blame him for finding this whole situation too incredible to believe."

"It still puzzled him that the President had so readily believed. It was only his own sixth sense and the knowledge that James McCann could not be swayed by anything but the truth that had convinced him."

They landed on the outskirts of Caplin without incident.

General Mitchell took his first look at the beleaguered town. The blackened, flattened buildings.

"My God! It looks as if it has been blitzed," he muttered to Major Price. Price was silently taking in the damage.

149

A figure walked towards them. The General recognised McCann and walked to meet him, hand outstretched.

"Mitch, it's good to see you." McCann said as he took the proffered hand and shook it emphatically.

"Good to see you Mac, you old walrus." General Mitchell studied the tired face.

McCann gave a rueful smile, running his hand over his clean shaven face. "I shaved it off a couple of years ago Mitch... made me look older."

"You are older Mac... We both are... What happened?" He swept his arm in the direction of the almost ruined town. McCann's expression wavered slightly, he then described the events that had taken place. Mitchell listened in silence until it seemed McCann had run out of words.

"As far as we know, she is on Battle Mountain, at least that's where Onotage is convinced she is."

He detected something in McCann's voice... Something he couldn't quite put a finger on.

"Yes... we figured that's where she was going. She came here first. In the space of thirty minutes... she left twelve people dead... incinerated. Karl Dorfson, whose father was an earlier victim. Three teachers. A lawyer. Two doctors. Two of my men and two of your men.

"Lieutenant Brady and Deputy Sheriff Jeff Ryan... are among the dead. All good men and women... All educated people... Almost as if she chose them for that reason."

Mitchell now recognised what he had detected in McCann's voice. It was the voice of a man still in shock.

"What in God's name is she?"

"I don't know Mitch. I only know she is getting stronger by the minute. When she first came into town, I didn't know who she was, I actually went to her, asking how she had arrived in town. She laughed saying that she travelled on the flames of dissension. I thought she must be some crazy lady who had wandered out of the hospital. Beautiful... Stunning... But crazy. I tried to take her back to the hospital. She turned those..." he shuddered. "She turned those eyes on me and a force like... like lightening hit me, sending me reeling across the street. I knew who she was then alright... I couldn't stop her."

Mitchell placed a steadying hand on McCann's shoulder. Price listened. A look of pure disbelief on his face.

"She entered the church where people were sleeping and made her first attack. Two teachers... women. These were not secluded attacks.

150

They were made openly and selectively with witnesses to each one. By this time, I had raised the alarm. My men fired on her... You know what she did?... She laughed... Maniacal laughter that turned my blood to ice... She melted their guns just by looking at them. I've got four men in hospital. What's left of it. With severe hand burns. Your soldiers fired on her. Two of them rushed her. They went up in flames like they were made of paper. She headed for the hospital. Mostly women and children sleeping in there. Lieutenant Brady and Jeff Ryan had figured she was heading for there, they were waiting for her. They must have decided to fight fire with fire and turned a flame thrower on her.

"She walked straight into the flames lifting her arms, her hair... like a woman will when taking a shower, laughing crazily at the shock on their faces. She was enjoying the entire horrifying incident.

"Then she stood in front of Jeff and Lieutenant Brady. She burned them... She burned them slowly. Not stopping until the two of them were... incinerated. She is the Devil incarnate."

Mitchell had listened to this in total silence. "What about the salt. Mallory said salt would help."

"It visibly slows her Mitch... But there's no way it's ever going to stop her."

McCann's eyes travelled from the General to the silently derisive Major Price.

"I'm sorry Mac. This is Major Ian Price."

McCann studied the Major as they shook hands. "You don't believe any of this do you Major?"

Major Price showed no surprise at the direct observation. "I'm sorry but..."

"Don't apologise Major, I'm not offended. On the contrary, I feel sorry for you. I didn't believe it when I first came here. But **you** are faced with all this destruction. With the word of a Chief of Police... myself. You are faced with the fact that your own senior officer, the General here believes it enough to have spoken of the situation to the President of the United States and that same man has sent your senior officer here. Yet you still disbelieve. When you finally have to face the truth Major Price... And you will have to face it... I hope your character is strong enough to take it, and I hope I am around." McCann didn't allow Price or Mitchell the time to pass comment.

"Come, we'll go to my headquarters, maybe between us Mitch we can devise some way of stopping her."

"That is what Onotage, Mallory and Kane are hoping to achieve...

even as we speak."

McCann was puzzled. "What do you mean... Who is Onotage?"

"I'll explain on the way to your headquarters." Mitchell turned around, looking for Joe who had stayed in the background during the conversation. He was unsurprised by the look of open admiration for McCann on Joe's face.

"I want you with me Joe." Joe nodded and followed in silence alongside an equally silent Major Price.

Once inside the building, the coffees appeared. Joe declined.

"May I have some spring water please, and is there somewhere quiet where I can relax away from all this activity?" he asked McCann.

Surprised, McCann instructed one of his men to show Joe to a small ante-room. "He sick or something Mitch?"

"No Mac, he may be our only means of communication with those three men on the mountain if the radio signals are still out. Thought transference through the Indian... Onotage."

Al joined them and was introduced to the two army officers.

"Where's Mike and Simon?" he asked.

"They've gone after her Al... They've gone up the mountain." McCann told him.

"What!" Al exploded. "You mean they're on that mountain... alone. No protection from that... That... she-devil. Whose idea was that? You're the one who should be up there General, you and your soldiers."

"They are not alone sheriff. They are with Onotage." General Mitchell answered firmly.

"Onotage! Who the hell is Onotage?" Al was livid. He had already lost one close friend, he wasn't going to stand by while he lost two more.

"Calm down Al," McCann said, understanding Al's anger. "Onotage is the Indian friend of Mike's. He's leading them."

"Indian... You mean Steve. He's only a kid, still in his teens. I know Mike placed a lot of faith in him... but he's still only a kid. How the hell can he protect them or himself from that female demon?"

"Sheriff," General Mitchell spoke patiently. "Believe me, if I thought that sending an armed force up there would be the right thing to do... I would do it, but your friends are against this kind of action. Frankly, after what I have seen and heard, I agree with them. Both Mallory and Kane trust this young man completely... So do I."

Al's outburst gradually subsided. "I know they do. I just hope they are right."

"Now." The General spoke emphatically. "We must decide what is the best plan of action for this town. Evacuation has to be considered."

"Well, I anticipated this kind of decision General when I heard that more soldiers were arriving. So I had a word with the townsfolk. They want the women, children, sick and elderly evacuated, but all able men want to stay... fight if necessary. It's their town General." Al sounded more like his rational self now.

"Under the circumstances, that is acceptable to me Sheriff."

"Then let's make plans and get this evacuation under way."

As there was insufficient fuel, it was decided with some trepidation to use the helicopters.

Like McCann said. "Let's face it, we don't have a choice. If the pilots stay low... they should be safe."

"My pilot has volunteered to take the first evacuees out." Even has he spoke, General Mitchell felt the nauseating attack of alarm in the pit of his stomach. An alarm that had saved his life and his troops lives on more than one occasion.

"Gentlemen." All eyes turned in his direction.

"Gentlemen... I know I have endorsed this method of evacuation... But I feel perhaps... We have been hasty in making arrangements. Under the unusual circumstances, it would be wiser to keep the people here... until we can arrange for land transport from Salt lake City."

He felt the full weight of the puzzled stares. If this had been active duty in a warring country, he wouldn't have hesitated to rescind his decision. But these were civilians in a situation not previously encountered.

Only McCann knew Mitch well enough to know that something was troubling him. He spoke carefully. "Mitch... You know we can't raise Salt Lake on the transmitters. We know from what Onotage has said that this bitch probably intends to make Caplin an example to the world. We have to try Mitch."

"The helicopters are stripped down and ready to fly sir." The voice from the soldier entering the church hall cut through the tension.

"We want our women and children taken to safety General." One of the townsmen spoke up... "They way I see it... there's an element of danger whatever we decide."

Words of agreement passed among the men. General Mitchell reluctantly acknowledged the logic in this last remark.

"Yes... you are probably right. Go ahead... Start the evacuation." The uneasy feeling stayed with him.

"The women with young children were to go first. Most of them in tears. Torn between not wanting to leave their husbands, and an inborn

153

urge to protect their young by taking them to safety. Al was upset at the sight of people he had come to think of as his family, crying in each other's arms. His upset turned to anger as he thought of the unspeakable suffering they were being caused by this maleficent being."

"He kept himself busy, helping to place the children on board.

"Come on Jamie," he picked the tousle haired youngster up.

"Stop your crying, you're upsetting your sister. See, Richie isn't crying."

"Richie's got the window seat, and I want it."

"Well, you can have it next time... I promise."

Al shook his head with a tired grin. "Kids."

He stayed, trying to make them comfortable. Clowning to make them laugh and reassuring them that they would be okay... But the memory of Jeff haunted him. Seeing his friend like a burning torch, hearing his screams of agony. It wouldn't leave his mind. It would never leave his mind."

"General Mitchell watched as the first helicopter rose gracefully from the ground. The Bell Model 205 was designed to carry fourteen fully armed troops, a pilot and co-pilot. Stripped of excess fittings, it had taken twenty six women and children easily. It had to. They only had five of these craft."

Mitchell glanced at his watch .. 02.10. Hopefully his pilot would be able to recruit some assistance in Salt Lake.

"Damn and blast the radios," he muttered.

"He was the first to see the piercing blue light reaching out from Battle Mountain.

"No!... Dear God... No!"

The light enveloped the helicopter illuminating it against the dark skies. He could see the terrified faces of children as they banged on the windows. The helicopter erupted in flames.

"He started to run towards the stricken machine. Then was forced to stop and watch in horror as the craft came down engulfed in flames. The screams of the women and children mingling with the explosion as it hit the ground... catapulting towards one of the other helicopters still being boarded."

The horrified onlookers surged forward. McCann and General Mitchell with them. A hurtling piece of rotary blade struck the general like a projected missile. He went down unnoticed by McCann in the havoc that surrounded them."

"The following thirty minutes would forever change the lives of the townsfolk of Caplin. The horror of it a permanent scar on their emotions. Courageous men and women oblivious to being scorched by the blistering heat in their frantic but useless efforts to rescue the writhing victims still trapped inside the stricken helicopters. The few lucky ones who were thrown clear were whisked off to the hospital along with the many burnt would-be rescuers. The rest perished. Thirty four women and children. Four pilots and ten men who had been with their families boarding the second helicopter. Forty eight lives in all."

"A silence had fallen over the stunned crowd, broken only by the sound of weeping."

Major Price suddenly broke the silence startling those closest to him. "Where is the general?"

McCann looked around him. "He was with me. We both ran to help."

"Over here," a voice called.

A man was knelt beside a still form lying on the ground. McCann raced towards them, dropping to his knees and reaching to feel for a pulse on the blood splattered general.

He looked up as Price reached him. "He's alive."

"Price made no answer. His gaze went from the general to the scene before him. Al was still supervising the fire fighting. It would be some time before the victims would be found and identified. Two soldiers dragged a struggling man away from the burning body of the second helicopter. The man threw himself to the ground, beating it with his fist. A group of silent townsfolk stood helplessly watching."

In the light of the flames, Price could see the shocked horror of despair in the faces of some. Anger in others. Above all he could see fear. He could smell fear. A smell he had come to hate in Vietnam."

The distraught man staggered to his feet and walked unsteadily towards Price. McCann stood, unsure of the grief stricken man's intentions. He stopped about two foot away from Price. Mixed emotions flitted across his face. Mouth mobile but no sound. At last the words came discordantly out.

"You!... Why... haven't... My wife... My... my two children... Why!... Why!" He pointed to the still burning wrecks.

"How... Many... More... Have... To die before you do... Something."

The man was choking on his words. He drew back his fist to strike at Price, but collapsed to the ground before he could deliver the blow.

Price looked down at the man, an unfathomable expression on his face. He straightened his shoulders, lifting his head.

"Lieutenant Skellern."

"Yes sir."

"Have this man taken to the hospital with the General. See that he is taken care of. Go with them. I want a full report on the General's condition as soon as possible."

Without another word, he turned and walked towards the church hall. McCann followed sensing that the Major had made a decision of action.

"Price. Price."

The Major carried on walking ignoring McCann. Al, who had been about to join them. Heard the agitation in McCann's voice and followed them. When they reached the church hall, McCann caught hold of the Major's arm.

"Answer me damn it. What are you going to do?"

The Major calmly loosened McCann's grip.

"I am going to do what has to be done."

"What do you mean?" McCann shouted again, blocking his path.

Al joined him. "Answer the man will you?"

"Sergeant keep these men here. I have an urgent communique to make." The sergeant and two soldiers stood at arms in front of McCann and Al.

Price sat at the transmitter they had brought with them. First turning on the scrambler, then without hesitation proceeded to send his message.

Captain Wesley: U.S.S. Medway:

Major Price on code name Triton stop General Mitchell injured stop I take full responsibility for this communique stop Request immediate assistance from aircraft stop Proceed with bombardment of Battle Mountain Repeat Bombardment of Battle Mountain urgent stop Heavy civilian casualties expect more unless assistance is prompt stop

End of Communique stop

Joe staggered into the room holding his head as if in pain.

"What have you done? Onotage tried to come through to me. Tried to warn me of danger. Then this crazy laughter blocked out the message. God it's driving me mad."

McCann grabbed the Major's arm again. "What was in the communique Price. We have a right to know."

"I am not obliged to tell you anything McCann but under the circumstances I will. I have arranged for Battle Mountain to be strategically bombed."

Something snapped inside Al, the pressures of the last few days. The horror they had just witnessed. The trusting face of little Jamie Stewarts. He went for Price, lashing out with both fists, knocking him

156

to the ground. Two soldiers pulled him away, pinning him to a wall.

He shouted in fury. "Have you forgotten the three men up there trying their damnedest to stop all this? Risking their lives for us."

"No sheriff I have not."

The Major got unsteadily to his feet. "Have you forgotten the screams of your dying townsfolk already? Most of them children. I will not allow more carnage. I am prepared to sacrifice those three men in order to save lives here. It was not an easy decision sheriff."

Price spoke quieter now. "I understand how you feel. It was not an easy decision but it is **my** decision and I will not retract it."

Joe, still dazed from the trance he had been in. Collapsed to the ground.

U.S.S. MEDWAY TUESDAY MAY 16th 02-50 hrs

"Captain Wesley checked the communique again. General Mitchell had informed him that Major Price would be his second-in-command. He also had informed him that unless the word "Firebrand" was included in any request for assistance, under no circumstances was he to allow nuclear weapons inside the designated area. So as discussed and agreed with General Mitchell. Fragmentation bombs would be used on Battle Mountain. The order was given and four Phantom aircraft departed from U.S.S. Medway watched anxiously by Captain Wesley and his crew."

BATTLE MOUNTAIN. TUES 02-05 hr.

"The three men rested a while. They had made good time and were more than half way up the mountain. They had neither seen nor heard Nemesis but each one was aware of her. Even Mike, the least susceptible to her presence. He glanced occasionally at the ring. Touching it."

"What kind of protection do you think they will give us Simon?"

"I don't know. I suppose that depends on how much faith you have in them."

Mike looked at him. "Have you got faith in them?"

"Yes I have," Simon spoke softly holding his hand out to Mike.

"Have faith in them Mike and in yourself."

As his hand came into contact with Mike's hand, the rings became prismatic. Mike rubbed his eyes. Maybe it was a trick of the light. He was sure the rings were made of metal, probably silver. Silver didn't create colours. He looked again. The variegated colours were still there. A kaleidoscope of colours dancing in the moonlight. Mike released Simon's hand. The rings became regular.

"It seems the strength is in keeping them close."

"Yes," answered Simon. "They belong together, so stay close by me when we hit trouble."

Mike's familiar lopsided grin appeared, cheering Simon for a moment. "I'll be so close... You'll think I'm part of you."

Onotage stood apart from them. Vigilance etched on his young face.

"Come, we must carry on."

The brilliant flash of blue light almost blinded them as they rose to their feet. Simon was upright first, binoculars to his eyes.

"Dear God! She has hit something in town." He lowered the binoculars. The orange ball of flame could easily be seen with the naked eye.

The peal of maniacal laughter echoed around the mountain. Simon and Mike turned to Onotage. Fear on their faces.

He stood with arms folded... eyes closed. Concentration etched into his face.

"It is no good," he said with a grim expression. "I cannot reach Joe. Whatever has happened, it is blocking my thoughts. I will try again shortly. Come, we must make haste, this could cause serious complications."

"You are so right my tedious, insignificant friend."

The words startled them. She sat on a boulder. Vivid turquoise eyes watching their reaction. Her beauty was awesome. She looked every inch... a goddess.

Mike stared at her. "Susan," he whispered.

His thoughts amused her. She smiled at him. "You are a pathetic imbecile, but I do find your desire to hold me, quite refreshing... Almost tempting. It is a long, long time since I was held in a man's arms."

Her smile was tantalisingly whimsical. Mike made the smallest move towards her... Her mood changed abruptly. The smile vanished.

"You dare to think I would allow this? I doubt there is a man good enough for me in this despicable world."

"What have you done to the town?" demanded Onotage.

She glared at him. "Be very careful earthworm... Or I will crush you." The softness of her voice did nothing to hide the venom in her words.

Swiftly she stood. Mike noticed that her feet were not touching the ground but were several inches above it.

"Follow me if you are brave enough. I promise you a splendid view of your dying earth before I depart and leave you to meet your God." With a peal of crazy laughter. She was gone.

"So she can levitate also. She really is capable of everything isn't she."

Onotage saw the bleak expression in Mike's eyes as he spoke.

"Do not despair Mike. She has lead this battle, showing all she can do. Our chance will come... and when it does... We will each grasp it with both hands."

They set off walking once again. Onotage leading, setting a faster pace. Mike and Simon close behind.

They had been walking in silence for almost an hour when Onotage suddenly stopped, scanning the skies anxiously.

"No," he said softly. "That fool Price... No... No." Mike and Simon also heard the drone of approaching aircraft.

"Eagle to base: Eagle to base: Objective in sight. ETA approximately nought point four minutes. Will advise when mission accomplished. Over."

"Why are we bombing a mountain skip? Is it a dummy run for something big?"

"No Del, it's not a dummy run. It's the real thing... Top secret.... even I haven't been told why."

"Tomcat to Eagle: We are in position for attack sequence. Over."

"Squadron Leader Glen Dorning glanced to his right and felt a deep sense of inner pride at the sight of the three Phantom aircraft accompanying him. He had been flying these aircraft ever since the US Navy had given them precedence in "58". It still caught at his breath each time he saw them in flight."

"The white and navy fuselage emblazoned with orange markings were impressive and distinctive. To his mind they were the finest fighting machines ever made. Anyone who thought they weren't streamlined killers, need only look at the skull and crossbones on the vertical stabiliser to remind them of just how wrong they were."

"Eagle to Tomcat: I read you. ETA now nought point two minutes and thirty seconds. Over."

"You read me Buzzard. Over."

"We read you skip. Over."

"You read me Falcon. Over."

"Loud and clear skip. Over."

"Dorning's pride went out to these young flyers who were part of his squadron. Part of his life. He gave a small laugh. They weren't part of his life. They were his life. He had trained and better trained these men and he loved them. They were the sons he had never had in the loveless, childless marriage he had endured for seven years. He was a proud and happy man now."

They were flying over Winnemucca. Battle Mountain was straight ahead.

"Okay Buzzard. Okay Falcon. Go. Go. Go. We'll be right on your tails."

He watched as the two aircraft swooped gracefully downwards. Moonlight dancing on their wing tips. Outlining the thirty eight foot span.

"Beautiful." Dorning whispered.

"You read me Tomcat. Over."

"We read you Eagle. Over."

"Let's do it."

The two aircraft swooped after the leading pair.

"The sooner we get this job over and done with... the better." Glen Dorning's words were still echoing round the cockpit when the beam of blue light extending from Battle Mountain took him by surprise.

"What the Hell..."

The two leading aircraft were caught in the beam of light and appeared to have come to a standstill.

"It's not possible .." He felt a sickening lurch as his own aircraft was also caught in the light.

"What the hell is happening skip?"

"I don't know Del... I don't know."

The radio burst into life as the pilots of the three aircraft tried to contact him at once.

"No control"... static... "Aircraft turning"... static.

"Heading east"... static... "Heading south west"... static...

Silence.

Dorning was stunned as he saw the two leading aircraft separate, flying in different directions. He desperately tried to contact them but received no response.

Del watched in white-faced silence.

Then the impossible happened. Del was thrown out of his seat as their aircraft did a complete turn. They saw Tomcat do the same.

"Eagle to Base: Eagle to Base: Aircraft out of our control. Buzzard

160

and Falcon heading in opposite directions."

Recovering swiftly, Del was frantically scanning the chart, tracing paths with his finger, showing Dorning who passed the information on.

"Possible courses. Salt Lake area. Reno or Sacramento."

Del was stabbing at the chart again and the compass heading. His face ashen. Not trusting himself to speak.

"Eagle and Tomcat... Dear God... On direct course for base... Repeat... Direct course for base... For Medway... Not of our perpetration... Repeat... Not of our perpetration. We have no control...."

Laughter... he could hear crazy skin crawling laughter.....

"Repeat... No control. Whatever is on that f.....g mountain has control of all aircraft. Over."

Dorning lapsed into silence, straing into the night.

"What's on the mountain skip. A flying saucer?"

He glanced at Del and didn't answer. The same thing had crossed his mind also. He could only **hope** that Medway had received his message for there was no response from the radio.

"What's happening skip?" Del asked again quietly.

"I don't know... Del, I want you to eject before we go over the Cascade Range."

Del was silent for a moment. "No skip, we are in this together. I'm staying with you."

Dorning gave a brief smile. "This isn't a request Del. It's an order."

"I've never disobeyed an order yet skip... but there's a first time for everything.

"Del. You've checked the chart and compass. Now check the radar. Where are we heading?"

Del checked, knowing already where they were heading.

"We're on a direct course for Medway skip... you know that."

"Yes. What I don't know is who or what is controlling this aircraft. I'm hoping to take her away from Medway... Somehow." He was thinking of the fifteen thousand pounds weight in bombs they had on board and the armoury on board Medway... Including nuclear weapons.

"I don't know if I can... I don't know if I can do anything but I have to try. I need you alive Del. I need you to say what has happened here. So no more arguments. Get ready to eject on my order. Take the tapes with you. They've recorded everything... They are your proof."

Del reluctantly nodded his head. "Okay skip, I'll do as you say... but I don't like it."

Dorning could see the pilot of Tomcat and signalled his intentions, hoping he understood. He received a thumbs up sign.

The Cascade Range loomed in front of them.

"Right Del. Eject now."

Del pressed the ejector button. No response. Again he pressed. Still no response. "Looks like you're stuck with my company to the bitter end after all skip."

The frantic signals from Tomcat suggested they had the same problems. Dorning tried the controls again but to no avail.

"Damn! The controls feel like they are stuck on auto. I don't understand what is happening... have to think of something fast... We'll jettison the fuel and the bombs when we are over the sea. Then somehow... I have to try blow the engines."

"We could use the Very Pistol skip."

Dorning looked into the calm eyes of his co-pilot and felt an overwhelming fear for him. Del was only twenty three, too young to die, and here he was suggesting an idea that would probably burn them both alive before the craft hit the sea.

"We'll use it if we have to Del."

"He again signalled his intentions to Tomcat, trying to keep his mind off the fact that the two men on board her were married with children. He tried the radio again... Still nothing. He left the radio open... just in case Medway could hear him. And prayed to God that they could."

"U.S.S. Medway. Carrier to the Phantom aircraft, lay some four miles out to sea."

"The carrier was fully armed with enough explosive to be disastrous to the coast, even at that distance. Three days ago, they had taken on board two nuclear missiles which were now being sealed and deposited on the sea bed as a precaution.

They would be recovered at a later date."

"Captain Wesley listened to the desperate conversations.

He could hear the men in the aircraft but not contact them. Glen Dorning was a good man. A man obviously convinced that the two aircraft were on a collision course for Medway. that was why he, Captain Wesley had made the formidable decision three minutes ago to launch an attack on his own aircraft."

"Four Phantom aircraft had taken off from the carrier. He could not allow sixty thousand pounds of bombs to explode on towns or any populated area. He could not take the risk of Dorning being unable to turn his aircraft.

The pilots of the four aircraft had been given explicit orders.

162

"Seek out and destroy Eagle, Tomcat, Falcon and Buzzard... At all costs."

BATTLE MOUNTAIN. 04-40 hrs

Nemesis rested, her eyes closed. "This mortal body may well be useful, but it is also weak."

A smile of deep satisfaction crept onto her face.

"Two hundred and eighty earth years taken from my life. Only my vengeance will absolve the humans from this outrage against me." She thought of the aircraft. "Oh how I enjoyed controlling their toys."

The smile quickly vanished. She frowned. "None of the aircraft had contained nuclear weapons, that is a great pity." The ship had contained two of the weapons.

"Curses on that interfering captain for placing them beneath the waves. Supreme as I am, I cannot penetrate water. You have joined them now fool... If you had not interfered, I would have spared your ship... for a short while."

Her strength was returning, she allowed her powerful mind to travel to the scene of the attack on Medway. Floating debris was all that remained of the once majestic aircraft carrier.

"I will teach all humans to respect Nemesis... " She suddenly fell silent... "What can I hear... Something is moving beneath the surface of the sea."

She stared hard into the depths, seeing a shape that she instantly recognised from the book Jeff Ryan had been reading.

"This is an underwater vessel... A submarine... They carry nuclear weapons... By the Gods!... If only it would surface."

Even as she spoke, the large dark conning tower rose gracefully out of the sea, foaming water spilling from it's centre. She laughed, intoxicated with power.

"Now! Humans. I will deliver a gift to your President... A gift from **Nemesis**."

163

THE THRESHOLD

"With Beauty like a tightened bow, a kind
that is not natural in an age like this,
Being high and solitary and most stern?
Why, what could she have done, being what she is?
Was there another Troy for her to burn?"

W.B. Yeats. (No Second Troy)

CHAPTER ELEVEN: THE THRESHOLD

"The room in which President Nixon had called the emergency meeting was deathly silent save for the President's tense voice.

All had been roused from their beds. The fear showing in their faces and in their hurriedly thrown on attire."

"I have explained the incredulous but dire situation we are now facing from a being previously unperceived by ordinary people. With the exception of those who have an interest in Greek Mythology, the name Nemesis will have little or no meaning at all."

"Each of you will see before you a detailed report on the events leading to this emergency meeting. You will also see before you a written copy of a telephone conversation held by me during the early hours of Monday the 15th of May. Yesterday. The man with whom I conversed with was Karl Dorfson. The son of the late Erik Dorfson."

A subdued murmur passed around the room.

"Yes." The President carried on speaking. "A very eminent nuclear physicist. A very close and dear personal friend."

"Karl Dorfson gave me an explicit account of the strange and unexplained deaths taking place in Caplin. His father's death was one of them. All this was prior to General Mitchell and Saul Kramer approaching me with the same account... with unnerving appendages."

The President cleared his throat looking gravely around the room.

"This... Nemesis... has taken up an offensive position on Battle Mountain. Four phantom aircraft were launched from the U.S.S. Medway. Their mission to bomb the mountain and hopefully destroy this being..."

"I received an emergency message from Medway stating that the pilots of these aircraft were no longer in control of their craft... That some unknown force had taken control of each aircraft. As a result of this, Captain Wesley of the U.S.S Medway, dispatched four phantom aircraft with orders to seek and destroy the four aircraft previously mentioned."

"Gentlemen, I have to inform you that at precisely four minutes past four, two Phantom aircraft... fully armed with fragmentation bombs...

crashed simultaneously. One on Salt Lake City. The other on Reno."

The murmuring was louder this time. The President resumed speaking. The murmuring hushed.

"They took with them in their death plunge, the two aircraft whose mission it was to destroy them. The casualties and destruction they will have caused has not yet been ascertained."

A man rose from his seat, intent on asking questions.

"Please be seated sir," the President's secretary spoke in a voice not to be argued with.

The President cleared his throat again.

"At precisely fifteen minutes past four the aircraft carrier U.S.S. Medway, situated four miles off Coos Bay, and from which all these aircraft had originally been launched, was hit and subsequently sunk by two Phantom aircraft in a kamikaze fashion. The two aircraft whose mission it was to destroy them also struck Medway. Again, I have not yet received a full report, but the results of this catastrophe must be... colossal."

"The tension in the room was a tangible, suffocating, living thing. A deathly silence had settled on the room. Then the questions started. The room became a furore of confusion. Voices striving to be heard. Three questions being repeated. "Who is Nemesis?" "How could the President believe this incredible tale?" "Which country is attacking them?"

"The loud banging of a gavel silenced the babble of voices. President Nixon stared at the faces in front of him.

"Have you not listened to my words? Have you not read the report? We are not under attack from a foreign source, as some of you would prefer to believe. To believe the easily believable at the expense of the truth... incredulous though it may be. Would be perilous for us. For America... Perhaps for the world."

"I have been in touch with the world's leaders, assuring them that I know we are not under attack from any of them, or the world's lesser countries. Understandably they are sceptical, as most of you are. Nevertheless, they are sending their most prominent scientists to assist us. To help eliminate this so called mythical creature. If I have received the support of foreign countries at such short notice... Surely gentlemen, I will receive your support also."

"The President slowly seated himself, wiping his forehead with a handkerchief. He was deeply worried. He had not succeeded in convincing all the major powers that America was under attack from a mythical being, and not a foreign source. Nor had he been totally successful in assuring all foreign powers that America was not trying to provoke a major incident.

Britain and France were open minded, but then both these countries were well acquainted with General Mitchell and Erik and Karl Dorfson. Because of these two powers, many of the smaller countries were more or less convinced that something strange was happening in America... No... His concern was with America's old adversaries... Russia and Japan. These two powerful countries were non-committal. With China and Germany waiting to hear their reaction."

Somehow he had to keep the wolves at bay.

He nervously wiped his brow again.

"The red telephone on the President's desk suddenly burst into life, startling all the occupants of the room.

The President stared hypnotically at it. He lifted the receiver and listened in silence.

At the end of the one-sided conversation the President, his face even more ashen, merely said. "Keep me informed," and replaced the receiver.

The expectant sea of faces wavered. He swayed a little, gripping the edge of the table before he spoke.

"Gentlemen. I have to inform you that one of **our** submarines have launched... three nuclear missiles. Their destination, the United States. Their targets, Washington DC, Salem and Jacksonville."

The President took a drink of water before carrying on.

"The launching controls were seized by an unknown power just as the controls of the Phantom aircraft appear to have been seized by an unknown power... An attempt is being made at this very moment to disarm and deflect the missiles... I pray to God that they are successful."

"The warning sirens outside could be heard plainly. Each person in the room could visualise the panic being caused in homes. Each one grateful for the fact that few people would be on the streets at this time. Each one allowing their thoughts to fly to their own loved ones. One man left his seat, reaching the door before realising the futility of this act. Turning, he sat down again, bowing his head. More than one head was bowed in tearful prayer.

"The ticking of the clock sounded deafening. One minute. Two minutes. Three minutes. Four. Five. Some heads were raised. Six. Seven... The red telephone rang shrilly. All heads were raised... All eyes riveted on the trembling hand of the President as he lifted the receiver.

"Yes."

A silken voice murmured into his ear.

"Your armies are so entertaining Mr President. Please accept the gift I, Nemesis, am sending you. I am sure you will find it... Uplifting."

"Who is this....."

A peal of loud, nerve wracking laughter caused him to drop the receiver, allowing all present to hear it. His secretary quickly retrieved it and listened... to static.

President Nixon raised fearful eyes. "None of this has been made public... none but the most trusted know of the events. I believe that person, gentlemen, **was** our adversary... Nemesis."

He sat down pressing the recorder, allowing all present to hear the words of Nemesis.

The telephone rang again. He nervously reached out, closing his eyes... listening... praying... not trusting himself to speak. His eyes sprang open, looking around the room....

"Thanks be to God."

"The sigh of relief was audible. The sound of someone weeping was comforting. The President allowed a brief, weak smile before speaking.

"That particular danger is over. The missiles have been rendered harmless and deflected. We must now decide how to proceed... and fast. This being has absolute powers. Gentlemen, I do not think it is unrealistic to say we are on the threshold... of Armageddon."

BATTLE MOUNTAIN

"The three men on the mountain watched helplessly as the pilots struggled for control of their aircraft. The maniacal laughter ringing in their ears. they saw the two leading aircraft separate and go in different directions. The two following aircraft did an about turn manoeuvre that no man could have achieved."

"She has control of them." Onotage spoke in a tight voice.

"I have underestimated this... this... Thing."

Mike felt a chill of fear in his heart for Susan. In spite of all that had happened, he knew he could never allow them to kill her. A hand fell onto his shoulder. He looked up, having involuntarily dropped to his knees. He saw Onotage's face through misty eyes and realised he was crying.

"I may have underestimated her Mike, but we are not defeated. I want you both to rest, it is a long while since either of you slept." Mike and

168

Simon immediately protested and were silenced by stern words.

"I need your minds fresh and agile, not woolly with fatigue. There is nothing to be done at the moment. Now rest close together. I will rouse you when it is time."

"What are you going to do Onotage?" Simon asked.

"We need help. I will contact my forefather."

Simon nodded his understanding.

"Now rest."

"Mike was shocked to realise how physically and mentally tired he was. As soon as he lay down, he felt the weariness creep over him like a heavy grey blanket. He was asleep in seconds. Simon, although he also felt tired, lay thinking. Regretting his past refusal to acknowledge the gift he had been born with. If only he had allowed his mother to teach him how to use it fully, maybe he would have been more help to Onotage. On these thoughts, he drifted into an uneasy sleep."

The first fingers of dawn were reaching out for the top of the mountain as Onotage sat cross-legged on his prayer mat, a little way from his companions. closing his eyes, he visibly relaxed. The tension left his body, creating an innocent expression on his face. Making him look much younger than his eighteen years.

Today was his birthday... Today he entered into the age of manhood.

Onotage was alone, walking through a thickly wooded forest. A voice called to him.

"Are you lost my son?"

Onotage turned in the direction of the voice and saw an impressive looking Indian in full headdress seated on the grass and he knew he was facing Hiawatha.

"Yes my father. I am lost. Lost in ignorance. I am in mortal combat with a being of infinite power. I need your assistance Great One. I have to know exactly what she is capable of and if she has a weakness. One I can use to defeat her."

"I know of your troubles my son. Be seated and I will enlighten you."

Onotage sat down on the soft grass opposite his forefather.

"Close your eyes my son and all will be revealed to you."

"Swirling mists clouded his vision. Then scenes slowly appeared before him. Unrolling like a film.

He saw everything from the burning of Rebecca Allen and her call upon Nemesis to avenge her. To the havoc and destruction Nemesis was now causing."

169

"The horrifying and lonely deaths of Pop Bailey and Cal Stevens.

"The attacks and deaths in Caplin."

"The attacks on the helicopters, both over the Indian lodge and in Caplin."

"The courageously futile attempts of the aircraft pilots as they tried to jettison bombs and fuel. The excruciatingly slow deaths of these brave men in their attempts to destroy the aircraft."

"The devastation in and around Salt Lake City and Reno."

"The horror of the sinking of Medway resulting in thousands of deaths along the coastal areas. The multiple explosions had caused a huge tidal wave to hit the coast."

"Tears flowed unashamedly down Onotage's face. He heard the voice of Hiawatha."

"These are atrocities she has already committed. Much greater atrocities have been averted through the vigilance of your fellow men. Now I will reveal to you what she is capable of."

"Onotage witnessed the destruction of mankind. The awesome spectacle of multiple nuclear explosions. Some created by Nemesis, others created by nation firing on nation in misconceived retaliation."

"He saw countries laid to waste with rotting bodies as far as the eye could see."

"He witnessed the elements react in a violent frenzy."

"The seas boil."

"Once dormant volcanoes erupt with fury."

"Then... Darkness. The death laden skies obliterating the sun.

"He saw pathetic remnants of the human race dying slowly. Some taking the lives of their loved ones and then their own lives in preference to the misery and agony of a slow and torturous death. And yet others bravely struggling to remain alive in a world that no longer could sustain life."

"It was with much relief that he opened his eyes and found himself back in the forest. His breath coming in short emotional gasps.

Hiawatha was watching him. Looking deeply into his soul.

"You have seen the possible legacy of Nemesis."

Onotage nodded, unable to speak.

He was alarmed when his mentor began to fade from his vision. His voice returned with fervour.

"My Father. You have not answered my questions. What is her weakness? What is the solution?"

The vision of Hiawatha was gone but his voice echoed eerily through the branches of the trees.

"Her weakness. The solution. And the reason for your being are one and the same my son.

"The Ultimate Act". With this you destroy her malice with the purity of Love....."

"Onotage was back on the mountain. Mike and Simon were still asleep. In those unguarded moments, the enormity of the situation showed on his young face like physical pain. His shoulders drooped allowing his forehead to rest on his knees."

".....The Ultimate Act....."

"He knew now what he had to do. He stood upright arms outstretched praying for strength and guidance. For although he now knew his purpose in life, the reason for his being, he did not know which path it would take."

"A breeze fanned his face causing his long dark hair to stir and drift outwards. The inscrutable smile of inner knowledge once again on his face. He could feel the vulnerability leaving him. Strength flowing through his veins."

"Thank you my Father for showing me the way."

"Turmoil no longer existed within his soul. He now knew who he was and why he was."

He did not wear a watch, but guessed it to be about five thirty am. He walked over to his sleeping friends and gently shook them.

"Come it is time to move."

The two men stiffly rose to their feet. Simon eyeing Onotage questioningly.

Onotage smiled. "Trust me my friend. We are not alone."

Mike looked as if he were about to ask questions, then changed his mind.

As they began walking, Onotage held out a hand to each of them.

"Eat this as we walk."

Mike examined what Onotage had placed in his hand. It looked disgustingly like a lump of mud.

"Onotage smiled again. "It is dried fish and cereal. Do not be put off by its appearance. You will find it quite tasty and nourishing."

"Mike grinned a little shamefacedly realising his thoughts had once again been made known to this young Indian. He took a bite.

"Mm Onotage is right, it is tasty," he mumbled to himself. He realised something else. He was ravenous. Onotage had been right about the need for sleep also.

"He studied the leading figure of the Indian. There was a reassuring

171

strength in the curve of his back. an air of confidence in the way he held his head and shoulders. Firm and erect."

(A born leader.) Mike thought. (But was he enough? Were the three of them enough to prevent this fiend from doing as she threatened? He didn't see how they could be.)

He shook his head trying to clear the frightening thoughts crowding his mind. He thought of Susan instead. "I **will** get you back, we will beat this creature." He muttered shaking his fist defiantly."

Simon bringing up the rear saw the unconscious gesture and smiled. (That's right Mike. Think positive. God knows it is the only defence we have.)

THE ULTIMATE ACT

"Fair Prototype of innocence,
Sleep upon thy emerald bed,
No coming evil vents
A shade above thy head."
Taken from The Dictionary of Dreams.

Gustavus Hindman Miller.

CHAPTER TWELVE: THE ULTIMATE ACT

BATTLE MOUNTAIN -TUESDAY MAY 16th

"The route they were taking was becoming rough now. Steeper, craggier. Some parts were a sheer drop. They could no longer rely on hands and feet, but had to use ropes. Mike was glad Onotage had insisted on their resting. As an inexperienced climber, he needed all his wits about him.

Simon coped easily. His agile body seemingly to thrive on the climb.

Onotage was like a mountain goat. Nothing insurmountable to him. Almost as if he and the mountain were kindred spirits. This just added to Mike's feeling of being a hindrance. Like being a third limb. Unnecessary and cumbersome. They even had him roped between them as a precaution."

(Odd.) Mike thought. (Onotage hasn't spoken of his "Spiritual Trip" as he had come to think of them. Certainly the young Indian had a more determined and confident air about him since the last one. This acted as a tonic to his wilting faith and raised his hopes for Susan's return and the defeat of Nemesis.)

His thoughts came to an abrupt halt. Ahead of them was a wall of what appeared to be sheer smooth rock, rising some seventy feet above them. Simon seeing the look of pure dismay on Mike's face, clapped a hand on his shoulder. "Don't look so alarmed Mike, you are doing well my friend."

"You... you mean we have to climb up there?" Just thinking of it made him feel dizzy.

"From the way Onotage is surveying it... I'd say yes."

Looping the rope so as he did not run the risk of tripping over it, Mike shortened the distance between himself and Onotage.

"Stand here Mike and look up. See. There are plenty of hand and foot holds and I will be using crampons. It is not as difficult as it looks."

Mike studied the rock face in silence.

"You could stay here," Onotage said, thinking of Mike's fear of heights. "Although it would be most unwise of us to split up."

"I'm going with you," Mike answered grimly. "I just hope you are right. About it not being too difficult I mean," he added with a tight smile.

Onotage made the climb first, hammering crampons home every ten foot or so. Scaling the vertical precipice with the skill of an experienced mountaineer.

"Right Mike." he called from the top. "You next and remember I have you on the rope. You cannot fall. Just take it steady."

Mike started the climb. Onotage was right. There were more hand and footholds than Mike had first thought. With the help of the crampons and the rope, he was more than half way up quicker than he expected.

"Need any assistance my sweet?"

The honeyed tones startled him, causing him to lose his grip. He fell ten sickening feet before coming to a sharp and painful stop.

"She was seated on a jutting outcrop of rock watching him with those exquisite eyes. Enjoying the terror on is face."

"Now, Mike Mallory. Shall I burn the rope and send you plunging to a possible death?" She tilted her head to one side and smiled.

"No... Too... Ordinary."

She smiled again as if inspired. "I know, I will burn you slowly, starting with your blood. I will cause your blood to become warmer and warmer until you feel it bubbling in your veins as it begins to boil."

He stared at her. Hypnotised by her voice. Paralysed with fear. Unable to move. Like a fly caught in a spider's web.

"Then perhaps I will start on your bones. I will create just the right amount of heat to bend them... slowly. Do you know what burnt human bones look like my sweet? I will tell you. They look exactly like charcoal." She smiled again, a smile that made Mike shudder.

"And finally I will burn your flesh. Your weak and rancid flesh." Mike began to feel hot. He could feel the perspiration running freely down his body.

"Christ." She was burning him.

Suddenly a strange feeling came over him. He was no longer afraid. He laughed up at her mockingly.

"What would you gain from that Nemesis? One less spectator to witness you lose the battle for the earth. One less witness to the defeat and downfall of Nemesis. Go ahead. Kill me. I am not afraid to die. I take with me the knowledge that Nemesis is nothing but an egotistical braggart. An arrogant dismal failure."

Her expression changed. Fury turning her beautiful eyes and mouth into vicious slits.

"How... Dare... You. You... Ludicrous... Savage. You think that I... Nemesis, am incapable of destroying your precious planet? You will live to regret your words Mike Mallory." She calmed herself now.

"You and your companions will live long enough to behold the power of Nemesis and the inane, futile struggles of your fellow humans. Then... You will beg to die."

She was gone. Mike managed to get a firmer footing and resting his face against the cool rock, he gave a sigh of relief.

"Are you alright Mike?" The concerned voice from above him broke into his solace.

"Yes. Yes I'm coming up." He reached the top without further incident.

"I faced her Onotage. I faced her and I won. I just hope I didn't go too far."

Onotage placed a hand on Mike's shoulder, a broad smile covering his face. "No Mike, you didn't go too far. You merely spoke the truth. We will beat this fiend. Now, let us haul Simon up before she returns."

They examined the area they had reached. It was a small plateau, concave in the centre.

"Almost like a stage." remarked Simon.

"Yes it is and not far from the peak. I think this is as far as we need to go." Onotage added quietly.

"Wise choice." She was back.

"You will be on the stage when I, Nemesis, bring down the final curtain on your world." She laughed, amused at her own words.

Mike felt a surge of anger. "No one will know it was you. Only the three of us and the people in Caplin."

"Why do you say that?" her mood changing again.

"Because you cut communications. No television. No radio. No audience for the great Nemesis. They will be blaming each other, not the all powerful Nemesis. No one would believe it anyway, because you Madam are a myth."

Simon and Onotage remained silent. Simon hadn't quite got over Mike's first verbal attack on this unpredictable being.

Nemesis was outraged. Her eyes glittered with white hot malice.

"Then I shall change that you... insufferable slug. You will see." Once again she was gone.

"Whew," Simon looked at him. "Is it wise to provoke her anger Mike?"

"Wise or foolish, I had to do it. We need communications back and

176

that was the only way. Can't you see? Her weakness is her ego, her hatred. Her strength is our fear. When I was at her mercy on that rope, that's when it came to me. It seems to be only weakness that she has and somehow we have to use it to stop her. What I said about countries blaming each other is true. You know this is exactly what will happen. She only has to start hostilities and they will finish it themselves... unless we can convince them of the truth."

"I don't know what she has done out there." He swept his arm towards the world below them. "I have a terrible feeling she has already started on her vengeance trail."

Simon was impressed, he'd never heard Mike speak so passionately before. Onotage was also impressed. Mike's words hit him deeply.

"You are right." He walked towards Mike and placed both hands on his shoulders. "She has already started wreaking her vengeance and you are right about her ego being a weakness. There is more to you than I first gave you credit for Mike Mallory. Your love for Susan seemed to make you weak for a while. Now you are stronger then ever... As always my grandfather was right."

"Enough philosophising now." He spoke to both men. "We have preparations to make."

Removing the bag he carried across his shoulder, he took out several smaller bags.

"Scatter this salt around Simon. Stay close to the ground so as the wind does not take it. Mike. You have set it in motion for communications to be restored. Try the two way radio. See if you can contact General Mitchell. Keep trying until you get a response.

"Are you going to contact Sarah Millar?" Mike asked.

Onotage shook his head. "When the time is right. She will contact me.

"Mallory calling General Mitchell... Do you read me. Over..."

Mike was both relieved and surprised when his signal was answered immediately.

"Major Price here. Receiving you loud and clear. All communications back to normal. Over."

"Figured they would be. What is the situation now. Over."

"Bad news all round. The President has called an emergency meeting of the world leaders. We are on the edge of a precipice... My fault I should never have sent in the aircraft. All started from there."

Mike's head was reeling as Price brought him up to date with events. Simon was listening also. They were alarmed by the news of Russia and Japan preparing to take offensive action at the least "provocation".

177

"Listen Price. What's done is done. You must prevent further attacks on this mountain at all costs. Take no further action unless you hear form us. Over."

"Have already advised the President as such... Mallory... two TV crews are on their way to you. Couldn't stop them. Over."

"Jesus Chri... How are they travelling. Over."

Mike needn't have asked. He could hear the whirr of their approach.

"They're here now, must go. Mike over and out."

"I don't believe this," groaned Simon as the two helicopters came into view.

"Try the radio Mike." Onotage shouted above the noise.

"Mountain to craft... Do you read me... Do you read me..."

No response.

The helicopters were close enough now to see figures inside.

"They are here to see me." Even above the noise of the craft, her voice had a startling clarity.

She walked to the edge of the plateau. "They want proof of my powers. I shall oblige them."

Mike walked calmly to her side.

"These are the television crews you wanted Nemesis. Right now you are being seen by millions of people in this country and possibly other countries. If you destroy them you destroy that also."

"Be silent fool. You dare to think that I need your advise?" Mike stepped back, he had no wish to antagonise her now. He hoped she could see the significance in his words.

"She elevated her body and floated gracefully towards the eagerly filming crewmen. Turning in mid-air and raising one hand, she pointed to the mountain peak.

A ray of laser-like power emitted form her fingers. The ground shook beneath the feet of the three men helplessly watching as the beam made contact with the peak. They flattened themselves to the rock face as an avalanche of boulders hurtled down the mountainside."

She returned to the plateau. Turning her back to them. Onotage placed his mat in front of him. The Pendant was around his neck.

"Do not move or speak," he cautioned Mike and Simon quietly.

Nemesis watched the helicopters. Her eyes glittering. She knew now that the satellites were for communication and not devices of war.

"So I cannot use them to destroy these miserable beings, but I can use them to bring terror to their infernal souls."

She levelled her gaze at the craft with the words "Local Sound and Vision" written on it. First giving the occupants a dazzling smile. Then to the horror of the onlookers. She annihilated them.

The updraft from the explosion as the helicopter hit the side of the mountain caused a thermal gale. Sending the second helicopter into a crazy dance.

Neither Mike nor Simon saw Onotage move slowly towards Nemesis until he was directly behind her.

The Pendant was now in his outstretched hands.

He almost made it. He was just inches behind her. The chain in position above her head.

Mike held his breath. (Now) he thought to himself.

He would never know whether or not she heard his thoughts. He would never know and so never forgive himself.

She sensed the presence. She moved quicker than the eye could see, shooting a beam of light at him.

"Onotage went over the edge of the mountain.

Taking the Pendant with him."

CAPLIN TUES MAY 16th

"The private room in the once spotless hospital looked more like an untidy conference room. Major Price, Jim McCann, Al Jackson and Joe Daniels were seated around General Mitchell's bed. Two soldiers were posted at the door. When General Mitchell heard that communications had been restored, he had insisted on the town being scoured for a workable television and having it installed in his room.

They all stared at the screen now in silence."

"What chance have we got now?" McCann's whispered words cut through the silence like a sharp edged blade.

"My God! What chance have we now Mitch?" he uttered the words again. McCann was as pale as the general.

General Mitchell, head swathed in bloodied bandages, threw off the bedclothes and stepped out of bed, catching hold of the supportive arm of Major Price as the room swam before him.

McCann jumped to his feet alarmed at the pallor of his friend.

"Mitch, you're not fit enough. Wait until you feel stronger."

"Stronger for what Jim... Armageddon?"

The general's words hit home to McCann. He turned even paler... thinking of his dream.

"You're right. Let me give you a hand."

"For God's sake Mr President, you have to convince them of the truth. Christ! Are they blind? Didn't they see what she is capable of?"

General Mitchell was speaking to President Nixon on the telephone. All idea of secrecy scattered to the four winds. Just the opposite was needed now.

Tension showed in the faces of the men grouped around him listening.

They could hear only one half of the conversation, the rest wasn't hard to imagine.

"How the hell can they think it is a set up....."

"What!.... A Film set... They're not on a film set. It isn't Steve McQueen and Paul Newman up there. It's now **two** very courageous men trying to save this planet from Doomesday. They're on top of Battle bloody Mountain and that young man...." General Mitchell took a deep breath, forcing himself to speak quieter, calmer.

"That young man... who went over the edge is dead... Dead Mr President."

"General." Major Price interrupted the heated conversation. He held out the two way radio. "It's Mallory sir. He wants to speak to you urgently."

"Excuse me for a moment Mr President... Yes... it's Mallory... I'll come back to you."

"Mallory... you okay... We saw what happened... God I am so sorry. Over."

"We're both okay General." Mike's voice sounded remarkably calm.

"We need some time buying, and from what I have just overheard, the world's leaders need more to convince them. I want you to send another camera crew up here. Just one helicopter and keep the crew to a minimum... You understand General. She will not attack as long as there is only one helicopter and as long as she knows she is playing to a world wide audience, I don't think she will go over the top... Not for a while at least. Over."

"I understand Mallory. I'll get a crew up there if I have to fly them myself. Over and out." He returned to the phone, glancing at the worried faces surrounding him, then repeated the conversation to the President.

"What Mallory means sir, is keep the camera crew to a minimum but include reliable witnesses. Witnesses who are in a better position to convince the world of the truth. I am going myself, so is Major Price, we are both known to foreign powers. We have to be certain that all world powers are aware of the truth...."

180

"What!..."

Mitchell signalled frantically to switch the two way radio off.

"They want to send a delegation..."

"Are they idiots... You have to stop them..."

"On their way..."

"How long..."

"Three hours... I see."

"No... I understand... There will be no stopping them. You understand there will be no stopping her either. She will annihilate the lot of them.... America will be blamed.... Russia and Japan will take action against us... Then it's God help civilisation anyway..."

"No sir, I do not think that is what she intends. This lady definitely wants to be chief executioner herself... at her leisure. Thank you sir. I'll keep you informed.

General Mitchell replaced the phone, his eyes going straight to the men around him.

"You understood all that?" The faces dumbly acknowledged him.

"Russia and Japan are sending their own men here... Mike and Simon have three hours to accomplish what they are trying to do... After that, it's... the nightmare of all nightmares."

Mitchell fell silent.

"There is a chopper ready and waiting sir."

"Good work Major. Contact Mallory... tell him we are on our way... No more than that. With luck... Nemesis knows nothing of this."

"Now... I need two camera men." Mitchell looked towards the American National TV crew who had just returned from the mountain. Two of the men stood immediately. "You can count us in General," one of the men said.

Mitchell shook each man's hand thanking them. "You have been up there, you already know of the danger. I don't need to spell out the fact that we may not return."

"No sir. It looks to me like we are at the redoubt... Or... "Custer's Last Stand" so as to speak."

"You could be right, but I hope you are wrong young man. I pray to God you are very wrong."

Mitchell led the way to the door, McCann joining him.

"I'm going with you Mitch." Al and Joe were about to follow them.

"No sheriff." Mitchell offered his hand. "I appreciate your offer, but your people will need you here. And you Joe, I think you should stay with Al. He will need your support if things start to get rough."

Al took a firm grip of the general's hand. "Good luck sir... Bring those two men back with you... Regardless."

"I'll second that General." Joe gripped the general's hand tightly. "Regardless."

They watched until the helicopter was out of sight.

SARAH MILLAR

"Held in slumbers soft embrace,
She enters realms of flowery grace,
Where tender love and fond caress,
Bids her awake to happiness."
Taken from The Dictionary of Dreams.

Gustavus Hindman Miller.

CHAPTER THIRTEEN: SARAH MILLAR

"Mike and Simon rushed forward. The stunned horror on their faces replaced by anger. Their cries of rage heard by the helicopter crew as it turned and headed back to Caplin."

Mike dropped to his knees looking down at the crumpled body seventy feet below him, pounding the ground with both fists.

"No! .. Oh God .. No!... You murdering bitch." Springing at Nemesis, he was an animal ready for the kill. Simon caught hold of him, pinning him to the ground.

"Mike! .. Mike!... It's no good that way. We can't do a thing for Onotage now. Save your energy man. Cool it. Cool it." Simon slipped into his high school speech idiom without even noticing.

"That is right," Nemesis screamed. "Save the impetuous fool. You will need each other to cling to when you witness my Revenge..."

Once again they were alone. Mike stopped struggling. Simon pulled him roughly to his feet looking closely into his face. He shook him.

"It's up to us now Mike. Don't freak out on me... I need you."

"I'm okay... I'm okay." Mike answered in a voice tight with emotion.

In those few moments he had realised that the woman was no longer Susan and that he not only could, but would kill her if the opportunity arose. He shook his head rapidly. His brain working now with cool clarity.

"We have to get that camera crew back. Play up to her infernal ego. It will delay her for a while. Long enough maybe to show the truth to the world before they start firing on each other."

Simon agreed, relieved that his friend seemed to be over his outburst.

"More than that Mike. We have to retrieve the Pendant."

"She made a mistake. A big mistake. If she saw the Pendant in Onotage's hands, then in the heat of your attack on her, it slipped her memory. She was taken by surprise... And it was forgotten... It's still down there. If she can make a mistake like that... Then she... **can** be beaten."

"I'll go for it now." Mike said moving to the edge of the plateau.

"No my friend. I will be quicker than you. I will retrieve the Pendant. You contact General Mitchell and get that camera crew back."

"Simon gazed down at the figure of Onotage. A mixture of grief and anger flooding through him. He quickly repressed the feelings. Now was not the time."

"Strange. The enigmatic smile was still in evidence even in death on the smooth face, unmarked by the fall. It had a calming effect on Simon."

He placed the Pendant around his own neck and turned to climb again.

"Have faith Simon... You can defeat her."

Simon swung around. The young Indian lay in the same position. One that Simon had gently adjusted. Legs straight. Arms folded across his chest covering the burn that Nemesis had inflicted upon him. Eyes closed in death. Yet Simon knew it was his voice he had heard. He walked back to the lifeless body of the young man.

"I swear to you Onotage... We will succeed."

"The two men sat close to each other. Eyes closed. Allowing the warm sun to ease the tension from their bodies. Mike earnestly hoped that Sarah Millar would contact Simon while he rested.

"God knows... We need your help."

He thought of Onotage and a fresh surge of anger spread through his veins renewing his strength. "Your death won't be wasted. We won't let you down. I swear it."

"What?" Simon muttered, stretching his long limbs.

"I'm sorry Simon." Mike said, giving his friend a concerned look. "I didn't realise I'd spoken out loud... Did she come to you?"

Simon sat upright, rubbing the life back into his arms and legs.

"Only briefly Mike... She said "Trust me.""

"He reached out grasping Mike's hand. The rings began to glow. A glow that grew in radiance as the grip of their hands became firmer. He felt a surge of strength coursing through his veins, renewing his determination, healing his battered emotions."

"Can you feel it?" Simon whispered, not wanting to break the flow with too many words, yet needing to know that Mike was experiencing the same feeling.

"Yes." Mike answered quietly, closing his eyes, allowing the strength to penetrate his entire being.

The whirring sound of the helicopter's blades shattered the precious respite. The leapt to their feet.

"I hope to God I'm right about Nemesis." Mike had to shout above the noise.

"Don't worry," Simon shouted back. "She won't destroy them yet."

He gave Mike a smile of confidence, but deep down he felt they were running out of time.

"The helicopter hovered in front of them. They could easily make out the figure of General Mitchell, head swathed in bandages. Major Price and Jim McCann alongside him. The radio held in Mike's hand crackled into life.

"Hello Mike and Simon... Do you read me. Over." Mike recognised the general's voice immediately.

"Mike here sir. Receiving you loud and clear. Over."

"Good... I don't know what assistance we can give, but we will do whatever we can. The priority here is to convince the world of the truth. Over."

"Oh I agree General Mitchell." The silky voice purred behind him. Startled. The general turned so sharply, only McCann's swift reaction prevented him from falling out of the craft.

"How in God's name...." His words were drowned by her nerve tingling laughter as the craft lurched dizzily, sending them all to their knees while the pilot fought to regain control. The craft steadied and General Mitchell took his first look at their adversary."

"She was seated with one leg crossed demurely over the other. Her chin resting delicately on the back of one hand.

(What ever else she was. She was beautiful.)

She gave him a dazzling smile. "Why thank you General. It is quite a pleasing body I have borrowed. I may decide to keep it for a while." She made a mockingly apologetic gesture with her other hand.

"Oh I startled you... I am so sorry. You were about to tell your two would be heroes of the situation your pitiful excuse for a world finds itself in. Do not waste your time and breath General. You have very little left. I can assure you, your friends on the mountain realise only too well that I hold your world in the palm of my hand."

"She held out her hand, palm upwards. A large grape materialised and lay in the centre of her palm. She closed her hand tightly, crushing the grape until the juice ran through her fingers.

She raised her beautiful but evil eyes to the general, studying him deeply.

Her eyebrows arched in genuine surprise."

"Ah! General. You have realised how I entered your craft. Excellent.

186

Your intelligent reasoning deserves to be rewarded. I shall allow you and your companions the privilege of witnessing the destruction of your world along with your friends on the mountain...." She was gone before the general could speak.

McCann and Price stared questioningly at the general.

"She doesn't become invisible. She can travel faster than we can see. The speed she moves at is swifter than our optic nerves can cope with. Obviously she can read our minds too. A very clever lady. But not clever enough to deal with all human traits thank God."

"What do you mean?" McCann asked.

"She planned to shock and that's exactly what she did. Shocked all other thoughts from our minds. I suspect she also allowed certain communications through to ensure her world-wide notoriety. Yes... a very clever lady."

Major Price stared at the mountain. His eyes resting on the still form of Onotage. "We are up against a violent creature who is hell-bent on destroying this world and everyone on it, and, I have helped her make a start... God forgive me."

McCann looked away from the Major's haggard expression. He no longer wished to witness this man facing his moment of truth.

"She would have done it anyway Major," the general said, picking up the handset. "She did not need any assistance."

"Mike, can you hear me? Over."

"Yes I hear you... We saw what happened. Over."

"She is on her way to you. Good luck. Over."

Mike and Simon stood close together... Waiting. She did not keep them waiting long.

"Gentlemen." She stood at the far end of the plateau. "It is almost time. I have enjoyed your company on this mountain, you have entertained me greatly. So, as a reward, I will show you what I have accomplished so far. I will acquaint you with my powers before I annihilate your world."

"Don't trouble yourself," retorted Simon. "There won't be anyone left to tell this to, so what is the point?"

She stared at him. "You dare to argue with me? You dare to argue with Nemesis? Why, I could split your world into two halves this very instant you fool."

Simon's temper exploded. The fear and anger caused by this destructive being, poured from him like water from a breached dam.

"It **is** what you intend to do, choose what I or anyone else say. All the power you have is wasted. You have no intelligence. You could have

187

ruled this world... But no. You are so intent on destroying it, you are blind to what you really do have in the palm of your hand... Go ahead, we are powerless to stop you... But I swear on everything I hold sacred... I'll see you in Hell or Hades before see you live through this..."

His outburst came to a sudden halt. A strange expression on his face. (Too late... Too late... Oh God... Too late.)

"Her eyes became like pools of blue fire. The energy flowing from her became a lethal field of force. She was now hovering a good three feet above the ground. The air around them was a writhing violent mass. The pilot of the helicopter struggled with the controls as the craft was tossed around like a balloon in the wind. The ground beneath the two men began to tremble. The whole mountain was lurching. Loosened rocks began a slow descent from their resting places. The skies darkened as if every thunderous cloud in the world had gathered around the peak of this mountain. A flash of lightening crackled and zig-zagged across their faces, blinding them for a terrifying moment."

"Dear God," Mike shouted. "This is it. This is the end." A savage animal like sound escaped from the back of his throat.

"Got to take the bitch with us."

"He staggered towards her, reaching out with hands that now looked like talons. His one driving thought was to grasp her beautiful neck and choke the evil life out of the body she had made use of. He felt a pair of strong hands pulling him back. Fury made him strike out blindly with his fists until he was free.

With the strength of an insane man, he fought his way to her.

The force surrounding her was too great, it tore at his body. A sharp rock bounced off his shoulder, ripping at flesh and muscle. The instant pain restoring his sanity. He fell to the ground, praying that the end would be quick."

Simon had first felt her presence. Then to his relief he saw her. a young and beautiful replica of Nemesis. The wind whipping at the flimsy white garment she was wearing. (Dear God... maybe... not too late.)

"Why have you not listened to the dark one Nemesis? He is right, you could rule this world."

Sarah Millar's voice was clear and strong enough to be heard even above the tempest that surrounded them.

Simon caught hold of Mike's arm, dragging him to his feet. Pulling him close. The rings immediately became luminescent.

Nemesis stared at the girl in shocked silence. The tempest gradually

188

subsided.

"Who... Are... You?" She demanded slowly.

"Do you not recognise me Nemesis? I am Sarah Millar."

The malevolence that flowed from her was more violent than the tempest she had caused.

She levelled her terrifying gaze at the girl.

"Then Sarah Millar. You will die for a second time on this hateful earth."

"So!... The man is right," cried Sarah. "You have no intelligence. Nemesis, goddess of Retribution. All powerful... But blind. Incapable of seeing what she has in the palms of both hands."

Sarah's voice grew in strength.

"You obviously have not taken the time to discover this world you would destroy. You will never see the awesome spectacle of Niagara Falls on the borders of this country and Canada or the Victoria Falls in South Africa. Both are wonders of nature that need to be seen to be believed and appreciated. Or the magnificent Taj Mahal in India. Built by the Emperor Shah Jahan. A monumental symbol of the love this man had for his wife. Or the glorious sunset on the Sahara Desert in North Africa, so rich in colour it is as if the very skies have caught fire."

"And Nemesis... When did you last see the Aegean Sea with the moonlight dancing across its surface?" Sarah's voice had lowered, a passionate ring to it.

"Do you realise that the Acropolis remains standing after all these years?" The eyes of Nemesis widened slightly, but she remained silently staring at the girl.

"Yes, you can actually walk through its magnificent splendour, and still feel the power of the Citadel of Athens."

"It is a beautiful world Nemesis, with many wonderful and mysterious places to visit, but you are too full of hate to see this. It is a beautiful world, and it could be yours to rule. All the riches it contains... all the peoples of the earth... Yours to command."

Nemesis glared at Sarah. "Do not waste your words girl. I will have my revenge on this world and go back..."

"Go back." interrupted Sarah. "Go back to what... Ruling the Furies perhaps? You are prepared to give up all that you could possess and risk being ruler of those snake haired venomous creatures..."

"Tell me... Do you think Zeus would allow you to hold a position, even one as lowly as that if you do return... Remember... Zeus has always had a benevolent leaning towards this planet."

189

For the second time since taking control of Susan's body, Mike saw a flicker of fear pass across the face of Nemesis. Sarah saw it too and took full advantage of it.

"Yes," she said in a quieter voice. "You have been so full of hate and revenge, you have lost sight of reason. You cannot go back, but it is not too late. You can still have all that I have spoken of and I can help you."

"You... Why would I need you. Nemesis needs no one."

"But you do," persisted Sarah. "You have already proven you need guidance."

"Nemesis was listening to Sarah, but she was thinking of Zeus."

(My fury in all its potency will be no match for his. The girl is right. I have gone beyond the boundaries. The Olympian Deity will crush me. I can never return.)

"Her fury reared again, this time at her own stupidity."

"Her body rose higher and higher above the ground. She raised her arms up above her head. A terrifying sound emitting from her open mouth. Like the dying cry of a mortally wounded animal. The air was charged with electricity as dazzling flashes of lightening radiated from her with a vivid intensity that would have dimmed the sun's radiance."

"Mike and Simon instinctively covered their faces, clinging to each other as they felt the mountain moving beneath them once again."

The helicopter, unbelievably still airborne, was again in danger of hitting the mountainside and veered away, rocking crazily.

"The sudden calm that followed the violent onslaught was equally frightening. Simon uncovered his face and looked around uneasily."

"Nemesis was once again stood on the plateau. The two women faced each other, standing about six foot apart."

"Simon was vaguely aware of the noise of the helicopter and fervently hoped they had been able to film what they had just witnessed, for he himself could scarcely believe it. Nemesis had floated twenty feet above the plateau emanating a cosmic light that had given the earth a phosphorescent glow. It had hurt his eyes to watch. He was convinced that the earth had moved. Not the mountain."

"The silence was broken now, only by the whirr of the helicopter. Nemesis finally spoke.

"You are right. I can never go back. Zeus would not permit it. But I do not need you foolish girl. You should never have returned."

She raised her arm slowly, until she was pointing one long finger at Sarah... an evil smile parting her lips... eyes glittering like twin beacons of death.

190

"Yes you do." Sarah spoke calmly. "You need my body. The one you now possess will age. It is already older than my body. You will be hindered by it. Remember... You can only possess a Millar. Susan is the only female Millar. The only direct descendant of Martyn Millar on earth at this time, with the exception of myself. My body will not deteriorate. It will never age. With my body you be timeless. Ageless and all knowing. All the knowledge I have of this world will be yours."

Nemesis slowly lowered her arm, looking suspiciously at Sarah, but showing great interest.

"And you. What would you hope to gain from this "union"," she asked. Acid-like scorn in her voice.

"Life." said Sarah. "You caused my life to come to an untimely end. Twenty years was all I had. Twenty short years. Through you I can live again and on a much grander scale than I could ever have hoped for in my previous life. Through you I can experience power. Through me you can experience human emotions. Together we will be supreme on all levels."

"You tempt me greatly girl..."

"Do not hesitate Nemesis. Do it now, before the holocaust you have set in motion escalates beyond redemption. I urge you to do it now... Now."

"Slowly Sarah moved closer to Nemesis, gazing steadily into the luminous eyes. Emerald green met emerald green... A potently charged meeting of positive and negative energy."

The effect. Simon later described. Was like the aftermath of a nuclear explosion. He and Mike could feel pinpricks of radiation on their skin. The air was alive with it.

Simon caught hold of Mike's arm. "Be ready," he hissed. "We will only get the one chance."

"They watched transfixed as the visible life force that was Nemesis, began to flow into Sarah Millar's body. The life force that had survived two hundred and eighty years... Sealed in rock."

"The two women were only three foot apart now. Standing so still they seemed to be suspended in time. The only movement, the snaking form of the ectoplasmic life force emitted from the eyes of Nemesis into the eyes of Sarah, joining the two women."

"A powerful living, glowing entity."

"Susan's body fell to the ground like a discarded rag doll. She opened her eyes and stared blankly at the scene before her, her expression devoid of recognition. Then mercifully... She passed out."

"Simon sprang forward kicking the open chest closer to Sarah and dragging Mike with him. Sarah was now directing through her hands, the living force that was Nemesis into the skull. She was staggering, reeling as if receiving physical blows from an unseen assailant.

"You... Must... Help... Me... She... Is... Too strong."

Her voice was weakening now. No longer vibrant with confidence.

"HELP HER." The voices of Vincent and Rebecca Allen echoed around the mountain.

"The rings." Simon shouted as he leaped to assist Sarah. The two men each caught hold of a flaying arm and taking a firm grip of her wrists, brought them together pointing them towards the skull.

"The rings took on a life force of their own. The prismatic light emanating from them with an intensity that startled Mike and Simon. A fast moving glowing force that joined the plasmic flow compelling it to enter the skull."

"The three human forms were staggering, writhing, lurching around as if they were indulging in some crazy dance. She was dragging them backwards... dragging them to the edge of the mountain. Simon felt the ground giving way beneath his feet as he teetered on the brink of falling."

"He gasped as two firm hands were placed on his back propelling him forward, away from the edge of the plateau."

"He was exhausted, convinced his very soul was being dragged from his body. He was being physically and mentally ripped apart."

"Mike could hear someone screaming and the sudden realisation that the screams were being torn from his bursting lungs, shocked him into total silence."

"The girl between them gradually faded from sight as the flow diminished. The two men no longer struggled to stay upright."

When there was nothing of substance left to hold on to, the two exhausted men dropped to the ground."

"Simon speedily encircled the chain around the skull, pushing the Pendant firmly into the now open jaws. Slamming the lid of the chest shut. He collapsed on top of it. Mike alongside him."

"After what seemed like an eternity, Simon raised his head to look at his friend. The sight of Mike's now pure white hair, caused only the faintest glimmer of surprise."

The air was filled with the sound of throbbing engines.
Simon looked towards the sound.

A dozen or more helicopters were approaching the mountain. The babble of several foreign languages striving to be heard came through the two-way radio. He started laughing hysterically.

"Would you believe it?" He spluttered between gales of uncontrollable laughter. "They've sent the Foreign Legion this time... And they're still too bloody late."

He threw his arm around Mike's shoulders. Both laughing until they dissolved into tears...

"They grasped trembling hands. The rings were gone."

A soft moan reminded them that Susan was alive.

THE GUARDIAN

"No motion has she now, no force;
She neither hears nor sees:
Roll'd round in earths diurnal course
With rocks and stones and trees."

W. Wordsworth. (A Slumber did my spirit seal)

CHAPTER FOURTEEN: THE GUARDIAN

THE GREAT SALT LAKE DESERT - THURSDAY 18th MAY 07.30 hrs

"The convoy of army vehicles made it's way slowly across the desert creating a billowing cloud of sand. The rising sun cast a warm but eerie glow on to the scene."

"A family of desert rats scuttled out of sight as the vehicles approached. With the exception of one.

The desert rat sat back on his haunches watching with alert interest. His keen eyes darting to each vehicle in turn. Searching.

Mike pointed him out to Susan, attempting to draw her out of the secret world she had retreated into. "Look Susan. He's a bold one."

"Susan stared at the desert rat in silence.

The desert rat stared back at her.

She turned her head as they past. Staring into the unblinking gaze of the rodent.

It sat perfectly still, the only movement being the turning of its head as they passed. The eyes holding Susan's until the convoy had passed. Then the animal rejoined its family, stopping once to look over its shoulder again directly at Susan. Baring its teeth."

Mike regretted pointing it out. He had the uneasy feeling that the animal had actually been watching Susan. He shrugged the feeling away hoping Susan hadn't noticed.

"They were in the second jeep. Simon, Susan and himself. Joe had stayed at the Seismology station. The leading jeep was occupied by General Mitchell, Major Price, Jim McCann and the secretary to President Nixon. Behind them the third jeep was occupied by four top officials. Two trucks brought up the rear, one containing a mechanical shovel. The other containing a small bulldozer."

Susan sat in between Mike and Simon. She looked strained and pale. Her fingers constantly plucking at the material of her dress.

Mike's arm tightened around her shoulders, his hand closing over both her hands. "Relax Susan," he said quietly. "It's all over now."

She looked up at him. The white hair although not unattractive, would take some getting used to. She tried to smile, but was too much aware of the metal safe behind them. The safe containing the chest... and Nemesis.

"(All over she thought. Then why do I feel.... What... What do I feel..)"

She couldn't put it into words, even to herself. She knew she was at breaking point.

"The look of fear she had seen in the eyes of men and women when they had arrived at the town had unnerved her greatly. She could not remember the journey down the mountain, but she would never forget the stares from the townsfolk."

"They hadn't stayed in town. They had flown back to the station. She knew this had been for her sake."

"(Oh God. Will I ever feel or be the same again?)"

The rodent had unnerved her. The rodent had... known her... Feared her."

As Simon watched his two friends anxiously, he allowed his mind to go back over the last couple of days.

"They'd had to wait until the air was free of the helicopters before starting to carry Susan down the mountain to where they could be picked up. It had been a nightmare enough journey without adding backdraft to the hazards, neither man in a fit state physically or mentally. Mike's torn shoulder muscle throbbed painfully with every move. Simon had suffered a cracked rib, during Mike's crazed attempt to kill Nemesis.

"You certainly pack a powerful punch," he'd tried joking with Mike. Mike merely gave him a miserable smile. He scarcely remembered the incident. He hoped Susan would remember nothing. She had been unconscious most of the time and judging by the way she had threshed around calling for Sarah, she had been plagued by hellish dreams. They'd had to secure her arms and legs to prevent them from dropping her.

"The arrival into Caplin... Seeing the devastated town, hearing how close the world had come to total war when Russia and Japan joined by Israel had insisted on going to the mountain. Hearing of the world wide destruction Nemesis had caused, finally brought Mike to his knees just before he passed out. Both he and Susan were detained in hospital and given a sedative."

"Simon had listened in silence as the full extent of the final wrath of Nemesis was related to him. Her unleashed fury had caused a total

196

eclipse of the sun and moon at such a speed that it had been followed by world wide tidal waves. The loss of lives would run into tens of thousands.

Simon refused to stay at the hospital with Mike and Susan. He needed to speak urgently with General Mitchell.

"The chest must be buried immediately. I have a fear that scientists may be interested in examining the skull. This would be highly dangerous."

"I realise this Simon. You can be assured that no one will be allowed anywhere near the chest. I have already been in touch with the President and impressed this fact on him. He was in total agreement. Having witnessed her incredible power along with the whole world. He has given me full authority to take whatever steps I deem necessary. I have informed the President that as far as I am concerned, the death of Onotage left you and Mike as the sole advisers."

"I have just one suggestion to make."

"What is that?" Simon asked cautiously.

"Just this," Mitchell answered with equal caution. "Much as I wish to see this chest buried as soon as possible. I think it is vital for Susan to witness the actual burial for the sake of her mental health. I suggest that we take her and Mike back to the station. We will fly you of course. I will accompany you... With the chest. I do not think it should be left here... too risky. Certain foreign powers have already expressed an interest in it. I suggest we allow Susan at least one full day's respite. Yourself and Mike also. Then early on Thursday morning... We will bury Nemesis and hopefully have done with her."

Simon gave this some thought. He would much rather have got the ordeal over with now. Reluctantly he saw the logic in the general's words, especially where Susan was concerned.

"Alright sir, we will do it that way." He suddenly realise how desperately tired he was. He needed a shower and a sleep. The general was right, they all needed to rest.

The spirit of Onotage had visited him that night.

"You and Mike have done well my friend, but guard against complacency. Nemesis is and always will be, a very dangerous entity."

The grave words were enhanced by the serious young face before him. Suddenly the smile appeared.

"I sense sadness in you my friend. Do not grieve for me. My earthly death was inevitable. It was the only way Sarah Millar could appear as a solid body. She needed my timespace on this earth."

"The weakness of Nemesis was her hatred of humanity and of her own selflove. Pure egoism. My death was the ultimate act. The total opposite of these vices."

Simon understood but was greatly saddened.

"But for you Onotage, we would have plunged to certain death. Fate played you a strange hand my friend. You deserved better." Onotage merely smiled.

"Tell me where should she be buried Onotage?"

"By the shores of The Great Salt Lake, where you first met Vincent, Rebecca and Sarah. You will recognise the area, there has been no great change. Now sleep Simon. Tomorrow you will understand everything and will be prepared for the final stage of imprisoning Nemesis and in answer to your unspoken question. Sarah's spirit is unharmed."

"Au revoir my friend." he said as Simon's eyes closed.

"Joe had come to him the following morning. A troubled expression on his face, fingers nervously clutching at the amber amulet he still wore around his neck."

"Simon. Onotage came to me in my sleep."

Simon smiled. "Then you are fortunate Joe. Do not be troubled by this."

"I'm not persisted Joe. It's what he said that troubles me. He told me I was the Keeper of the Rings and that I would understand shortly. That you would soon be able to explain."

"Then trust the words of Onotage as I do Joe." Simon gave him a reassuring smile, but was himself puzzled at the words.

The crackle of the radio brought Simon's thoughts back to the present.

"It's General Mitchell sir," the driver said. "He says we are in sight of the lake. He wishes to know how close we should be to it."

Simon stood, scanning the terrain. His eyes quickly found what they sought.

"A sizeable hill with the slopes running gently down to the shores of the lake. A scattering of large rocks worn smooth by time and the constant attack from the wind and sand. Onotage was right. He did recognise the area from his dream..."

(His dream. Was that **really** only four days ago....)

"The large hill driver. Just to the left of us."

The driver relayed the information back to the general.

Mike could feel the tension mounting in Susan as they alighted from the jeep.

"He and Susan had been married that morning. Mike had wanted to wait until Susan was over the ordeal, but Simon had insisted that marrying her now would be beneficial to her. An added protection."

"So in a simple and short ceremony with Simon as best man. Joe, Al and McCann as witnesses and General Mitchell standing in for Susan's father. Susan had become Mrs Michael Mallory shortly before this exodus."

"Now they stood before the cavity created by the mechanical digger and witnessed the lowering of the safe into the depths. The bulldozer speedily filling it with the loose rock and sand taken from the excavation."

Susan returned to the jeep and watched in silence as a six foot high pillar of rock and boulders was placed over the tomb.

"Oh," She put her hand to her throat. "Hard to... breathe... Stop .. stop... panicking."

General Mitchell walked over to Susan, alarmed at her pallor. She stepped out of the vehicle as he approached her.

Holding his arms out to her, he embraced her tightly.

"It is over now Susan." He spoke softly and reassuringly to her. "Place all that has happened behind you. Look forward now to a happy future with Mike. You are going away aren't you?"

She gazed up at him. "Yes, we are going to my parent's" A haunted expression filled her eyes.

"I wish I could be as certain as you seem to be. God knows I want to believe that it is all over, but... I cannot. I feel she has left something of her being in my body and this feeling scares me."

She began to cry. The first tears she had shed since being brought down from the mountain.

"Cry Susan. It will be good and cleansing for you. Give yourself time. I am sure that is all it needs for you to realise that it **is** finished."

Mike and Simon had stayed where they were. Allowing the general the time to speak to Susan alone.

Mike turned his eyes from them and stared at the pillar of rock. His gaze travelled slowly up the hillside... "What the!..."

He caught hold of Simon's arm pulling him, pointing to the top of the hill.

"Look."

There was nothing to see but rocks and a few scattered bushes.

"Simon. I'm going crazy. I swear I saw Onotage." Alarm sounded in his voice.

Simon gave a smile that reminded Mike unnervingly of the young Indian. "You did Mike."

Mike stared at him. Alarm giving way to a look of bitter uncertainty.

"How on earth could I? I saw him die didn't I. I saw that murdering bitch kill him."

"Yes, you did see him die Mike."

He told Mike of Onotage's visit to him. Repeating all that Onotage had revealed to him. How he, Simon, now understood as Onotage had promised.

"He had to die Mike. Something pre-ordained at his birth. Probably the reason for his birth."

"Even his name "Onotage" was pre-ordained. Translated it means... "The top of the Hill." That is where he will stay. At the top of the hill. He is "The Guardian." It was his destiny. Just as it was ours to be involved."

"Who was he Simon...What was he?"

Simon smiled... remembering his own same questions of Onotage.

"He was just a man Mike... A man with a gift."

"He decided it would be wiser not to reveal to Mike that he, Simon, was the earthly Guardian, also pre-ordained. He did not reveal to Mike the visit of Onotage to Joe.

Joe had wandered into his favourite area of the garden, still pondering over the words Onotage had spoken to him. Seated beside the pool, he had seen the Rings.

They lay close together in the water, under the shadow of the moonflowers. There they would stay protected by the watchful eyes of Joe."

"So now you can relax Mike. Knowing that she will always be under the surveillance of Onotage. Come, it is time to leave. Take Susan away from here. It is over."

"As they neared the jeep, Simon felt rather than heard the sigh.

A sigh that rippled through the earth until it reached the surface."

He stopped walking. Fear creating cold shivers through his body.

He turned and was relived to see the lone figure stood with folded arms on the top of the hill.

The voice of Onotage came into his mind.

"We must always be vigilant Simon."

He turned and joined Mike and Susan in the jeep.